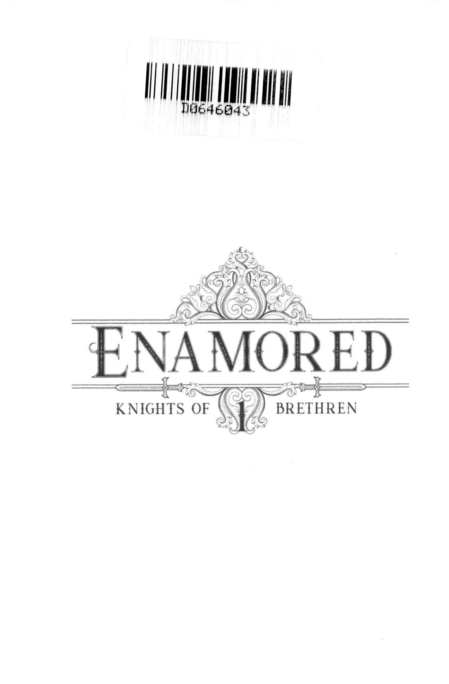

ENAMORED

KNIGHTS OF 1 BRETHREN

D0646043

Books by Jody Hedlund

Knights of Brethren Series
Enamored
Entwined

The Fairest Maidens Series
Beholden
Beguiled
Besotted

The Lost Princesses Series
Always: Prequel Novella
Evermore
Foremost
Hereafter

Noble Knights Series
The Vow: Prequel Novella
An Uncertain Choice
A Daring Sacrifice
For Love & Honor
A Loyal Heart
A Worthy Rebel

Waters of Time Series
Come Back to Me
Never Leave Me

The Colorado Cowboys
A Cowboy for Keeps
The Heart of a Cowboy

The Bride Ships Series
A Reluctant Bride
The Runaway Bride
A Bride of Convenience
Almost a Bride

The Orphan Train Series
An Awakened Heart: A Novella
With You Always
Together Forever
Searching for You

The Beacons of Hope Series
Out of the Storm: A Novella
Love Unexpected
Hearts Made Whole
Undaunted Hope
Forever Safe
Never Forget

The Hearts of Faith Collection
The Preacher's Bride
The Doctor's Lady
Rebellious Heart

The Michigan Brides Collection
Unending Devotion
A Noble Groom
Captured by Love

Historical
Luther and Katharina
Newton & Polly

ENAMORED

KNIGHTS OF BRETHREN

JODY HEDLUND

NORTHERN LIGHTS PRESS

Enamored
Northern Lights Press
© 2021 Copyright
Jody Hedlund
Jody Hedlund Print Edition

ISBN 978-1-7337534-8-7

www.jodyhedlund.com

All rights reserved. No part of this book may be reproduced, stored in a retrieval system, or transmitted in any form, or by any means, electronic, mechanical, photocopying, recording or otherwise, without prior permission of the author.

Scripture quotations are taken from the King James Version of the Bible.

This is a work of historical reconstruction; the appearances of certain historical figures are accordingly inevitable. All other characters are products of the author's imagination. Any resemblance to actual events or locales or persons, living or dead, is entirely coincidental.

Cover Design by Roseanna White Designs
Cover images from Shutterstock
Interior Map Design by Jenna Hedlund

Chapter 1

Elinor

"Whom do you choose as your husband?" The king leaned closer to me in our spectator box. "Surely amongst so many gallant noblemen you have your sights affixed on one by now."

"I would that I did, Your Majesty." The melee unfolded in the tournament field before us, but I took no pleasure in watching grown men fight, even with blunt weapons. "I fear the choosing is more difficult than I expected."

For a man of fifty years, the king maintained an aura of strength and purpose in his large, muscular frame as well as a benevolent spirit that had earned him the enduring title Ulrik the Good.

I prayed his benevolence would hold fast toward me, but as he rubbed his fingers through the light-brown hair of his beard, I sensed his patience was running thin.

I shifted in my cushioned seat, the pleasant warmth of the autumn day suddenly stifling and the gold laces at the sides of my gown constricting me. "I regret I have not yet developed fondness in my heart for any of the men—"

Queen Inge's touch on my arm halted me. In the chair on my other side, she wore a stunning blue velvet gown and a circlet with a sheer veil covering her blond hair. Though she wasn't my mother by birth, I was glad we shared the same hair coloring. The resemblance allowed the populace to accept me as a daughter of the king and queen when I was really only their niece.

The queen leveled a censuring look at her husband before she patted my arm. "You need not apologize, Elinor. The king knows how difficult this royal courtship tradition is."

He raked a gaze over the queen. "I had no trouble selecting you from amongst the dozen noblewomen who came to court me."

The queen smiled, her cheeks turning rosy at the king's compliment. "Even so, you must be patient with Elinor. She wants to choose wisely."

The king released a long sigh. The golden crown circling his head tilted precariously, as if to remind me of the precarious nature of the transfer of authority.

I wouldn't assume the full rulership of Norvegia until after the king's death—hopefully, not for many years into the future. Nevertheless, upon my eighteenth birthday in two days, the time would come for me to be crowned the heir apparent.

According to royal tradition, the naming of the heir to the throne was contingent upon the successor becoming betrothed to either a royal or noble bloodline from within Norvegia to prevent undue influences from other countries infiltrating the ruling class. The successor was also highly encouraged to make a heart match to ensure a strong marriage.

The twelve most eligible men or women were invited to the capital city for a weeklong courtship process. The festivities culminated in the eighteenth birthday feast, where the royal princess or prince officially chose a heart match.

In theory, the courtship tradition was reasonable and fair. I might not have complete freedom in whom I married, but at least I was given some say in the matter.

However, I had not developed fondness for any of the twelve noblemen during the past week. Now I felt the king's frustration, for it matched my own.

If only we didn't have the added pressure from King Canute of neighboring Swaine. While our ambassadors had clarified Norvegia's long-held tradition to the young Swainian king, he'd asked for my hand in marriage anyway, insisting we would co-rule our countries side by side, that he had no intention of usurping my authority in Norvegia.

As my birthday drew nearer, the threats from Swaine and King Canute had steadily mounted. But King Ulrik and his advisors hadn't bowed to the pressure. The weeklong royal courtship had commenced as planned, and now my future husband was among those fighting in the mock battle before us.

"I beseech you not to worry, Your Majesty." I spoke with as much confidence as I could muster. "I shall surely develop fondness erelong." I had done little else over the past days but spend time with the men, praying I would be able to pick the worthiest candidate and develop a heart match with him.

The king motioned toward his cupbearer, who quickly approached with a chalice of mead. "You always have thought deeply, Elinor, an excellent quality for a leader. But this week you must let go of the need to analyze everything and allow your feelings to grow."

"I shall try, Your Majesty."

A cheer arose from the crowds of nobility sitting in open stands along the fence line as well as from the commoners who watched at cordoned-off areas. The level field sat to the east of the city limits, where the terrain flattened into fertile farmland. I was used to seeing the sprawling eastern land from the castle turret every morn and was more interested in taking in my surroundings than in the melee.

Nevertheless, I attempted to concentrate on the dozen men fitted in armor from their great helms down to their chausses covering their leather ankle boots. The clank of sword against sword as well as the clashing of weapons against shields rang in the air.

The knights deserved my attention and utmost respect. After all, they were performing for me to demonstrate their strength and courage, and in so doing, prove themselves worthy to be my husband.

"Lord Torvald Wahlburg, Your Majesty." Rasmus bent down with another update. "He's eliminated his third opponent." The Royal Sage stood behind the king's chair, his usual scholarly black robe draped with a purple embroidered stole designating him as one of the seven Royal Sages. His black cap circled his head but was long and hung down one side, coming to a tasseled tip.

The king nodded toward the fierce knight swinging his sword at another opponent. "What about Torvald, Elinor? He would make a good husband, would he not?"

"He is indeed a worthy man." But he had not captured my affection. Truthfully, he had not even tried, unlike the other noblemen. I could only conclude he had no aspiration to marry me and become the future king of Norvegia.

"He is the best." The king took a drink of mead. "The best after Sir Ansgar, of course."

Though I willed myself not to gaze at the knights congregated below the spectator box where we sat, I couldn't help myself. My attention strayed too oft to Sir Ansgar, much to my embarrassment. Outfitted in chain mail and a gambeson, he stood amidst his companions, tall and strong, holding himself with the bearing of a man who feared nothing.

Even though Sir Ansgar was among the Knights of Brethren and had earned the position of Grand Marshal, the highest knight in all the land, he was but a commoner, the third son of a chieftain, and not eligible for consideration as candidate for the future king.

His lowly birthright didn't make him any less appealing to me and nearly every other young maiden in the kingdom. With his light-brown hair, warm brown eyes, and chiseled features, he was a handsome man. And he was renowned for his great victories in battle.

"It is settled," the king said. "You feel some affection for Torvald. You shall marry him."

"You cannot decide, Ulrik." The queen's interjection was firm but gentle. "'Tis Elinor's choice to make and hers alone."

"Yes, but Torvald is an excellent swordsman and is most suitable." The king nodded at the young knight knocking another nobleman's feet from under him.

I knew better than to protest outright. Instead, using a more tactful approach with the king would work better. "What if Kristoffer is more suitable, Your Majesty? After all, he won the joust yesterday."

"Excellent point."

"Or perhaps Sigfrid is the best. He defeated his opponents in archery."

The king nodded, his gaze alighting on each of the young knights as I listed them. "You are astute as always, Elinor. I suggest you continue to get to know them all."

"That is a wise decision, Your Majesty."

"What say you, Rasmus? Do you have words of wisdom for the princess?"

Rasmus bowed his head, then met my gaze steadily. "She is wise to show the world she is choosing carefully. Let us pray King Canute hears of her caution and accepts her selection."

I heard what Rasmus wasn't saying, that King Canute could very well reject my decision and wage war against Norvegia to claim me for himself.

Rasmus pursed his lips and then scanned the distant harbor of Vordinberg and the sea beyond as he'd done throughout the festivities this week.

What was he looking for?

Vessels of all shapes and sizes crowded the waterfront, some with sails aloft but most at rest. The turquoise water gleamed with midday sunshine, revealing the depths that descended so endlessly that never was a sunken ship or lost item ever recovered along Norvegia's southern coast. Offshore several hundred feet, numerous islands protected the capital city from wind and waves, making Ostby Sound a safe harbor and Vordinberg one of the richest port cities in the world.

I saw naught that was out of the usual. Naught that should cause Rasmus to fret. Was he afraid King Canute would attack by sea? Surely not. Swaine had far less coastline and lacked the ship-building industry and fleet that Norvegia possessed. The neighboring country wouldn't dare try a sea invasion, not against Norvegia's naval superiority.

The noise from the crowds crescendoed again as more knights succumbed to their opponents and fell to the ground in surrender. In a final move, Torvald swung his sword, bringing down the remaining opponents wearing the blue heraldry, leaving only those in red standing.

As the trumpet blast signaled the end of the melee, the king pushed up from his seat, his velvet cloak flapping in the breeze drifting from the sea, the air laden with the scent of fish and brine.

I rose from my position of honor between the king and queen. The crowd continued to cheer for the victors, but as royalty we remained neutral in our display of emotion, as was the custom in the tournaments.

Torvald was the first to extend a hand to the men he'd defeated, lifting first one and then another to his feet. His team did likewise, extending grace to those who'd lost. When finally, the dozen noblemen were standing, the winners approached the edge of the field in front of our raised seats.

The men removed their great helms and bowed their heads. I didn't need the game master's whispered remarks to know which of the noblemen was the champion. Even so, I listened and accepted the holy laurel I was to place upon the winner's head. Although the king usually did the crowning, this week the duty belonged to me.

"I congratulate each of you on your feats of valor." My voice rang out over the now-silent spectators. All eyes were fixed upon me, including those of Ansgar, facing the royal seats only a few feet away.

"One man has demonstrated unyielding courage in the face of adversity. His gallantry was evident on the battlefield today." I paused and let my gaze linger on each bent head, wondering as I had a hundred times already during the past week, why Providence had chosen me to become the next ruler of the great northern country of Norvegia and not someone else.

Although I had spent my entire life preparing for the task of reigning, a small part of me had always hoped the king and queen would have a child of their own to fulfill the obligation.

Alas, Providence had not supplied a substitute. Now upon the cusp of adulthood, I could no longer deny the reality of my destiny—that I would become the ruling queen of this nation.

I pushed aside my reservations and continued. "Thus, in honor of his noble enterprise and his combat to glorify the king, I crown Lord Torvald Wahlburg as the victor of the melee."

Cheers rose into the air. Torvald was the decisive winner. Should he also be the decisive winner of my hand in marriage? Could I somehow conjure feelings of affection for this man?

The Knights of Brethren standing below us parted ways, making room for Torvald to approach the raised seating box. When he took his place directly below us, I stepped to the railing.

Grit and dirt and grass from the melee coated his armor. Perspiration flattened his dark hair to his head. A slight scar on his cheek confirmed that this brave knight fought as heartily in a real battle as he had today in this mock tournament.

Torvald was a brave and good man. I had no doubt of that. But would his bravery and his goodness be enough to satisfy me if he were to become my husband? And would I satisfy him?

I settled the laurel upon his head, then stood back.

As was the custom, he removed his leather gauntlet and held it out to me as a token of his devotion.

Although his face remained expressionless, his eyes relayed a message I could read all too well. He did not relish this exchange between us.

Perhaps he did not wish to be king any more than I wished to be queen. But he was doing his duty just as I was.

I accepted his glove and brought it to my lips. I brushed a kiss upon it, tasting the dust of battle. Then as custom demanded, I lifted the glove into the air and waved it grandly.

The crowd surged to their feet shouting and clapping and whistling. I did not deceive myself into thinking their accolades were for me. Yes, they accepted me as the next in line to the throne. But 'twas no secret the people of Norvegia loved Torvald.

Almost as much as they loved Ansgar.

Torvald was also one of the ten Knights of Brethren. As prestigious as the king's knights were, only titled firstborn sons of nobility who were in line to inherit their family's estates could participate in the courtship week, thus enhancing the king's lands and coffers through the marriage union.

I fought to keep a smile in place as I lowered the glove and tucked it into the golden circlet belt riding low on my hips. I nodded one final time to Torvald before I spun away, letting all pretense dissolve.

The queen slipped her hand into the crook of my arm and squeezed gently. "'Tis time for you to begin preparations for tonight's ball." Although I had not expressed my concerns, the kindness in her eyes told me she understood the heavy weight upon my heart.

As the queen and I crossed to the stairs, my ladies-in-waiting hastened to follow. The women who attended me were my closest companions. They were more thrilled with the weeklong celebration than I was, and their excited chatter had filled my chambers in recent weeks.

At a shout and commotion from beyond the bystanders, Rasmus paused in speaking to the king, his keen eyes homing in on several riders galloping toward the competition field, black cloaks billowing in the wind behind them.

"Who is approaching, Rasmus?" The king followed the Sage's gaze.

"Maxim, Your Majesty."

Maxim? My heartbeat stuttered to a stop, as did my feet, and I clutched at the railing to keep from stumbling.

The queen also halted, her fingers tightening on my arm. "Maxim is home?"

I searched the riders, looking for Maxim's familiar form—his bony shoulders, lanky body, and hair as black as a winter night. But with hoods shielding the riders' faces, I saw none who reminded me of Maxim.

As they reined in, the now-silent crowd watched them. Rasmus focused on the tallest of the three as they dismounted. For just a moment, I glimpsed something sharp in Rasmus's eyes before his expression schooled into one of usual passivity.

The taller man strode forward with a confident step and proud bearing. As he drew near the royal spectator box, Ansgar and the other Knights of Brethren raised their swords in warning. The newcomer seemed as though he had no intention of stopping and only did so when the tip of Ansgar's sword pressed against his chest.

Without flinching, the newcomer tugged away his hood and let it fall to his back.

My pulse started up at double the speed. It was Maxim. Home. After ten years, two months, and twenty-eight days. Yes, I had been counting how long he'd been gone, although angrily.

"Maxim." The queen's whisper contained a note of excitement. I had become her daughter, but Maxim had been the son she'd never had, and she'd loved him dearly.

As Maxim lifted his face, I sucked in a startled breath. Gone was the boy with thin, sallow cheeks and a toothy grin. In his place was a darkly handsome man. His shoulder-length hair was wavy and unruly. His skin was swarthy and his features rugged with a layer of scruff covering his chin and jaw. His expression was hard and unfriendly, and his dark brows furrowed.

"Your Majesty," Rasmus said. "May I present to you my son, Maxim Gandrud. You may remember him from his childhood."

"Yes, I do." The king eyed Maxim with wariness.

Who could forget the intelligent boy who had grown up alongside me in the king's household?

"Your Majesty." Maxim's voice rang out with an authority that sent prickles of more surprise over my skin. "I am your humble servant." He had changed much in the years of his absence. So much so I could not reconcile this man with my childhood best friend.

Rasmus narrowed his eyes upon Maxim, scrutinizing his only son from his head down to his leather boots, laced up his legs with twine. "I called him home to begin his Erudite training."

"Very good, Rasmus." The king finished his study of Maxim and seemed satisfied. "I have no doubt someday he will follow in your footsteps and become a Royal Sage."

"He has many years of training ahead of him, Your Majesty."

"Of course." The king's gaze flitted to the queen, taking in the eagerness of her expression. "We are celebrating the princess's courtship week. You will join us for the remainder of the festivities, Maxim. I know the queen would like that."

The queen smiled at her husband, her eyes radiating her gratefulness.

Maxim bowed his head in subservience. "I would be honored, Your Majesty."

The king glanced in my direction. "You do

remember Elinor, do you not?"

I held my breath and waited for Maxim to look at me for the first time in ten years. What would he think? Would he recognize me? Or would he find me so changed that he wouldn't be able to hide his surprise?

"I do remember the princess, Your Majesty." Maxim bowed his head. "I pray her choice of a husband will bring happiness to all the land."

My nerves tightened with anticipation. What would this reunion with Maxim be like? I'd waited so long for it that I'd lost hope it would ever happen.

Maxim raised his head, but he didn't spare me a glance and instead kept his focus solely upon the king. Almost as if I wasn't there. Almost as if he didn't care.

The spark of indignation that had festered for years flamed inside my chest. He had not once in all the time he'd been gone visited or replied to the many letters I'd written to him. The day Rasmus sent him away was the last I'd heard from him.

An ache swiftly pushed into my throat. I finally had to acknowledge what I'd suspected for years, what I'd tried to ignore.

Maxim no longer cared about me.

When the queen moved down the steps to depart, I tore my attention from him and allowed her to lead me away, vowing to extricate him from my thoughts once and for all, the same way he'd cut me out of his.

Chapter 2

Elinor

The guests waited below for my entrance to the ball.

"You will do well, my love." The queen pressed a hand to my cheek, her bracelets and rings clinking together. "Do not forget how beautiful, intelligent, and kind you are."

"Thank you, Your Majesty." I leaned into her palm, grateful for her tenderness and constant understanding.

Donned in an intricately embroidered purple gown that was trimmed in black fur, the queen was still one of the most beautiful women in the land. She wore her golden crown studded with large amethyst and topaz gemstones along with smaller rosettes and pearls surrounded by gold rose leaves.

The king, too, was attired in his royal robe, wearing his taller and more elaborate official crown that matched the queen's. He took his place in front of me out of sight of the grand staircase, placed both hands on my arms, and appraised me.

"Elinor, though you were born of my sister, I consider you my own flesh and blood."

His words stirred emotion within me, but I'd learned long ago not to show my feelings and think rationally instead. "You are too kind, Your Majesty."

"You have become my daughter, and one day you will be a great queen." His words were filled with warm affection.

I thanked Providence every day for giving me parents like Ulrik and Inge to replace the ones I'd lost. Of course, I couldn't remember my real family. I'd been but a newborn when my mother disappeared with my sister, only a year older than me.

I was told my father had been frantic with worry, had scoured every corner of the land and followed every clue to find my mother and sister. But tragically, during one of his voyages, a violent storm had assaulted his ship in the Dark Sea. He and everyone aboard drowned.

For years, King Ulrik had continued the hunt for his sister and niece and offered rewards to anyone who found the missing members of the royal household. But in the eighteen years since their disappearance, no one had discovered a hint of their whereabouts.

Eventually the king had given up hope of finding them. But I had never been able to relinquish my desire to learn what had happened. I questioned travelers and visitors who came to the royal court and was always seeking answers about my mother and sister.

For my whole life, their disappearance had been a mystery I couldn't solve no matter how hard I tried. Logic and rationale pointed to the fact that they couldn't have survived for so long without anyone's knowledge.

But another part of me wasn't ready to let go . . . the part recognizing that, as the second-born daughter of the king's sister, I shouldn't be next in line for the throne. I'd been given the position by default, not because I'd proven myself capable.

Now standing before the king in the hallway, just moments before my coming-of-age ball, old insecurities flooded my soul. Was I suited for this? Especially when I wished for a different life, one of studying and learning and pursuing wisdom.

I squared my shoulders and straightened my chin. I would do my duty. I wouldn't shirk the responsibilities placed upon me.

The king leaned in and pressed a kiss against my forehead. The queen did likewise, leaving the waft of her lavender oil in her wake. Then the king held out his arm, and the queen linked hers there as they positioned themselves at the top of the wide stone staircase.

A trio of trumpeters announced their presence, and the music below in the grand hall faded to silence. I had watched them descend the staircase from below many times over the years. But tonight I would be the last to arrive to the festivities. The king, queen, and the entire court would watch me glide down in my stunning gown made of swan feathers that had been dyed a vibrant purple.

The skirt was rounded and full, and I was half tempted to test whether the feathers would allow any sort of floating. But I'd studied the science behind flying and knew much more was necessary for soaring than mere feathers.

Even if I couldn't fly, I felt as graceful as a swan, especially since my long hair was styled loosely, the flowing waves hanging about me in unfettered beauty, setting me apart as the most coveted maiden at the ball.

What would Maxim think when he witnessed my descent?

I gave myself a shake, loathing my weakness in considering him at this moment. Since leaving the tournament field hours ago, I'd vowed to put him from my mind. Even so, images crept in unbidden, as if they had a will of their own. "No, I shall not dwell on him."

"On whom, Your Highness?" At Rasmus's voice behind me, I startled. I'd believed I was alone—except for the master of ceremonies standing nearby and the guards on duty at each end of the long passageway.

I was not the blushing type. If I had been, my cheeks would have flamed red. As it was, I drew in a steadying breath before I pivoted.

"Has someone finally caught your attention, Your Highness?" Rasmus's dark brows rose, his eyes filled with curiosity.

Except for the angular lines and aristocratic features, I had never been able to see Maxim in his father's face. From what I'd gathered, Maxim's appearance resembled that of his mother, who had died after giving birth to Maxim. She'd apparently been a beautiful and intelligent woman. It was rumored Rasmus had loved her passionately, and after she died, he'd never been able to love again.

During the years Maxim had lived at the royal residence, I'd never witnessed Rasmus interact with

Maxim in any way other than to interrogate him on his studies or criticize him. And after Rasmus had sent Maxim away, he'd seemed almost relieved his son was gone.

I'd concluded Maxim reminded Rasmus too much of the woman he'd lost, and as a result, he never wanted to see his son again. I'd accepted that even if Maxim eventually returned to Vordinberg to attend the Studium Generale for Erudite training, Rasmus would make sure the young man stayed away from the royal court and castle.

Had my theories been wrong? Rasmus had almost seemed relieved that Maxim had ridden up to the tournament field earlier. Had he been awaiting Maxim's return after all?

"Forgive me, Your Highness." Rasmus tilted his head in obeisance. "My question was impertinent. You do not need one more person pestering you about whether you're developing feelings for any of the men."

I nodded but said nothing, never certain what to say or do around this wiseman. Sometimes his concerns seemed genuine. At other times, I sensed he was wise beyond anyone's good.

"A weeklong courtship isn't easy, Your Highness." His voice softened, and this time when he met my gaze, his eyes held empathy.

"The pressure, indeed, weighs heavy. What if I do not form a heart match by the final feast?"

"In sensing your plight, I have been scouring the laws and texts for another option."

"And have you found any?"

"I am close."

Tonight's ball was the grandest event of the week and would last well into the night. On the morrow, after everyone was sufficiently rested, the noblemen would engage in a hunting expedition to again prove their worth. On the final day, the day that marked my birth, we would have a feast to rival all feasts. Afterward, I would be expected to announce my choice. A betrothal ceremony would quickly follow, and then I would be crowned as the heir apparent.

I considered myself an intelligent woman. After all, I did have more education and learning than most men. But in this matter of selecting my husband, I was learning I was woefully inadequate.

The master of ceremonies beckoned to me from the other side of the staircase, my signal that the king and queen had finished their entrance and that my turn, my moment, had arrived.

An invisible hand clutched my heart as if to root me in place. In fact, it seemed to urge me to flee before I made a terrible mistake.

I briefly closed my eyes and pried the grip loose. I might not find a man I adored or a man who in turn adored me, but I would do my best to pick the nobleman who was worthiest for the task of becoming king.

If only I could know for certain which one that was.

With a final intake of breath, I started forward, making sure each step was measured just as the master of ceremonies had instructed. When I reached the top of the wide staircase, the grand hall spread out before me, crowded with guests clad in their finest attire, all silent and watching me expectantly.

The three trumpets sounded again. Then the herald

called out, "Her Royal Highness, Princess Elinor of the house of Oldenberg."

The guests clapped as I began my descent with meticulously timed steps. I was also careful to keep my hands at my side and my toes pointed forward as etiquette required.

The king and queen waited at the bottom, watching me with love radiating in their eyes.

I am doing this for them. I am doing this for them. I am doing this for them. If I repeated the declaration enough times, would I quell the doubts that had been plaguing me with increasing intensity in the days and weeks leading up to my eighteenth birthday?

Behind the king and queen, the honored noblemen stood in their finest garments, their eyes fixed upon me as well. I was scheduled to dance with each man once. For the final dance, I would be expected to honor one—and only one—of them with a second dance.

If only this process were simpler, easier.

"Those who aim at great deeds must also walk a difficult path." The words of the ancient philosopher flitted through my mind, one of the many wise sayings I'd memorized during my schooling—wise sayings both Maxim and I had learned together.

From my periphery, I glimpsed a tall, darkly handsome man. Maxim. Standing on the perimeter of the room. Unlike at the melee, this time he was watching me. How could he avoid doing so at this important occasion when I was the center of attention?

Instead of the black robes of those attending Studium Generale, he wore a fine suit with a tight-fitting doublet of blue—a blue that matched his eyes.

I'd always loved his eye color, which reminded me of the waters within a deep northern fjord. The surcoat over the top was a shade of brown, almost black, as were his leggings.

I wanted to turn my full attention upon Maxim and revel in the changes time had wrought. But since I meant so little to him that he hadn't taken a moment earlier in the day to greet me properly, I kept my focus upon the king and queen, unwilling to let Maxim think I harbored any interest in him.

With each step closer to the loving presence of the king and queen, the grasp that had been holding me back began to loosen. I even managed a smile at the two as I stepped from the last stair.

The queen wiped tears from her eyes, her smile filled with pride and joy. As was the custom at the coming-of-age balls with the mother bestowing upon her daughter a bangle, the queen unclasped the bangle she wore, studded with amethysts that matched the purple swan feathers of my dress. The queen wrapped the bracelet around my wrist, the symbol I was no longer a child but would take my place now in the world of adults.

She kissed first one of my cheeks then the other, her tears continuing to spill over.

Although not part of the instructions I'd been given by the master of ceremonies, I brought the queen's hand to my lips and kissed it, letting everyone know without a doubt that I loved her like a daughter.

At that moment, the other bangle on my upper arm—the one that had once belonged to my mother— squeezed my flesh. My guilt squeezed just as tightly that I'd hung on to the bangle all these years, had always secretly worn it. Inge didn't deserve my disloyalty, not after how unreservedly she'd accepted me as her child. If only I could bring resolution to all my questions about my long-lost mother and sister . . . Then maybe I could just as unreservedly accept the queen, the king, and my fate.

The king spoke the words everyone had been waiting for: "Let the dancing commence."

As I took my place at the center of the room with my first partner, I curved my lips up in the gracious smile expected of me, which I managed to hold in place with each new dance and each new partner. With so little time left in the courtship week, I did my best to elicit deeper conversation with the men, hoping some interest or commonality would arise to spark attraction within me.

But I was ashamed to admit—even to myself—that all the while dancing with the noblemen, my thoughts shifted to Maxim, especially whenever I caught a glimpse of his frame in my line of vision. He mingled among the courtiers who kept to the outer edges of the hall, drinking and eating but never joining in the dancing.

During one of the breaks between dances, I stood surrounded by the noblemen, talking with them and accepting their compliments. I didn't realize how close I was to Maxim until I glanced up to find him only a dozen feet away.

In the glow of the candles in the crystal chandeliers, his hair gleamed a blue-black. It was neatly combed and tied back with a leather strip, unlike earlier when he'd worn it free and wind-tossed. The style made him look older, more mature, reminding me again of all the missed years between us. Up closer, every one of his features was sharper, darker—and breathtaking.

As I took him in, it was almost as if he sensed my attention upon him. He shifted and looked directly at me, zeroing in as if I were the only one in the room.

For the space of several heartbeats, our eyes remained locked. His were full of the same admiration I'd seen in the eyes of the noblemen, acknowledging my fair beauty, womanliness, and grace. Of course, I had been told many times in my life what a pretty princess I was, and my suitors had lavished me with praise this week. If I'd been a vain maiden, the flattery might have turned my head. Instead, I'd always longed to be esteemed for my intelligence more than my beauty.

But now, at the glow of appreciation coming from Maxim—a glow that told me he saw me as a desirable woman—a shiver of pleasure whispered through me.

Perhaps he wasn't as oblivious to my presence as I had first assumed. He was interested, at the very least curious about me. What did he think of all the noblemen surrounding me and attempting to win my heart?

As though hearing my unasked question, he glanced at the men. Then before I could read the answer in his expression, he pivoted, turning his back upon me.

Heat flared in my chest. Maxim had just dismissed me. After all these years, could he not be bothered to give me a nod or a smile or even a small wave to acknowledge the friendship we'd once shared?

I returned my full attention to the men surrounding me, outwardly remaining composed while inwardly, mortification mingled with anger.

This was not the Maxim I had known and loved like a brother. This was someone entirely different, someone I didn't like, someone I had no wish to reacquaint myself with. His action had communicated quite clearly that he had no desire to be my friend any longer.

If that was how he felt, then I'd grant him his wish.

Chapter 3

MAXIM

DISLIKE PUNCTUATED EACH RAP OF MY KNUCKLES AGAINST Rasmus's door. I'd known this confrontation was coming from the second I received his summons to return to Vordinberg. I'd only hoped to have more time to mentally prepare myself after my arrival.

Instead, the moment the ball ended, a scribe had delivered the message that Rasmus was summoning me to visit him in his study.

Visit.

I swallowed the oath on the tip of my tongue and stood back from the door in the passageway to await his acknowledgment to enter.

We had never *visited*. A visit, by definition, involved a back-and-forth exchange of pleasantries and information. It contained a degree of conversation and getting to know one another more personally. None of that had ever happened during any of my so-called *visits* to Rasmus's study in the past.

At the sound of laughter and voices down the hallway,

I lifted my candle. No, I wasn't hoping for a chance encounter with Elinor. Certainly not. I was only checking to see who of the guests, if any, dared to venture into the wing of the royal castle that was dedicated to the Sages.

But as the echo of laughter faded, I shook my head. Why was I thinking of Elinor again? She wouldn't be wandering around the castle at this early hour of the morn. Her ladies-in-waiting had likely accompanied her back to her chambers and assisted her to bed. From what I'd gathered, she still had another day of festivities and spending time with her special noblemen as they fawned over her.

I released a scoffing breath as I'd done every time I pictured the way the men had positioned and maneuvered themselves during the dance, practically throwing themselves upon her, making fools over her every word and deed. It had been sickening to watch.

I'd never been more eager for an event to end. If I'd had to watch one more man dance with her, I would have vomited the little sustenance I'd managed to take in. The entire night had been nothing but an exercise in holding back the contents of my stomach.

"Wise men speak because they have something to say; fools because they have to say something." I'd repeated the Greek proverb many times throughout the evening to keep from speaking my mind about the entire process of finding a husband for the princess. It was nothing short of ridiculous.

To be fair, I'd sensed Elinor's discomfort with the attention. And I felt a little bit sorry for her. I'd been with her when our tutor informed her of the courtship tradition. I'd witnessed her tears and felt her fear as if it were my own. She obviously still retained her reservations.

I lifted my fist to knock again but then just as quickly dropped it to my side. I couldn't forget Rasmus loved to test a person's patience by making them wait an unnatural amount of time. The one incident as a child when I'd tired of waiting and departed, Rasmus had punished me by making me stand outside his door for twenty-four hours without respite.

I'd learned my lesson well. Rasmus always made sure I learned a lesson well.

Familiar bitterness burned in my throat.

The day I was sent away from Vordinberg, I'd prayed I'd never have to see him again. God had granted my request, and I hadn't seen him over the past ten years. But then, with only three months to go until my twentieth birthday, I'd received a missive from him.

At the time, I'd been finishing my Sagacite education, the first level of training to become a wiseman. I'd been at St. Andrew's Abbey in the city of Finnmark and had started studying for the entrance examination to the Studium Generale.

I'd ignored Rasmus's letter for two days before gathering the strength to open and read it. In his usual impersonal and haughty way, he ordered me to return to Vordinberg in time for the princess's eighteenth birthday celebration, well ahead of my scheduled arrival. I crumpled the letter, threw it against the wall, and let it gather dust under my bed for a week.

But my faithful manservant, Dag, had swept it out, unraveled it, and placed it on my writing table, where it had stared at me for another week. Dag hadn't needed to say a word. His action had been enough to remind me I had no choice but to obey a Royal Sage, especially when he had the power to keep me from being admitted to the

Studium Generale. If I didn't go to the studium, I'd never complete the education required for becoming an Erudite. And if I didn't reach the Erudite level of wiseman, I'd never have a chance of becoming a coveted Sage.

Though Rasmus's letter explicitly instructed me to arrive no later than seven days before Elinor's birthday, at the start of her courtship week, I'd delayed my departure to ensure that I would most definitely not reach Vordinberg on time. Among the many lessons from early in my life, I'd learned I might not be able to refuse Rasmus's commands, but I could thwart them in an underhanded manner.

I stared ahead at the familiar door, at the patterns I'd memorized in the oak panel. I'd even concocted a maze through the wood grain lines, starting at the top and ending at a knot somewhere in the middle.

"You may enter." Rasmus's voice was low and calm. He never spoke in a raised tone, though I'd been the brunt of his anger oft enough to know it existed deep within his heart and could be expressed innumerable ways other than yelling. The glint in his eyes when I arrived at the tournament earlier had warned me of the anger simmering beneath the surface for my tardiness.

As I opened the door to the dimly lit room, I rehearsed the excuses I'd formulated on the ship during the voyage from Finnmark to Vordinberg.

What punishment would he contrive this time? Would he make me memorize another ancient script, copy hundreds of pages of Holy Scriptures, or postulate theories for riddles that had no answers?

He sat in a cushioned chair at his writing table, several old scrolls open, the brittle parchment held in place by crystal paperweights. He was peering through an ocular lens at the fine print on the page before him.

"Your Excellency." I bowed my head but inwardly remained as straight as a pike. "Your scribe said you wished to see me."

"Shut the door and come closer."

Never a greeting, never a preamble, never any warmth. Maybe somewhere in my subconscious I'd hoped he would see me differently now that I was an adult. But I wasn't surprised he intended to treat me as poorly as he always had.

I did as he asked, but even when I moved to take my place in front of his writing table, he continued reading for several long minutes. Nothing about his appearance had changed, except for a few more lines in his face. Nothing about his study had changed either. It was as dark and melancholy as I remembered. The floor-to-ceiling shelves were still crammed with ancient relics along with stacks of scrolls and tomes. Even the scent of exotic spices remained heavy in the air from the incense pot he kept burning on a tall stand in the corner.

Finally, he placed the ocular lens directly over several markings on the paper—strange patterns of lines and dashes. Then he reclined, folded his hands, and shifted his dark eyes upon me. "I expected you to arrive five days ago."

"We experienced several storms that caused delays." It was the truth. We had faced storms off Norvegia's rugged western coastline. But the delays had been in hours, not days.

From the pinch of Rasmus's lips, I surmised he knew the truth, had likely already queried the ship's captain.

"When needling someone, do not yelp when they needle you back." Another line of ancient wisdom, the reminder

to live with whatever might come my way as a result of defying Rasmus.

He narrowed his eyes, and I could almost hear his mind at labor, coming up with a form of torture that would teach me he was in control, just as he'd always been.

The silence stretched once more, and my muscles tightened in preparation for his judgment.

"You are attracted to the Princess Elinor."

A current of surprise zinged through me. I opened my mouth to deny him but immediately closed it. In the same instant, I regretted my hesitancy.

By switching subjects so abruptly, Rasmus had purposefully thrown me off guard. It was a tactic used in conversation to gain insight into the truth of a matter, giving the other person little warning or time to come up with a false narrative.

My mind quickly sharpened, and I worked to compensate for my mistake. "Of course I'm attracted to the princess. What man wouldn't be? She has grown into a stunning woman."

Stunning didn't quite describe Elinor. The rumors that had reached all the way north to Finnmark hadn't exaggerated her beauty. She was exquisitely lovely. When I'd ridden in from the harbor and gained my first sight of her at the tournament field, my emotions had battled in a swordplay of their own. First, surprise and admiration for the beautiful young woman she'd become. Then, sadness for the loss of our friendship. Finally, resolve for what must be.

After all, it had taken years of trying to erase her from my memory, years until I'd stopped caring about and missing her. I wouldn't let the time and effort be for naught.

By the time I'd dismounted, I'd had the inner clash well under control. I'd put her from my mind, far away where she belonged.

But seeing her descending the staircase at the ball in her extraordinary gown had drawn every thought, every dream, every infatuation, and every desire for her out of captivity. The sharp pain in my chest had been too much to bear. I'd spun to leave only to find Rasmus across the grand hall watching my reaction intently. Apparently, he'd seen enough to understand just how conflicted I was.

Though I'd tried to keep out of his sight for the duration of the dance, 'twas possible he'd continued to surreptitiously watch me, scrutinizing my every weakness, looking for anything important to use as leverage against me.

Even now, his inspection was calculated, and I composed my expression into one of indifference.

"You still care about her, though you have tried not to." Rasmus spoke as if he'd read my thoughts.

It was another tactic, one of stating a fact with such assurance and authority that the other person believed his emotions and thoughts were entirely readable.

Though I'd only just completed the first phase of training to become a wiseman, I was already more learned than most of my teachers. I knew the best way to parry Rasmus's tactic was to counter with one. "You are all-seeing, Your Excellency. Thus, you surely can also see my *care* for the princess arises from the heart of a loyal subject and nothing more."

Pretending to believe in the other person's exaggerated skill, flattering them for it, and then playing upon the false skill—I could do this well.

His eyes narrowed. Did he realize I was capable of

joining in his games of the mind, that he could no longer easily back me into a corner?

He studied me a moment longer before picking up his ocular lens and dropping his attention back to the scroll.

Though I had no clock to count the passing of time, I'd learned to do so internally, organically by the pace of my breathing and the pulse of my heart. Long minutes dragged by as he scrutinized the text, until thirty, forty-five, and finally sixty ticked past.

If Rasmus thought to weary and frustrate me in order to weaken my instincts, he would learn I'd grown stronger, that I could wait for hours and remain just as alert.

Before the striking of the sixty-first minute of silence, he spoke without breaking his inspection of the parchment. "The Sword of the Magi. Tell me all you know about it."

Again, his change of subject would have caught someone else off his guard, but I was prepared, my mind quickly able to locate the information I'd stored there from the many facts I'd memorized about ancient relics—especially this one, which was kept in a special case at the Stavekirche of Vordinberg.

"The Sword of the Magi was a gift from the eastern wisemen who visited the Christ in Bethlehem. They anointed the sword with oil, bequeathing upon the weapon the power of Providence so that the bearer of the sword would not perish but have strength to defend himself against the unjust, the unfaithful, and the untruthful."

"What else?"

Was there more? I rapidly searched the archives within the recesses of my learning to uncover more information.

"Joseph used it to defend the Christ child against the Roman soldiers who were following Herod's orders to kill the babe."

"And?"

"When escaping Bethlehem, Joseph is believed to have taken it with him to Egypt and hidden it there. Later, pilgrims discovered the sword and returned it to the Holy Land. With the increasing turmoil and fighting in the Holy Land, eventually all the ancient relics were sent to various abbeys and monasteries for safekeeping. And the people of Norvegia were given the sacred task of protecting the sword."

Rasmus stood abruptly, the hem of his black robe pooling on the dusty floor and the wide sleeves falling over his hands. He crossed to the farthest shelf, next to an arched window with its shutter battened tight. Shadows shrouded him as he lifted an object from a center shelf, but enough light from my candle and the lone candle on his desk revealed a long slender case.

My pulse jolted forward. Did Rasmus have the Sword of the Magi here? If so, why had he taken it from inside the altar in the Stavekirche?

As he stepped down and turned, I forced myself to remain impassive. I couldn't afford to show any emotion, though excitement pulsed through me.

Rasmus crossed and held out the box draped in a velvet black cloth. "Open it."

Although no one had opened the case in my lifetime, I didn't hesitate. I relished the opportunity to try. I set aside my candle, then drew off the covering and let it drop to the floor to reveal a polished red cedar box. I touched the small gold clasp locking the lid to the base. The keyhole was tiny and intricate, and I obviously had no key.

My opening of the box was another test. Clearly, Rasmus wanted to gauge my ability to solve problems, perhaps even my worthiness to be trusted with an ancient relic—if what lay inside truly was the Sword of the Magi.

He was likely already timing me, no doubt having started the clock from the moment he'd uttered the command to open it.

I ransacked my mind for the most viable options for picking a tiny lock. What would work? A pin? The tip of a quill? A stiff piece of hay? No, picking a lock would be too easy. Any petty thief or curious historian would have done so by now, and the contents inside would no longer be there.

Instead, this case had been cleverly designed, the lock secretly hidden, and was more complicated than it appeared. In fact, I suspected that with so important an artifact, traps had been laid in the opening. Perhaps the lock was laced with a deadly poison.

I glided my fingers across the smooth top, searching for any depressions or lines that would indicate an opening. I did the same thing to the underside but found nothing. The wood itself was impenetrable, or someone would have hacked it open long ago.

Gingerly, I studied the three hinges at the back. The tiny gold pieces were scratched, a sign someone had attempted to get in by removing them. Again, as with the keyhole, the method was too easy.

Although I was tempted to move faster and prove to Rasmus my quick reasoning, sometimes haste could create more problems. As the old Norvegian proverb advised: *"Hasten slowly."*

The best strategy was to put myself in the mind of the person who had developed the case. What steps would he have taken to ensure the difficulty of getting inside? He would have eliminated the most obvious methods first and gone with a secret opening, one protected by a riddle or secret code.

I turned the box over and studied each of the ends. The place where the lip met the case was slightly bigger on one end. I slipped my fingernail into the slit, opening it enough to feel an engraving. I traced first one tiny picture and then another. Egyptian hieroglyphics. Randomly placed. Which meant I would not only need to remember the hieroglyphic alphabet I'd once learned, I also had to unravel the pattern and put the letters in the right order.

With only the tip of my finger, I tried to decipher each tiny engraving. Within seconds I had it figured out. There were four small letters: *g-a-i-m*. In my head, I rearranged the letters until I had the right word: *magi*.

With a prayer that I'd deciphered correctly, I tapped the *m*, the *a*, then the *g*. As I pressed against the *i*, something clicked, and the lid rose.

I'd done it. I'd solved the riddle for how to open the box.

I wanted to breathe out a sigh of relief that I hadn't failed, but doing so would only reveal weakness and uncertainty to Rasmus.

"Two minutes, eighteen seconds." Rasmus's voice contained no indication whether my time was poor, average, or excellent.

Did it matter what he thought? I didn't want to care, had tried to stop caring long ago. But I couldn't ignore the small prick of frustration at failing to earn his acceptance.

As the lid reached its pinnacle, wonder filled my chest. There, against a faded red cushion, was a silver sword. The pommel was round and studded with gemstones.

Shorter than the arming swords most knights and noblemen wore, this was more like a long knife: thicker, stouter, but no less sharp. The blade was engraved with an ancient language.

"Read what it says." Rasmus's command was casual, but I recognized it again for what it was: a test. And this time, I wouldn't be able to pass it.

"Your Excellency, I cannot pretend to know how to read this ancient language." I nodded at the scroll upon his desk. The tiny markings on the parchment matched the engravings on the sword. Now I understood what Rasmus had been studying. The right thing to do in this test was to defer to him and acknowledge his wisdom. "I cannot decipher the words, Your Excellency. But I am certain you can do so."

"You will learn the language and then read the engraving on the sword. By dawn."

Chapter 4

MAXIM

Dawn?

Rasmus was only giving me until dawn to learn an archaic language?

He began to lower the lid, allowing me no time to question his decision or my ability to complete the task. I was already fluent in four languages and knew at least a dozen more reasonably well. But was it possible to learn another in so short a time? How many hours did I have? Three? Maybe four at best?

Quickly, I studied each tiny mark on the sword, attempting to memorize them in the few remaining seconds. As the case closed, I knew Rasmus would expect me to translate without seeing the engraving again. His expectations had always been high. When I was but a boy, I'd rarely been able to accomplish the lofty goals he established for me.

But now? I'd show him I was beyond failure—that I could do everything I set my mind to, no matter how difficult it might be. In doing so, would I finally gain his respect?

He placed the cedar container on his writing table and rolled up the scroll he'd been studying. He tied a piece of soft twine around it, then handed it to me.

Even as I took it and retrieved my candle, I didn't move to depart. He hadn't dismissed me, and until he did, I had to remain rooted to my spot. Was there more he had to say? Or was he planning to have me stand for another hour to reduce the amount of time I had for learning the new language, making the task infinitely more difficult?

The true riddle was why Rasmus was showing me this ancient relic in the first place. What did it have to do with me? And my return to Vordinberg? It was becoming clearer by the minute that everything was intertwined.

"You must befriend her."

His words were so unexpected that I fumbled with my candle, tipping wax so that it dropped against my thumb and seared my flesh.

Thankfully, Rasmus had his back turned as he made his way to his writing desk and didn't witness my reaction. By the time he seated himself, I'd regained my composure.

I didn't need to ask who he was referring to. 'Twas clear we were talking about the princess again.

He unraveled another scroll. "You have behaved coldly toward her thus far." He paused in the unrolling, a sign that he expected me to respond.

"I am but a simple Sagacite. A man of my lowly position doesn't deserve, and certainly wouldn't assume, to have any contact with the princess."

"A simple Sagacite of a lowly position would not be invited to the princess's ball."

He was right. I scrambled to find another excuse. "I was invited because of the queen's fondness for me." I was aware I'd been like a son to the queen for many years. She'd favored me and given me privileges most children never had. Even last night, when we spoke briefly at the ball, she'd invited me to accompany her on the upcoming hunt.

Rasmus finished laying out the scroll, smoothing it gently into place before anchoring it with the crystal paperweights. The longer he dragged out the silence, the more my muscles tightened with dread.

This was why I'd crumpled his missive commanding my return. This was why I'd neglected it for so long. This was why I'd even considered sailing in the opposite direction, to St. Olaf's Abbey in the Frozen Wilds. Because I loathed every second of every minute I was with Rasmus.

I focused on the stub of my candle, not daring to look at him lest he see the loathing in my eyes and find a subtle means of punishing me.

"From now on, you must enamor her."

"Yes, Your Excellency." I would avoid her at all costs and thus have no occasion to worry about how I treated her.

"You will seek her out at every opportunity you have."

My respectful acquiescence stuck in my throat. Maybe he did have the capability of reading minds after all. While rumors abounded regarding Sages and magic, such a thing wasn't truly possible. Rasmus had perfected the art of reading faces and body language, and he'd clearly done so with me.

"Your task is to make her fall in love with you." His tone contained finality.

Make her fall in love? My rebuttal fell entirely away. I couldn't respond even if I'd wanted to. All I could do was stare at Rasmus. His cold eyes surveyed me in return, victory glinting in their dark depths. He'd gotten what he'd wanted. He'd turned me speechless.

"If you'd arrived on time, you would have had a week for the task. Now you have two days." He dropped his attention back to the scroll in front of him. "You may go."

Though I wanted to figure out something to say, some means of extricating myself from the situation, I had to leave while I could, before he changed his mind and came up with another reason to make me stand there longer.

I bowed my head. As I turned and crossed to the door, I waited for him to tell me he was mistaken, that he was merely testing me.

But only silence followed, even after I stepped into the corridor and closed the door behind me.

⤜✥⤏

I retired to my chambers, the same few rooms that had been mine when I'd lived in the royal residence early in my life. Tucked away in a corner of the wing belonging to the Royal Sages, it was a solitary place with sparse furnishings, unchanged from my boyhood, almost as if Rasmus had decided long ago that I would return and have need of my rooms again.

I would have preferred to lodge at the school or even an inn. But when I'd first arrived, I'd been given little choice in the matter. Now I knew why—because Rasmus wanted me to be close to the princess.

But what could come of such closeness? Of making the princess fall in love with me?

My silly childish dreams and aspirations toward the

princess had caused my misfortune to begin with, were why I'd been sent away. Now that I was back, I didn't want to get into trouble again. But it was possible Rasmus was endeavoring to do just that: disgrace me.

I tried not to think on Rasmus's strange commands regarding the princess while I memorized the intricate language on the scroll, which I soon realized was an early form of cuneiform. Even though I was already versed in Sumero-Akkadian cuneiform syllabary, I had to maintain my focus if I had any hope of learning the symbols and being able to read the script on the Sword of the Magi by the time day broke.

As dawn started to lighten the sky, I labored feverishly. Thankfully, I'd learned various methods for rapid memorization over the years and could quickly retain information. I pieced together the translation: *For a worthy king.*

I didn't have time to contemplate the meaning as I gathered up the scroll and headed out of my chamber into the tower stairway. With a sense of urgency prodding me to return to Rasmus's chamber, I descended the steps two and three at a time. A door swung open, and before I could halt, I collided with someone stepping into the stairwell.

The force of my body knocked the person—a woman—into the wall. My momentum propelled me against her, and I grabbed her arms to steady her.

"My apologies—" My words froze at the sight of startling green eyes—green the color of a moorland meadow, green that belonged to only one woman.

Hastily, I released her, backed up, and bowed my head. "Your Royal Highness. I didn't realize anyone else would be walking about. Please forgive me."

She said nothing. But even with my head bowed, I could feel her gaze upon me. What did she think of me? Especially after the way I'd avoided her thus far.

Rasmus had indicated my behavior was cold. If I was completely honest with myself, I knew he was right. I had been rude to her. For no reason other than my own self-protection. It wasn't her fault I'd always cared about her more than I should. Though I feared caring for her again, I couldn't punish her for my weakness.

Based on the friendship we'd once shared, at the very least, she deserved my kindness and respect for this reunion after so many years apart.

"Your Royal Highness, I—" Rasmus's commands also pressed to the front of my mind—the commands to enamor her, seek her out at every opportunity, and make her fall in love with me. "I beg you to forgive me for earlier, for not renewing our acquaintance more properly."

She remained silent.

I couldn't do as Rasmus ordered. Fostering such familiarity with the princess was out of the question, wasn't it?

Yet how could I refuse him? If I deviated even slightly from what he'd requested, he'd find many miniscule ways to make my life miserable. Not only that, but he'd likely obliterate my ambitions and carefully laid plans for the future.

The simple truth was that I needed Rasmus as my ally and not my enemy.

I lifted my head and cocked it to the side, making a show of studying her, as if I hadn't yet had the time or desire, although I'd had both. "When I left, you were but a child. You have grown and changed much."

She cocked her head—clearly imitating my move—and studied me in return. "Who has changed more, Maxim? You or I?" Neither her eyes nor voice held any warmth. Had I already ruined my chances at connecting with her? I would have to labor diligently to ingratiate myself with her.

But the very idea of ingratiating myself was both frustrating and humiliating. I had more important matters needing my attention than winning over the princess. And for what? What exactly did Rasmus intend to prove by thrusting me back into the princess's life? Did he hope to make the chosen noblemen jealous? Would they work harder at wooing her?

Her hair hung in unfettered waves over her shoulders, falling nearly to her waist. The glow from my candle highlighted the golden sheen, turning the waves to satin. Though her hair wasn't yet styled, she was already dressed for the day in a lovely gown cinched at her slender waist with a belt. The velvet bodice fit snuggly, outlining a womanly form that indeed showed her to be very much changed.

I let my lips curve into a slightly off-center grin. Over recent years, I'd perfected the smile—had learned I could wield my good looks like a chisel to mold maidens into doing my bidding. Not that I'd spent much time in the company of women. I'd only done so on occasion with my friends. However, I easily understood my power.

But here . . . now . . . I didn't seem to have any sway over the princess and didn't cause her to smile back. If anything, her beautiful eyes turned colder.

"Who has changed more?" I repeated her question lightly but with a touch of flirtation. "We have not been reacquainted more than a few minutes, and you're already giving me a riddle to solve?"

"'Tis no riddle." Her chin jutted, lending her an imperial look, reminding me she would someday be queen of Norvegia and my sovereign.

One thing was becoming abundantly clear. I had offended her with my lack of warmth earlier. And now she was angry with me.

"I have changed more." I dropped my tone and infused it with contrition. "I've been away from court life too long and have become as uncouth as a boar."

Her fingers clutched at her skirt, and she remained pressed to the wall. Where were her ladies? Her guards? She oughtn't be out of her chambers alone lest trouble befall her. She might collide with a ruffian who would think nothing of causing her ill will.

Perhaps I had become a ruffian now that I was at Rasmus's beckoning. Was I the one who would ultimately bring her ill will? I loathed the thought. I couldn't— wouldn't—harm her. Never.

I glanced up and then down the stairwell. As far as I could tell, we were still alone. Did I dare tell her the truth, that I was afraid to resume a friendship with her, that losing her once had been unbearable and I couldn't go through such pain again?

And what about telling her the truth about Rasmus's strange command to spend time with her and win her love? Did I dare mention it?

The young boy I'd once been would have confided everything. But I was no longer so naïve. *"The path is made by walking"* as the old saying went. Even though my journey had been difficult, I'd grown more careful with each step, learning that trust was not so easily earned.

The memory of the morn of my departure ten years

ago shifted to the front of my mind. I'd stepped into the schoolroom I shared with Elinor, a solar in the private royal chambers. A cozy room filled with all variety of books—geography, science, mathematics, history, languages, logic, politics, and more. Maps and charts were tacked to the walls. Three-dimensional models of the solar system, a skeleton of the human body, jars of dried insects, and so much more filled the room, supplying Elinor and me with much delight during the hours we spent learning and experimenting and soaking in knowledge.

The queen had allowed us to enjoy an infinite amount of time there—or so it had seemed to my young mind. She'd enlisted the best Sages from the Studium Generale to tutor the princess and had included me in the education. We'd shared nearly every waking moment, had been inseparable.

But when I arrived for our usual lessons that particular day, Elinor was absent. In her place at our table sat the king. Rasmus stood a short distance behind him, his countenance severe.

I braced myself against the closed door, ready to flee.

"Come, sit, Maxim." The king patted the spot beside him, the chair Elinor always occupied.

I hesitated, but one sharp nod from Rasmus was enough to prod me forward. I crossed the chamber and sat. I'd only spoken directly to the king a few times, had never been as close to him as I was to the queen, so I tried not to tremble as I waited for him to inform me why he was there.

He regarded me a moment, almost sadly. And I couldn't keep from thinking that he might be wishing he had his own son instead of a substitute like me. "You know the queen loves you dearly?"

"Yes, Your Majesty." My words were barely above a whisper.

"You have been good medicine for her these many years."

I didn't understand how I could be medicine for the queen when she wasn't sick. I nodded anyway.

"This arrangement with Elinor"—the king waved around at the solar—"it has come to our attention you may have gained aspirations that go beyond your role as Elinor's companion."

I didn't know what *aspirations* were, but I shook my head, knowing it couldn't be good.

The king shared a serious look with Rasmus, who cleared his throat before he spoke. "You told Elinor you would marry her when you grow up."

My mouth dropped open. How had the king and Rasmus learned of my declaration? A declaration I'd spoken privately yesterday when we'd been studying the history of the royal family and memorizing the names of the previous kings and queens. She'd grown distressed after the tutor informed her of the weeklong courtship tradition that would take place before her eighteenth birthday.

When the tutor stepped into the hallway a moment later to request more ink, I'd reassured her she had nothing to worry about, that I'd marry her, that surely the Royal Sages would approve of me.

Had Elinor told the king of my offer? 'Twas the only logical explanation.

"You do know, Maxim," the king said slowly, "you can never marry Elinor?"

I looked again to Rasmus for direction. Once again, he

nodded, confirming the king's words—that I would never be able to save Elinor from the anxiety of courting unknown suitors.

"Elinor must marry a Norvegian of royal or noble blood." The king's tone turned more forceful. "The laws prohibit royalty from marrying commoners."

"Yes, Your Majesty." Some part of me had acknowledged I was a commoner even though I lived among royalty. Rasmus had never discussed my origins other than to tell me he was a chieftain's son and my mother had been a merchant's daughter. I also knew Rasmus had an older brother with several children—cousins I'd never met.

The king folded his hands on the table over an intricate drawing Elinor had sketched of the various parts of a flower. I wanted to scoot the drawing away before the king smudged it. But I remained still and silent, somehow sensing the worst of the conversation was yet to come.

"Your father and I both agree you are growing too old to remain as Elinor's companion."

I couldn't keep from glancing around the beloved classroom where I'd spent many happy hours, days, and years. Would Elinor and I have separate rooms now? Different tutors?

"Though you are yet young, this arrangement, if continued, may contribute to fostering false ideas and feelings between you and Elinor."

"Yes, Your Majesty." Though I'd spoken the words already, I knew of no other acceptable reply.

"Very good. I'm glad you understand." The king stood, and I did too, as the rules of conduct demanded.

With Elinor's absence, perhaps my schooling would

take place earlier than hers henceforth. I would miss studying together, but we would surely have time later in the day, after our tutors dismissed us, for discussing and debating all we learned separately.

The king started toward the door. "Your father has made arrangements for you to leave this morn."

My heartbeat crashed to a halt. "Leave, Your Majesty?" I lurched after him, but Rasmus snagged my cloak and pulled me back. I knew better than to struggle.

"Yes." The king paused at the door but didn't look back at me. "You may say farewell to the queen, but you must refrain from further interaction with the princess."

Two hours later, I'd been aboard a ship and sailing away from Vordinberg. I hadn't been back since.

Now, in the stairwell, the princess pushed herself away from the wall. "Since your identity is clear, I shall be on my way."

"My identity?"

"Yes, that you are an uncouth boar." Straightening her shoulders, she slipped past me and started up the stairs.

I shifted the scroll in my hand. Rasmus would be expecting me by now. I couldn't delay any longer. Even so, I watched her for several steps. "Should you not have attendants, Your Highness?"

She paused, her back rigid. "How long have you been back in Vordinberg, Maxim?"

I rapidly calculated the passing of time. "Eighteen hours and twenty-three minutes." I hoped she would appreciate my preciseness, reminiscent of the way we'd always measured time.

"Of that eighteen hours and twenty-three minutes, you have spent less than one minute with me. Such an ambitious amount of time does not qualify you to speak as my Sage." With that, she continued on her way, her footsteps light, almost as if she was barefoot.

Was she barefoot?

She disappeared around the spiral before I could ascertain the state of her feet. But I suddenly didn't have to see to know what she was doing. She'd maintained our tradition these many years of sneaking up to this particular turret with an unobstructed view of the eastern horizon. We'd done so at dawn on clear mornings to calculate the exact time of sunrise, always removing our shoes so no one would hear us. Somehow, the queen had figured out our adventure—at least, I'd assumed that was why the princess's faithful guard Halvard had watched us from a distance and kept himself hidden.

Impetuously, I unlaced my boots, extinguished my candle, and followed the princess. When I reached the top, she was already outside on the top of the turret, the door wide open and letting in the chilled autumn air.

Though dawn illuminated her outline, I couldn't see her expression. And I wanted more than anything to see the wonder in her face and eyes as she glimpsed the first arc of the rising sun.

I took a deep breath and started through the door only to feel the bite of a knife in my back. A glimpse into the shadows of the tower behind me told me Elinor wasn't alone after all.

"Nary one disturbs the princess if he values his life." The gruff whisper belonged to Halvard, her burly, gray-haired guard. Though I couldn't see his face, I glimpsed the long beard he'd always had.

"'Tis I, Maxim." I held myself motionless. "You remember me, do you not?"

"Aye." Halvard didn't remove his knife. "But the

princess told me not to let you disturb her."

She'd expected me to follow her? And she'd instructed Halvard not to allow me onto the turret? The news should have discouraged me, but for a reason I couldn't explain, I was all the more interested in finding a way to see her again.

"Very well." I let my gaze linger upon her one last moment before I turned from the guard and started down, my steps light, my pulse tapping with eagerness.

Perhaps following Rasmus's order to spend time with Elinor wouldn't be as much of a chore as I'd believed. In fact, I might even enjoy it.

The trouble was getting her to enjoy it too.

Chapter 5

Elinor

After resolving to keep my distance from Maxim, why did I have to meet him in the stairwell, of all places?

I watched the horizon, the pale light creeping up from beyond the distant fields. I added several numbers to the list on the open page of my leather-bound journal, then focused on the angle of the sun against the earth.

Normally I found beauty and peace in my early morning venture to watch the sunrise. But today, only turmoil swirled through me, and my thoughts kept returning to my encounter with Maxim.

I was surprised he'd spoken to me at all. After he'd ignored me thus far, I'd only expected more of his coldness not less. I'd believed he would pass by with a quick nod but nothing more.

Perhaps in seeing me alone, he felt more freedom to speak and interact with me. Perhaps he knew how rude he would be if he said nothing at all. Or perhaps without anyone else around to judge his interaction, he was more comfortable acknowledging the relationship we once had.

"Stop making excuses for him." My frustrated whisper rose into the air only to be snatched away by the breeze.

I'd made excuses for Maxim for years, telling myself there were valid reasons why he'd left Vordinberg and the royal residence without saying goodbye. And surely he had valid excuses for why he'd never written to me—likely, he'd been too busy with his traveling and studying and the many adventures he was having.

Making excuses was easier than admitting he'd never cared enough about me.

Was it time to accept that Maxim and I had been childhood friends and nothing more? That we'd shared a short portion of our lives together, but that was all I could expect? That I'd placed more confidence in our friendship than he had?

If only my treacherous heart would stop admiring him. Even harried and tired with disheveled hair, he was a handsome man to behold, and the collision with him had robbed me of breath. Especially when his hands folded around my arms to steady me. The contact left me entirely too aware of the strength and energy coursing through his body.

With a sigh, I lifted my face to the sky, taking in the last of the stars and the half-moon that hung low and shone brightly over Vordinberg along the harbor. The distant calls were the signs that the city was stretching into wakefulness. 'Twould not be long before the fishing crews put out to sea and the busy capital was fully roused.

The fishing industry kept the country well supplied with the dozen or more varieties of fish that flourished off Norvegia's long coastline. Many small towns and villages thrived with the business of salting and drying the fish. To the north, in the Golden Plateau and Frozen Wilds, the chieftains provided seal and whale meat for consumption.

I turned my attention again to the east, to the lowland fields ripe for harvest, the grains waving in the sea draft as if to welcome the sun. Like the fishermen, the tenant farmers and their laborers would soon head out for the day to cut and bundle the oats and barley that the people of Norvegia and the livestock needed to survive the bitter-cold winter months ahead.

Even with the storing away of food and supplies, the winters could often be difficult for Norvegia, and as much as my encounters with Maxim were unnerving and distracting, I needed to remember what was truly important—choosing a worthy husband, one who would feel as strongly as I did about protecting and providing for this land and the people.

I wanted to live by the old saying: "He who is not a good servant will not be a good master." To be a worthwhile queen, first I had to be a worthwhile servant of the people.

But what if I selected a man who didn't have the same philosophy, one who took the power away from me and ruled as a tyrant in my stead?

With all my education thus far, I considered myself a good judge of character. But I didn't have the depth of training that Erudites and Sages had in understanding the inner workings of a person's mind. The Erudites had at least ten years of schooling and the

Sages ten more.

Few women ever accomplished such a feat. I'd read about only two or three accounts in the early history of our country. Some women with education became healers, although they were oft shunned, and I knew of only one ancient healer woman who lived in the Snowden Mountains.

And then there was my mother, Blanche. . . . She'd been studying to become an Erudite when she disappeared. I'd always hoped I could follow in her steps.

"Halvard?"

He shuffled inside the stairwell near the door but didn't come out. "Aye, Your Highness?"

"Tell me something about Blanche."

"Well now. Let's see." Halvard had been one of the palace guards when my mother lived in the royal residence long ago. He was the only one I ever asked about her. Everything I knew about her was because of him.

"She had a heart match with your father, that's for sure."

I smiled. Halvard had already shared as much. In actuality, he'd shared every detail he knew many times over. But I asked oft anyway.

"The Princess Blanche adored her husband," Halvard continued. "And he—well, he loved the princess more than life itself."

A heart match in Norvegia was considered important, especially among the royalty, because the Sages had determined that marriages based on mutual love and respect tended to bring more stability and peace within the kingdom and cause less conflict.

After a disastrous arranged union several decades ago, a Norwegian princess ran away and found refuge with a prince in Swaine. King Canute's grandmother was that princess, and now he was making the claim he had more right to the Norvegian throne than I did. Of course, the Sages asserted that as a niece, I had more right to the throne than a distant cousin.

"If Blanche were here, Your Highness," Halvard said, "she'd want you to find a man just like your father. Someone who loves you more than life."

I swallowed the lump in my throat. "Thank you, Halvard."

If only such a heart match were possible. Maybe I could petition for more time to make my decision. From studying the history of the royal lineage, I knew extensions had been given on rare occasions. But in my case, with King Canute's proposal of marriage and his threats hovering, I couldn't prolong the courtship week. I couldn't let my insecurities or anything else prevent me from doing my duty.

Maxim's handsome face flashed before my mind. Just as soon as it did, I tossed it into the breeze, praying the wind would carry it far away. Thinking on him wouldn't help matters. I couldn't allow myself to feel any attraction to him—not even the slightest twinge—lest it undermine how I felt about any of the twelve noblemen.

As the circumference of the sun rose above the horizon, I jotted a final note into my journal, tucked the lead between the pages to mark my spot, then slipped the book through the layers of my skirt into my pocket.

I'd faithfully kept detailed records of the sunrise for

years, always looking for patterns among my notes so I might understand the movement of the celestial body more accurately. I'd done it to learn, to investigate, and to make advances in the study of weather patterns that could affect our crops. I certainly hadn't done it to hang on to memories of Maxim.

The orb rose higher, its blooming pink and lavender petals unfolding. The first rays finally touched upon the slate rooftops of the tall homes painted in bright red, blue, and yellow that crowded together on the hillsides along the sea.

Moments later, the first rays spilled through the arrow slit of the crenellation. I glanced behind me to find the light forming a cross on the bricks, just as it had since the first day I'd come to the top with Maxim.

As had become my custom, I lowered myself to my knees, bowed my head, and lifted my prayers. I needed the guidance of Providence now more than ever.

"Please help me to find the man who is worthiest to become king."

Maxim

Rasmus made me stand outside his door one hour for each of the minutes I was late. By the time he issued his command to come into his study, four hours had elapsed.

The room was as dark and smoky as it had been before, the shutters always closed to keep out the light of day. Rasmus sat at his desk where I'd left him.

Did he ever sleep? If so, when?

I'd wondered the same thing as a boy and had never been able to discover anything about his personal habits. I'd concluded he had none.

He made me stand for five minutes before acknowledging my presence. "Well?"

"There is no excuse for tardiness. But I hope you will take consolation in knowing I was late because I encountered Princess Elinor, and I did as you requested. I interacted with her warmly."

I stood next to his writing desk and felt a strange unraveling inside. I'd spent years with the help of my mentors along with my manservant, Dag, weaving strong threads through the fibers of my being and working out all the weak ones left behind from Rasmus stretching them thin.

Would I now be undone by a few simple confrontations with him?

I closed my eyes briefly. Exhaustion was weakening me. I had no doubt that was Rasmus's intent—to lower my defenses even further, to make me susceptible to his manipulation, to stain me with his influence.

No, I couldn't let that happen. I had to stay strong and prevent him from twisting and knotting everything inside me.

Rasmus flicked a glance my way, as though warning me not to resist his efforts. "I would hardly call your interaction in the stairwell with the princess a worthwhile effort. Surely you have more charm and wit than what you used?"

Did Rasmus have spies everywhere? How could I forget his intrusiveness and how he made it his goal to be all-knowing? At the very least, he was making sure I was aware he was keeping a close watch over my efforts to enamor Elinor.

"It was but a chance meeting. I shall do better next time."

"You must. Your task is to keep her from gaining feelings for Torvald or any of the others."

This, then, was his purpose for me and why he'd wanted me to return earlier in the week. So that he might have more time to prevent the princess from falling in love with one of the noblemen. But why? As one of the seven Royal Sages, he'd played a significant role in picking the men for the courtship. Why did he not want the princess to marry any of them? Surely he'd placed his favorite among the dozen, someone he would support, someone he wanted to be king.

Rasmus tapped the red cedar box that still sat on his writing table where he'd left it. "I trust after diligent studying, you are now able to read the engraving on the Sword of the Magi?"

"'For a worthy King.'" The Christ child was indeed a worthy King. But I suspected the engraving held multiple meanings, as many symbols and prophecies did.

"I have studied the writings of the eastern magi extensively." Rasmus nodded at several more scrolls on the floor beside his writing table. "Tell me any other details you know of the prophecy regarding the sword."

I'd already quoted to Rasmus everything I knew about the Sword of the Magi, but I mentally flipped through the pages of my mind, searching for an obscure fact about the sword I hadn't yet spoken. "The sword has only been used once by a Norwegian king, Stefan the Worthy."

"Yes, King Ulrik's great-great-grandfather, the first of the house of Oldenberg."

I didn't know Rasmus's destination with the discussion, but he never spoke idly.

He shifted his ocular lens to the middle of the parchment on his desk, more of the ancient cuneiform writing that matched what was on the sword. Was he highlighting it and expecting me to read it? To prove I had indeed learned the entirety of the language and not just enough to read what was on the sword?

I centered on the writing and rapidly read the section under the ocular lens. "'When the sword is secured, only the man worthy to be king will be able to pull it free.'"

Rasmus said nothing.

I studied the long cedar case on the writing table. Did the cryptic words mean the sword was somehow permanently affixed to the case and unable to be taken out except by a man worthy to be king?

"What makes a man worthy?" I asked, not caring any longer if I showed my ignorance.

"The sword decides upon the worthiest, breaking free for the man of its choosing."

"And that's what happened with King Stefan long ago?"

"When he touched the sword, it came loose in his grip. In doing so, no one could contest his right to the throne."

More likely, since the unraveling of a riddle had opened the case, another riddle must be solved to free the sword from its resting place. But if Rasmus wanted to perpetuate a mystical power behind the freeing of the sword, who was I to contradict him?

The real question was, why was Rasmus showing this to me?

My mind leapt easily to the conclusion. "So, you would have me foil the princess's attempt to develop affection with one of the noblemen so that the sword can be used to determine her husband, the next king?"

I didn't need his answer to know I'd guessed the truth of his scheme and my part in it. In fact, I suspected I'd likely only touched upon the surface, that the intricacies of his plans went much deeper than he would reveal.

I couldn't go along with him, could I? It was the same question that had plagued me earlier, except now he was pulling me further into his scheming.

"The princess is already having difficulty deciding who will make the best king." As always, Rasmus spoke as though he could hear my thoughts. "She will gladly embrace another method that ensures only the worthiest man will rule by her side—a method no one can refute."

Worthiest? Was I wrong to think a riddle could separate the sword from the case? Was there a deeper blessing in the sword, one God himself would honor with the right man? The legends—and the ancient cuneiform writing—attested to the power. But how could a sword— a piece of metal—have the ability to both know and choose?

"The sword will determine the one worthiest to be the next king." Rasmus spoke with a certainty I didn't feel. "And no one will be able to argue against it."

"Even so, the king won't take kindly to my interference in the princess's courtship process." Did I need to remind Rasmus of why I'd been forced to leave Vordinberg? All it had taken was one innocent declaration by a boy too young to understand the implications of his words. This time, if the king suspected I had even the slightest of aspirations toward Elinor, he'd ban me from Norvegia altogether.

Rasmus dismissed me with a wave of his hand. "You need not worry about the king. He'll do as I bid him to."

As I left, one thought troubled me above all: Why did

the king trust Rasmus? No doubt Rasmus had made himself indispensable to the king, encouraged him in the belief that he would be crippled without the Royal Sage's advice and wisdom.

Sadly, I didn't see the king doing well if he continued to place his trust in Rasmus. In fact, I feared it would only lead to his demise.

Chapter 6

Maxim

"I am glad we can make up for lost time, Maxim." The queen patted my hand as we reclined on cushions under one of several canopies the servants had erected on the open hilltop. Surrounded by a thick forest against the backdrop of the Snowden Mountains, the area allowed for a stunning view while we rested.

Even though I'd forced my body to relax, my mind was still hard at labor. "I pray my many tales haven't been tedious, Your Majesty."

"Of course not. I have loved hearing every detail of your life from these past years." Attired in a practical riding gown, the queen radiated youth and health, her lovely features aglow with her delight in spending time with me.

I did not have to conjure any affection for the dear queen. I had enjoyed passing the afternoon with her too. The only difficult part was that it served to remind me of the motherly tenderness and care I'd lost after leaving Vordinberg. Although I'd missed her greatly in those early days—nearly as much as Elinor—I'd soon realized I wasn't the only boy who'd severed motherly ties. The other Sagacites had also said farewell to families to pursue their education. It was the way of things.

A servant bent to refill the queen's goblet with a spicy apple cider. She held up her hand and refused. When the servant tipped the leather jug toward my goblet, I accepted. I was in no hurry to bring my time with the queen to an end. In fact, I needed an excuse to linger longer under the canopy.

I had quickly realized the advantages of spending the day with the queen. First, it had appeased the king. He hadn't needed to entertain his wife, since I was keeping her well-occupied. If he remembered my long-ago transgression in offering to marry Elinor, he no longer seemed concerned about it. The few times he'd spoken to me, he'd been pleasant.

Not only had the afternoon as the queen's companion smoothed over my past transgressions with the king, but it served to bait Elinor.

During the ride out of the city into the hills, the princess had stayed busy mingling with the noblemen and watching them chase after prey. But throughout the hunt, I'd caught her looking my direction and showing more interest in my interactions with the queen.

When eventually the noblemen had finished the competition and Sigfrid had been declared the winner for bringing down the biggest prey, a reindeer, everyone had gathered on the hilltop clearing for refreshments while the prize buck was roasted over an open fire pit.

I'd spent the entirety with the queen. Now, if my calculations were correct, Elinor would join us erelong. She'd made her way closer and was only a dozen paces away, vibrant in a blue riding dress that once again highlighted what a beautiful woman she'd become.

I tried to maintain a balance of interest in her, glancing at her once in a while. I didn't want her to think I was being cold, since I was already guilty on that account. Yet I didn't want to appear too eager. With how eager the other men were, I'd never stand out and win her attention if I behaved as they did.

The king and half a dozen of his closest courtiers were reclining on cushions in another pavilion across the fire pit with several of the queen's ladies. I was glad she'd given them permission to leave her, allowing us more privacy.

From the serious expressions of the king and his men, I gathered they were conversing about Ice Men from Swaine crossing over the border and attacking Norvegian communities and farmers. The news had arrived just that morn from a courier who had escaped slaughter.

The vicious warriors had long past earned the nickname Ice Men for living in the icy heights of the Snowden Mountain Range. Norvegia had a long history of combatting the rugged fighters. Surely the aggression this time had come at the behest of King Canute in retaliation for the rejection of his proposal of marriage.

King Ulrik had been in meetings before leaving on the hunt, first with Rasmus and the other Royal Sages. He'd also convened with the Knights of Brethren, and during the hunt, he'd spoken to Sir Ansgar Nordheim on occasion.

Ansgar had gained renown four years ago when the Ice Men had attacked farms and towns in the moors and plateau. During the months of defending the land, he almost single-handedly put an end to the invasions. He became popular for his valor and fierceness in battle as well as his compassion and loyalty. When he also saved the king from an attack, he won the king's favor.

His rise to leadership as Grand Marshal had caused dissent among the older Knights of Brethren, so much so that two had schemed against Sir Ansgar. Rasmus had uncovered the plot, and the king had sent the two knights to their homes in disgrace.

The scent of roasting venison filled the air, and my stomach gurgled with hunger.

Upon hearing it, the queen pushed a platter toward me. "Eat more, Maxim." The abundance of the Norwegian harvest was on display with grapes, apples, plums, and pears along with several types of cheese including the brown goat cheese Norwegian farmers produced in abundance.

"Thank you, Your Majesty." I plucked a ripe pear. As I sank my teeth into the sweet fruit, from the corner of my eye, I could see Kristoffer speaking with Elinor. I'd learned that he, along with Torvald and Sigfrid, were three Knights of Brethren who had been chosen to participate in the courtship.

Kristoffer was a decent-looking man of wealth and influence. While I didn't know much about him or any of the other king's knights, I did know that as firstborns they would inherit their families' estates and titles. They had much more to offer the princess than most men.

After watching the Knights of Brethren most of the afternoon, including those who weren't a part of the weeklong competition, I had no doubt they were everything a knight should be: strong, brave, honorable, dependable, kindhearted, chivalrous, and more. They were about as perfect as a man could get. Truthfully, they were so perfect I'd found myself irritated at the fact, mostly because I wasn't half as good.

So far, the princess hadn't found a heart match with any of the chosen noblemen. While she seemed to be making a good effort, her strained attention, stilted smiles, and short conversations made clear that none had yet captivated her. Rasmus need not have brought me to Vordinberg to thwart the courtship. The princess was doing that well enough for herself. But why?

I'd pondered the perplexing problem since we stopped to rest. Yet I hadn't come to any conclusion other than forming the hypothesis that Elinor had a secret love interest elsewhere, a man who had already captured her heart.

"So, Maxim." The queen studied my face. "You have not yet spoken of whether a young maiden has caught your attention. In all your traveling, surely you have met many women."

At the queen's question, Elinor tilted her head our direction. Though the noblemen swarmed around her, talking to one another and vying for her attention, could she hear our conversation from where she stood? What if she'd purposefully positioned herself nearby so she could listen?

"You're right, Your Majesty. I have met many women." Did I dare fabricate a story to make Elinor more curious? As soon as the thought came, I put it from my mind. With Rasmus pressuring me to help him foil Elinor's interest in the noblemen, I was already having to be more deceptive than I would like. I couldn't add more guilt to my conscience.

Nevertheless, I took heart that her interest in me was growing. How much longer before she came and sat down? One minute? Two?

"I admit," I continued, "I haven't yet found anyone special."

The queen reached over and patted my hand. "One so kind and wise and handsome as you, Maxim, will surely find your heart match in due time."

Truthfully, I had not thought about taking a wife. Perhaps in seeing how my mother's death had so affected Rasmus, I'd resolved subconsciously not to have my heart broken the way he had.

"Good afternoon, Your Majesty." Elinor ducked under the canopy, leaving Kristoffer behind but bringing Torvald with her. "I trust you have enjoyed the hunt along with the refreshments."

Less than a minute. Apparently, Elinor's interest in my relational status matched that of the queen.

The queen scooted over and motioned to the cushion beside her. "Please join us, Elinor. Torvald. We are having a delightful afternoon."

"You are radiant with happiness, Your Majesty." Elinor smiled at the queen. "I have not seen you this happy in a very long time."

Until now, I'd yet to see Elinor smile, and the sight of her lips curving up did something strange to my chest. A tightening, as if I didn't have quite enough air in my lungs. She was already lovely today, her cheeks flushed from the fresh air, her eyes bright, and her hair kissed by the sun. Now, her smile made her more beautiful, if that was even possible.

The perfect gentleman, Torvald assisted Elinor to her cushion before he lowered himself to the place beside her. Again, I worked at trying to have balance in my expression, one of welcoming Elinor and one of mild indifference.

The tactic seemed to have been effective so far, and now if I displayed too much enthusiasm, she would surely see through my duplicitous behavior. I couldn't forget just how brilliant Elinor was and that she noticed and understood things on a deeper level than most people.

"Maxim, this is Lord Torvald Wahlburg." The queen gestured toward the nobleman.

The solidly built giant-of-a-man nodded at me, but the movement was perfunctory. One did not have to be an expert in body language and facial expressions to realize Torvald was reluctant to be here, clearly had no aspiration to be king.

"Maxim is the son of His Excellency Rasmus," the queen said. "After many years away, he has returned to Vordinberg to finish his training to become a wiseman."

I nodded at Torvald. "My lord, you are indeed a skilled hunter. I was surprised when your prey slipped away."

Perhaps no one else had noticed, but I'd realized at once that Torvald had purposely slowed down and lost the challenge today.

"'Twas unfortunate." Elinor slid a narrowed look at Torvald, one that led me to believe she was also aware he'd foiled his hunt.

A servant approached with goblets for both Elinor and Torvald, and for several moments the queen chatted with Elinor about the afternoon's events while Torvald and I sipped our cider and ate in silence.

Elinor finally glanced at me. "Maxim, since you are still interested in riddles, I implore you to tell us one about hunting." Although her tone was friendly, her eyes contained something sharp. She was obviously referring to our meeting that morn in the tower stairwell, when I'd accused her of giving me a riddle.

"Very well, Your Highness." I didn't quite know what she was up to, but I had no choice but to indulge her whim. I paused and reviewed the various riddles I'd learned since leaving Vordinberg, wanting to give her one she didn't know while likewise offering one easy enough for the queen to solve.

The queen sat up straighter, her eyes brightening. "The two of you always did enjoy challenging each other with riddles."

At the innocent comment, Torvald's gaze bounced between the princess and me as though he was attempting to sort out our connection.

"We were once like siblings until Maxim left." Elinor offered the explanation for Torvald, but her sharp gaze never left my face.

Maybe she wasn't merely upset at me for my aloofness upon my arrival. Maybe her anger went deeper, to my leaving of Vordinberg. However, if anyone should be angry, it should be me. She'd betrayed me by telling the king or queen about my comment to marry her, and I'd been the one sent away.

Regardless, I had to continue my charade. Even though Rasmus wasn't along on the trip, I hadn't figured out yet who he was paying to give him information. He likely had numerous servants doing his bidding, which meant he had eyes and ears everywhere.

"If a hundred birds are sitting in a tree," I began the riddle, "and a hunter comes along and shoots his arrow at one, how many are left in the tree?"

"It cannot be ninety-nine," the queen answered. "That would be far too easy."

"You're correct. It isn't ninety-nine."

From the quirk of Elinor's brow, I could tell she knew

the answer. I'd seen the quirk many times in the past and almost smiled at the familiar sight. I gave her a cautioning shake of my head, and she simply lifted her chin in response, understanding that this riddle was meant for the queen.

"What say you, Torvald?" Elinor turned to the nobleman, studying him, clearly trying to will herself into being attracted to the man. "Have you an answer to the riddle?"

Torvald ran his finger around the rim of his goblet as though contemplating his response. No doubt the princess was testing the man's wit and intelligence, both of which would be important qualities for a woman of her mental acumen.

"I believe how many birds remain depends upon the skill of the hunter." Torvald spoke slowly, possibly sensing how important a well-thought-out answer was to the princess. "For example, a skilled archer like Sigfrid would no doubt kill two birds with one arrow."

"Very keen." Elinor's compliment contained warmth and sincerity—qualities she'd once directed toward me. "I like your answer, Torvald."

The burly knight glanced to where his fellow Knight of Brethren Sigfrid had joined Kristoffer standing beside the fire pit, awaiting a portion of the roasting venison. If either was upset Torvald had taken the place of honor with the princess, they hadn't shown it. 'Twas clear the three were close and highly respected each other.

"And what is your answer, Your Highness?" Torvald asked politely. "How many birds do you think are left in the tree?"

"Yes," the queen echoed. "Tell us your answer, Elinor."

"Very well." Elinor folded her hands in her lap, likely to

keep from waving them dismissively as she'd always done when something was too easy for her. "If one bird was shot from a tree, none would be left. The single arrow, whether it killed one or two or more, would have scared all the birds off their perch."

"You are correct, Your Highness." I gave her what I hoped was a look of affirmation, but again I sensed she could see past my pretense to the truth, to my soul laid bare. How was it Elinor could see me for who I truly was even after so many years apart?

"Incredible." The queen began to reach for Elinor's hand but jerked back as screams and shouts rent the air outside the tent.

Before I could react, a screech resounded above our camp, the sound resembling that of a giant eagle or vulture.

Torvald bolted to his feet with his sword drawn. Even slouched, his head brushed against the canvas canopy. Fierceness radiated from his muscular body and face.

Outside, the others who were part of the king's elite group were rushing to surround the king and his canopy, their weapons drawn with Ansgar in the lead.

Torvald stepped out from underneath our tent but fell back as a whoosh of hot air fanned over the canopy. For a second, the heat was suffocating. In the next instant, the roof burst into flames.

What was happening?

I jumped to my feet, eyeing the rapidly disintegrating canvas overhead. Were the Ice Men harassing us? Surely not. Vordinberg was far enough away from the Snowden Mountains and Swainian border that we would have had an alert of their nearing presence if they'd launched a campaign. The same with King Canute and his army. If he carried through on his threat to forcibly take Elinor, we would have an advance warning of their attack.

Another birdlike shriek filled the air. More shouts and screams arose from those standing outside. Some stared up into the sky. Others covered their heads and ran.

I rapidly added up the clues and solved the riddle. A red draco was attacking us. Some called the creatures dragons, reminiscent of ancient days when supposedly all manner of vicious dragons had existed. In fact, the Valley of Red Dragons had been so named long ago.

In reality, the dracos were nothing more than flying lizards. They could grow bigger than a white-tailed eagle with a wingspan larger than a full-grown man and talons as long as an arm. They had papery-thin wings, black on the top with a translucent red on the underside. Their backs were covered in impenetrable scales, but their undersides were soft and had a checkered pattern with each box outlined first in black, then red, with a white center. Altogether, the effect made the flying lizard bodies appear as though they were covered in eyes. Lore referred to the spots as demon eyes.

Worse than their frightening appearance, the dracos had breath containing a combination of chemicals that caused things to combust. Like the canopy overhead. While most flying lizards ate small mammals and reptiles, the largest of the species were known to swoop down and capture bigger animals. Once in a while, farmers along the Blood River complained of losing sheep to the creatures. The old tales told of the flying lizards even carrying away women and children.

Whatever the case, the one attacking us today was wreaking mayhem. And we had to do something to keep the royals safe.

As the flames crackled against the canvas, Torvald lunged for the queen, shielding her with his broad body. At the same time, he shouted at me, "Protect the princess. And follow me. We need to get the queen and princess into the forest under cover. Anon."

I couldn't agree more. As the canopy burned, it would weaken and eventually collapse. We couldn't be standing underneath when that happened.

Elinor was already on her feet, peering out at the destruction. I grabbed her arm and drew her close, my pulse starting to pound with the need to find safety for her, especially before the draco breathed on the tent again.

Torvald hastened the queen out from underneath the canopy. But another screech filled the air, and a bush nearby exploded, knocking several noblemen backward and throwing them to the ground.

With Elinor tucked against my side and my arm draped around her, I halted at the tent's edge even as the flames soared in the air above us and pieces of canvas began to fall. If we moved out onto the open hilltop, we would exchange one life-threatening danger for another. But what choice did we have?

Torvald rushed the queen toward the dense forest area. Others were also running for the woods, as if there they might find safety within the brush and trees. But if the draco was intent upon gaining a meal, the woodland might slow it down but certainly wouldn't prevent it from capturing anyone within sight.

As I guided Elinor away from the canopy, I crouched low, continuing to cover her as best I could. Several servants were freeing the horses, which would allow them to seek shelter rather than face death by fire. I lauded their compassionate efforts, since we had no hope of outriding a flying lizard.

The king seemed to be well guarded by the Knights of Brethren, and the noblemen were doing their best to assist the other ladies. There was naught else to be done except ensure Elinor remained safe. I guided her after Torvald and the queen, running as best I could, glancing over my shoulders to gauge the position of the flying creature.

All the while, my mind replayed the ride up into the hills, searching my memories for a place more secure than the woodland. What about the outcropping of rocks we'd passed on the last part of the climb? The cleft would provide shelter. The way there would leave us exposed longer, but in the end, we would find better protection under a rock than a tree.

I shouted to Torvald, but the noise from the chaos prevented him from hearing me. With the smoke rising from the various fires burning around us, I could hardly see him anyway.

As the draco circled overhead, a volley of arrows flew through the air. The knights were doing what they could to thwart the creature. I prayed they would succeed in sending the hungry reptile on its way. But at the very least, the lizard's distraction with the arrows might allow everyone to scatter.

"Where are you going?" Elinor slowed her pace and struggled to veer back toward the queen and Torvald. "Should we not head into the forest?"

"On our way up the hill, we passed by several large boulders. We'll be safest there."

She began to question me but then inhaled smoke and was overcome with a fit of coughing.

"'Tis not far, Your Highness." I picked up my pace and was half-tempted to haul her up into my arms and carry her. But I also sensed that if I did so, she would only struggle against me all the more. "Trust me, Elinor. I remember seeing a place." I wasn't sure if she could hear the fear and earnestness in my voice, but she ceased her resistance and stumbled along beside me.

After descending the hill partway, we came upon the rocks. Tucked out of sight as it was, I doubted the others would have seen it. But I'd been trained to notice details most people didn't.

As we scrambled to reach the spot, a shadow with an enormous wingspan swirled overhead. I glanced up to find that the draco had sighted us and was now diving our way. My pulse picked up speed. "Make haste, Your Highness."

At the telltale screech, I dragged Elinor the last of the distance. I wrapped my arms around her and dove under the rocky ledge, positioning her on top of my body while my back took the brunt of the impact against stone and earth.

I hit hard, and the air swooshed from my lungs. But as the shadow hovered closer and a screech sounded nearer, I scrambled backward, bringing Elinor with me until we were within the tight crevice of the cleft and out of sight of the draco.

For long seconds we didn't move. Only our labored breathing filled the air, along with the heavy thud of my heartbeat against my chest.

When I could ascertain no further shadows or sounds, I attempted a normal breath.

Above me, Elinor peered down, her eyes tender with concern. "Are you hurt, Maxim? You landed quite hard."

I shook my head but felt a sharp pain and warmth trickling from my scalp. I lifted a hand to a spot behind my ear, and when I drew it back, blood coated my fingers.

She pushed up against my chest but bumped her head on the jagged ledge above us, causing her to wince.

"Careful," I managed.

"You are the one who is hurt. Let me examine you." But as she bent in, the tight confines limited her movement. Even so, she gently probed. "Here." She fingered a sharp rock next to my head. "You must have scraped your head here."

"It can't be too severe. I'm still conscious."

She narrowed her eyes on the spot. "'Tis bleeding quite profusely. But I do believe you are correct, that 'tis not a deep wound."

Suddenly I was conscious of her warm breath upon my cheek, the soft cadence of her voice near my ear, and her fingers in my hair, combing by my wound. The touch was beyond exquisite, making me forget entirely about the stinging cut.

As her chest rose and fell against mine, my body awakened to the realization that she was pressed against me. Every single beautiful inch of her.

My arms were still wrapped around her waist, holding her in place. Strands of her hair that had come loose during the mad dash to escape the fire and fury of the draco dangled across my face. I caught a whiff of jasmine, the unique scent I remembered from our childhood, from after her baths, when she'd snuggle on the queen's lap next to me with damp hair laden with the exotic flowery smell.

"I shall attempt to rip a piece of my shift to staunch the flow." Before I could caution her against moving, she hoisted up her skirt.

Though the rocky enclave prevented me from observing her, everything about our predicament was indecent. I'd only meant to shield her and keep her from harm, but now I was quite possibly staining her reputation, and I urgently needed to put proper distance between us.

Even as I released my hold, Rasmus's voice echoed in the corners of my mind, his order to become close to the princess. What better way to do that than to leverage the situation in which we found ourselves?

No. I couldn't.

As she stretched lower to gather her shift, her head rested against my shoulder. I was tempted to slip my arms around her once more. This time, not because Rasmus wanted me to but because I wanted her close, just like I always had.

Fondness swelled up from deep inside, a fondness I hadn't allowed myself to feel in so many years, one I'd closed away, one I'd forced myself to forget.

But in this moment, with my defenses crumbling more with every passing moment, I wanted to recapture the friendship that a ten-year-old boy once had with an eight-year-old girl. Was that even possible when she'd turned into an alluring woman who had the power to make a man forget to breathe?

Chapter 7

Elinor

I jerked at the linen beneath my skirt and tried to rip it, but I could hardly move, even though Maxim had loosened his arms from around me.

"I'm fine, Elinor. Truly." His labored breathing brushed my forehead.

"Regardless, you need a bandage." I slipped my knife from the sheath on my belt and sliced through the material.

"I do believe the space is large enough to accommodate both of us lying side by side." As he rattled off his calculation of the convex quadrilateral space, he shifted, as though preparing to lift me away.

When his hands settled against my hips, tingles shimmied around my middle. He had strong hands, long fingers, and a grip that seemed to perfectly fit my waist.

Maxim was grown up. The thought pummeled into me as it had yesterday when I'd first seen him and earlier this afternoon when he'd ridden next to the queen. Upon his steed in his tight-fitting cotehardie, his handsome physique had been distracting, and I'd become enamored with how different he looked.

Now with him so close, my free hand had a will of its own. In the next instant, my fingers glided over the ridge of muscles on his bicep.

He abruptly ended his complex mathematic problem and lapsed into silence.

Did my touch affect him?

I traced a line to his shoulder.

His body stilled, and his breathing halted.

Yes, my nearness was affecting him.

Fascinating.

My intuition was telling me Maxim was hiding something beneath the attentive façade he'd donned for the queen. Though I'd been away from him for years, I could still discern his inner workings. His words and actions were too calculated.

Should I use this moment and my proximity to entice him into revealing his true motives?

He slipped his hands to my arms. The movement sent heat along my nerve endings.

His face was so near—had it been so near before? His cheek brushed against mine, the slight stubble tantalizing. He needed only to lean in and his lips would be against my ear. Did I want his mouth there? Just the prospect sent my heart into a dizzying tumble.

In the next moment, he drew a line up my arm, his touch searing me through my sleeve.

It was my turn to grow motionless. Clearly, he was testing the power of his touch upon me in equal measure. It was only fair. Yet I feared he would be able to win me over much too easily, just as he had when we'd been children. Then when he was tired of me, he'd cast me aside once again.

The hurt of the past prodded me, and I started to slide away from him.

Before I could roll out of the crevice, Maxim lifted and deposited me within the confines of the interior so that my back was pressed against and protected by the rock while his body shielded me from the cleft opening. If the draco returned and aimed a breath at us, Maxim would suffer from the scorching while I remained untouched.

"Maybe we should return to our previous position," I suggested. Even if the close contact had stirred up strange new feelings, at least we'd both been safe.

With his broad shoulders blocking out most of the sunlight, his face was shadowed. But I could still see his brows rise and his forehead pucker.

"You're too exposed." I looked pointedly at the opening behind him.

"This is for the best." He didn't move closer but instead straightened his shoulders to shield me even more.

I started to protest, but when he tugged at my belt, the words got lost. He slid my knife into the sheath slowly, almost languidly. I didn't know how he'd ended up with the weapon, and I didn't care. Instead, my lungs once again ceased functioning until the knife was firmly in place. Even then, I couldn't draw in a full breath, not with his hand lingering on the hilt.

How was it possible Maxim could walk back into my life and upend my thoughts and emotions in just hours, but none of the noblemen had moved me in the slightest after an entire week?

After several heartbeats he withdrew his hand and rested his head on his arm, which exposed the blood-slickened wound on the opposite side.

His injury. How could I have forgotten about it so quickly?

I wrenched at the piece of my shift dangling by threads. It tore away, and I lifted it to his head. He didn't stop me as I pressed the wound. The only sign of his discomfort was a minor change in the rhythm of his breathing. It was almost imperceptible. No one else might have noticed it. But I'd always been attuned to his every nuance, and apparently that hadn't changed.

What was it about him that had always been my undoing?

In the dimness of the cleft, I studied his face, taking note again of the maturity in his features, the defined lines of his cheeks, the angular strength of his jaw, the purposeful tilt of his chin. And his eyes . . . they were a bottomless abyss that even now beckoned me to lose myself there. I could lie beside him and look into his eyes all day and never tire of it.

If only I could dive past the defenses he'd erected and discover what he was truly thinking and feeling.

"Maxim?"

"Yes, Your Highness?"

I wanted to give him leave to drop my title and address me by my given name as he always had when we'd been children. But we'd had little occasion to speak to one another since his return and had yet to become reacquainted. I couldn't assume we would renew our friendship where we'd once left off, although my keen longing to do so took me by surprise.

"Why did you leave without saying farewell?" The question was out before I could stop it. Yet, once spoken, I sensed it was the right approach. We might as well stop ignoring the chasm between us and instead labor to bridge it.

His blue eyes searched my face in turn as though he, too, was trying to acquaint himself with my changes—for surely ten years had altered me as much as it had him. As his gaze skimmed my cheek, temple, and then brow, a strange warmth pooled inside, almost as if his fingers were doing the tracing and not just his eyes.

"I wanted to say farewell." His eyes connected with mine, and this time the barrier was lowered. I could see the hurt and sorrow and angst clouding the depths. "But I was forbidden to do so."

"Forbidden?" I nearly recoiled but had no place to go with the cold stone against my back. "By whom? And why?"

"Why do you think?" An edge of bitterness laced his voice.

My mind spun in an effort to respond. But I had no answer now any more than I had in the days following his departure when I'd wondered what had happened—what I might have done—to drive him away. "Was it me? Did you leave because of me? Something I said or did?"

He held my gaze, intently probing as though he needed to see the truth.

I had nothing to hide from him. "You had to leave on account of me?"

He didn't deny it. In fact, his silence confirmed it.

"Why?" I asked.

"The day before I left, do you remember what happened?"

I went back in time, replaying a school day like all the others. "I can recall nothing out of the ordinary."

"Do you remember telling the queen or king that I offered to marry you?"

"You offered to marry me?" As the memory of his sincere words came back to me, I smiled. "I had forgotten. But yes, I started crying over the prospect of enduring the courtship week, and you gallantly proposed to marry me so I wouldn't have to go through with it."

"That's right." His tone and expression were devoid of humor. "You told the king of my proposal—"

"I did no such thing."

"Then you told the queen."

"I spoke of it to no one."

Maxim pushed up to his elbow. "How did the king learn of our exchange?"

I could hardly remember the instance myself, much less who else had been present. "Perhaps one of the servants or the tutor?"

His eyes narrowed upon me, almost as if he didn't believe me.

I pushed up to my elbow too. "Why would it matter if I spoke of your kind offer to anyone?"

"Because neither of us understood the reality of our different stations."

He was right. I hadn't comprehended at such a young age that Maxim wasn't royalty like I was. In fact, he wasn't even nobility. His kin had come from common stock. And as a commoner, he wasn't considered my equal in any way. "Someone heard your statement and assumed you were aspiring above your station?"

"Apparently so."

"And the king learned of it and decided you needed to be sent away?"

Maxim hesitated but then nodded.

My heart sank with the revelation that the king had been the one to separate me from Maxim. Although the queen had handled losing Maxim with more grace and poise than I had, she'd always lamented his parting. Seeing her joy today in being with Maxim again brought back the painfulness of those first weeks and months after he'd gone. We'd both grieved.

"He was wrong to send you away like he did, without an explanation, warning, or farewell." A tide of hurt and frustration threatened to erupt, but before I could vent any further, Maxim reached up and silenced me with a finger to my lips.

The touch was soft but firm, and I reveled in his nearness. For an achingly sweet moment, he held his finger there, as though he, too, liked the contact.

Finally, he dropped his hand. "'Twill do no good to dredge up old regrets and make them new again." He was quoting an ancient philosopher, one we'd memorized together. "The time had come for me to go away and begin my Sagacite training. If not that day, Rasmus would have sent me another day not long after."

"At least then I might have been able to say farewell." My voice caught, mortifying me. I didn't want to get emotional in front of Maxim, and I rushed to cover my sadness. "With some closure, perhaps I would have resigned myself to your leaving instead of wondering why you were angry and cut me out of your life so completely."

"I wasn't angry."

"Yes, you were. You believed I was the cause of your leaving. As a result, you chose not to respond to my letters."

"Letters?"

Had he not received them? Had someone intercepted them before they could be sent? Indignation swirled again, this time faster. "How could the king deny us letter writing? What purpose could be served by prohibiting communication betwixt friends?"

Maxim was silent for a beat, resting his head on his arm again. "Friendships between children are much easier to control than those between adults."

Another ancient philosophy quote? I didn't recognize it. But Maxim had a memory like an endless wellspring.

"Perhaps the king acted out of compassion more than spite." Maxim glanced unseeingly at the wall behind me, the sign that his mind was spinning faster than a tundra whirlwind. "'Tis possible the king sensed the bond between us was strong and thought to separate us before the severing became even more painful."

As usual, Maxim's conclusion made perfect sense. If our childhood friendship had continued, would it have shifted into something more?

I let my gaze linger over his strong brow and the strand of dark hair that had come loose from his leather band and flopped across his forehead. My fingers twitched with the need to comb it back, to feel his hair, to brush his skin.

If I was already battling an attraction to him so soon after his return, what would have happened if we'd stayed together? Perhaps we would have fallen in love.

Was it possible the king had hoped to prevent that, knowing it would lead to even greater heartache?

Maxim returned his attention to me. "I admit, I would have encountered great difficulty in relinquishing a maiden with your intelligence as well as your grace and beauty."

Somehow this compliment coming from Maxim meant more to me than any I'd received over the past days. His words filled up the empty places in my heart—perhaps even starting the process of healing it.

"Thank you, Maxim." I couldn't contain a smile, the thrill of being with him at long last pushing out the angst of the past. Neither of us had wanted the parting. Now that we were together, we needn't worry about having to go our separate ways again. "We can be friends now, can we not?"

Chapter 8

MAXIM

Friends?

Her meadow-green eyes watched me expectantly, and her smile remained wide enough to reveal her dimples. Dimples I'd not yet seen since being with her. Dimples I'd once adored. Dimples that I now wanted to see every day.

"How can the king or anyone else look askance on the renewal of our friendship if I am betrothed?" She spoke the words as if her upcoming betrothal would negate the attraction flaring to life between us. Surely she wasn't naïve enough to think so. As much as she might want to downplay that attraction, magnetic energy had most definitely sparked. While it could never become anything beyond a few sparks, a powerful pull toward each other was still there.

"I missed your smile and your dimples." The honest words were out before I could stop them.

The green of her eyes brightened. "And I missed the quirky way you always made every situation into a mathematical problem."

"Quirky?" I smiled in return, letting go of all my other concerns and simply basking in this reunion. "I didn't realize my wizardly mathematic abilities were quirky."

"How many other men have you met who calculate the square footage of a rock crevice just for fun?"

"I have met quite a number, actually." I missed the friends I'd made. Many of them would end up joining an abbey. A few might become tutors or teachers among the nobility. Only the most privileged and brightest would start the next phase of training and become Erudites.

"Tell me about your life these past years, Maxim." She settled back as though intending to stay for a while.

"'Twould take me days to tell you all. 'Tis best left for a time when you need tales to put you to sleep."

She laughed lightly at my attempt at humor, which had never been a particular strength of mine. But I had improved some in my wit and strangely wanted her to know it.

"Please, Maxim." She reached for my hand, clasping it between hers.

At the innocent touch, the beginning of an avalanche rumbled inside. I fought to quell the desire, knowing if I pushed for anything beyond friendship, I'd scare her away.

I glanced over my shoulder toward the hillside and the sky. I didn't see any signs of the draco. "We have a little time before we can chance returning to the others. Tell me what you'd like to know most about my past years. All of the exciting mathematical equations I've so brilliantly solved?"

Her laughter filled the small space between us again. "Tell me about where you lived first after leaving and then where you went after that."

"The tale is a long one with many bends in the road."

"I would like to hear it anyway."

"Very well." When Sagacites started their training, they traveled from abbey to abbey, learning under the best teachers and reading the treasured scripts at each holy place. The Sagacite was only ready to move on when he'd read and learned everything the abbey had to offer and when the abbot deemed that the Sagacite was surpassing the headmaster in knowledge and wisdom.

Very few Sagacites were able to travel to all the abbeys throughout Norvegia. But I had accomplished the feat, the same that Rasmus had. I'd spent the longest at St. Olaf's in the Frozen Wilds. The monks there had been devout and yet welcomed me like a son. Even when I surpassed my superiors, I'd stayed a year beyond what I needed to.

As I finished my shortened version of the past ten years, Elinor squeezed my hand, which she still held between hers. "I am glad to know you were happy."

I loved the feel of her fingers surrounding mine and didn't want our time together to end. But I feared at any moment, one of the king's knights would come searching for the princess and find us lying together. They would prod me back before the king at the tip of a sword, making all kinds of accusations. I would lose my chance of attending the Studium Generale and of being greater someday than Rasmus.

This situation with the princess was more than a little precarious. I couldn't anger the king, who had long ago forbidden me to develop a fondness for Elinor. And I couldn't anger Rasmus, who had commanded me to make Elinor fall in love with me. How could I possibly satisfy both authorities? Especially without hurting her in the process?

At a nearby shout, I pulled my hand free from Elinor's and scooted out from the hiding place, scanning the sky as well as the surrounding hills for any sign of the dangerous draco.

Before I could reach into the cleft and assist her, she was crawling out. "The draco has departed?"

"'Twould appear so." I offered her a hand in climbing to her feet, but once she was standing, I put a proper distance between us.

"We have never before had a draco so close to the city." She surveyed the land. Her hair was loose, and soot and dirt stained her gown, but she stood with her chin level and shoulders braced, as though she would face whatever came her way with bravery and dignity.

"Dracos don't typically leave the safety of their hunting grounds, unless they've been provoked."

"Or unless they fear for the safety of their young."

I couldn't forget Elinor had copious amounts of knowledge and was more intelligent than many of my fellow Sagacite friends. "'Tis also possible this draco was under the command of the Ice Men."

The mountainous group was known for capturing and training dracos. Was it possible they were working with King Canute and sent the draco to snag Elinor?

At another shout, our attention turned to several Knights of Brethren riding our direction. They'd apparently rounded up the horses—or at least their mounts—and deemed the conditions safe enough to be out in the open.

As they neared, I could see that the lead rider was Ansgar.

"Your Highness." Ansgar reined in his warhorse and bowed his head to Elinor. "Are you unharmed?"

"Yes, thanks to Maxim's sharp mind and quick thinking. He hid me amongst the rocks during the danger." She glanced to the cleft to indicate the place.

The other two knights halted beside Ansgar, and all of them took in the obscure spot before their attention swung back to me. They hadn't paid an unimportant man like me heed earlier in the day other than to note my presence with the queen. But now they assessed me with keen interest.

"'Twas a much safer place to hide than the forest, do you not agree?" Elinor spoke to Ansgar, her tone and her expression filled with admiration for the knight.

I narrowed my gaze upon the man. Did Elinor prefer Ansgar? Was this the secret affection keeping her from giving her heart to one of the noblemen?

Ansgar nodded politely at the princess. "I agree, Your Highness. The rock ledge was more protective. We owe a debt to Maxim for keeping you out of harm's way." At his words, he shifted his attention to me and bowed his head.

I sensed nothing pretentious in this man. Everything about him radiated genuine humility and kindness. Even so, a strange surge of jealousy pricked me, and tension crept into my shoulders and back.

Ansgar slanted another look at me, but I avoided his gaze, unwilling to let anyone see how Elinor was affecting me. Besides, what was I thinking? The jealousy was ridiculous. I didn't need to remind myself that nothing could come of such an attraction to Ansgar. Just like nothing could come of her attraction to me.

"The king has tasked us"—Sir Ansgar motioned to his riding companions—"with finding and returning you to the royal residence in Vordinberg with all haste."

"Then the king and queen are unharmed?" With her forehead creased in worry, Elinor gazed at the smoke curling into the sky in the direction of the resting area.

"Yes, they're shaken but well protected."

"I am relieved to hear it."

Ansgar dismounted and held out a hand to the princess. "I shall guard you myself on the ride back, Your Highness."

Elinor allowed Ansgar to aid her ascent into the saddle. As he mounted behind her, a hard knot formed in the pit of my stomach regardless of my attempt not to care that another man was touching her. Thankfully, Ansgar didn't place his hands upon her and instead held both reins.

With a final nod at me, Ansgar prodded his horse with his heel. His nod held his thanks and a transparency I hadn't expected. It contained an assurance he was doing his job to guard the princess and nothing more.

Though my envy still needled me, I couldn't begrudge this knight my respect. I could see why the king had chosen him. He was indeed a worthy leader.

My pulse came to a halt.

Worthy?

Worthy to become king?

The cool autumn breeze wrapped around me and sent a chill to my bones.

I was getting closer to solving the riddle that had been puzzling me since my meetings with Rasmus. He intended to use the Sword of the Magi among the general population, perhaps even to gain a king like Ansgar.

For as much as Rasmus claimed the sword would do the choosing of only the worthiest, I had no doubt he'd find a way to influence the sword to choose the man he most desired to be the next king. But how? And whom had he chosen?

Chapter 9

Elinor

Someone was searching for me. The door to the schoolroom squeaked open on its hinges, and I sank farther into the cushions hidden behind a low shelf, hoping to escape detection.

I'd performed my courtship duties at supper and well into the evening, and now I needed an interlude, time away from the constant effort of trying to decide who should become the next king.

After the draco attack during the afternoon hunt, the atmosphere throughout the evening meal had been subdued, and the conversation had centered around the attacks of the draco as well as the Ice Men on the southeastern border.

When the king had announced the need for another meeting with his closest knights, I'd used the opportunity to escape.

Now in the familiar, cozy chamber where I still spent great portions of my day learning, I'd curled up with a text on the draco, intending to refresh my memory on everything I knew about them. If only whoever it was would leave me in peace.

For several seconds, silence settled. I could picture one of my ladies-in-waiting peering into the room, intent on finding me. As the door squealed again and then clicked closed, I released a breath and returned my attention to the handwritten text on the parchment before me.

I carefully turned the brittle page to find a diagram of the flying lizard, amazed again that a reptile had the ability to fly like a bird. The hollow bones in the wings—

"I thought I might find you here," a voice whispered above me.

I jumped, pressing a hand to my chest.

Maxim bent over me and stared down at my book. "Studying dracos, are you?"

I hadn't seen him since leaving the hilltop hours ago. Though I'd asked Ansgar if we could locate an extra horse for Maxim so he might ride with us, the knight had informed me regretfully that the king had commanded him to deliver me back to the royal residence without delay. While Ansgar hadn't said so, I'd understood that everyone else would have to find their own way back, that his task was to protect me, that perhaps they'd concluded the draco had been sent specifically to capture me.

While I'd watched and waited for Maxim's return, I hadn't seen him. My discreet inquiries had finally afforded me the news that he'd stayed behind to help the servants clean up the damage. With the late hour, I'd given up hope of seeing him again today.

Now I couldn't keep from smiling, my heart leaping

at the sight of his handsome face, especially now that the blood and dirt had been scrubbed away and his hair recently washed and pulled back.

Before I could stand, he rounded the half shelf and dropped onto the cushion next to mine—the one he'd always used, the one I'd never had the heart to remove. Except now he was too big for the velvet square. The reading corner that had once seemed enormous was suddenly crowded. Or perhaps his presence was simply larger than life.

I wiggled farther back into my corner, my thoughts returning to earlier when we'd been together in the cleft. I couldn't deny I'd enjoyed the closeness. In fact, I'd relived those moments more times than I cared to admit—his arms holding me tight, the feel of his breath near my cheek, and then the pressure of his fingers at my waist.

"How is your wound?" I needed to divert my attention from this physical reaction to Maxim and focus on being friends.

He gingerly touched the side of his head. "I do believe I shall live."

I laughed.

His grin worked its way out, adding crinkles to the sides of his eyes.

I liked this older version of Maxim. Yes, I'd loved the friend he'd once been, but he'd always been so serious, almost as if he'd been afraid to do anything wrong. I suspected he'd lived in constant fear of his father's discipline. Rasmus had been harsh, pushing Maxim to be the best in everything.

Had the years away from Rasmus freed him from that fear, allowed him to be himself and enjoy life more? I truly hoped so.

"I see the company of a draco, even in diagram form, is more preferable than your suitors." His tone teased me, but something in his eyes hinted at more.

How honest could I be with Maxim? Of course, when we were children we'd been truthful with each other about everything. But how did I know I could truly trust him?

"Either that," he continued, "or you've already made your choice and have no more need to concern yourself over the men."

I released a weary sigh. "You are correct on the first count. I would prefer the company of a draco. But you are wrong on the second, as I have not yet made up my mind."

He leaned his head back and watched me through his lashes—dark, enchanting, long lashes.

What was he thinking? I wished I could read his thoughts and emotions, but he'd clearly become the expert at masking them. "You must think me pathetic, that I cannot choose from amongst so many fine men."

"Not at all."

"Then what, O wise one? Lend me your perspective, I beseech you." Though my tone was playful, I truly did covet his wisdom.

"*O wise one?*" He cocked a brow.

"Yes. 'Twill be my new name for you."

"I only answer to *O extremely wise one*."

A tender shoot of joy sprouted through the dry ground of my soul, as though he were both the sunlight and water sent to revive me. "Very well. What say you, O extremely wise one?"

He hesitated. "Do you fancy another man? If you

have already given your heart to—"

"No. No, that is not the case. My heart is still very much my own."

"Then you have no one you are secretly admiring?"

I shook my head. Although I'd enjoyed the company of many noblemen at court in recent years, I'd never felt overly attracted to one over another. "Allowing myself feelings for someone else would have been futile, since I knew I must wait for the courtship week."

He was silent another beat. "Then I say you are an honorable and dutiful princess who would marry any man whether or not you have a heart match, so long as you are assured he will be the king this country needs."

"Precisely." How could Maxim know me so well? Better than anyone else?

"Your fear of choosing wrongly is holding you back from choosing anyone at all."

"Yes." I sat forward, loving that someone could give voice to my dilemma. "'Tis too important a decision. If I pick the wrong man, 'tis not only I who will suffer but the entire country."

"Do you not trust that the Royal Sages have carefully selected the twelve so that you could not go wrong with any of them?"

Did I trust the Royal Sages? The wisest men in all Norvegia? Men like Rasmus, who'd spent their lives devoted to the process of learning and gaining wisdom?

On the one hand, I appreciated the emphasis in Norvegia on the rulers receiving direction from the wisemen as well as the warriors. The balance kept the country from being fooled by either peace or war.

My arm brushed against Maxim's. "Whom do you think I should choose?"

He didn't move to break the contact as he'd done earlier in the day. "If you cannot rationally and logically narrow down your choice, then perhaps you can decide upon whomever your heart beats for the most."

"What if my heart does not beat for any of them?"

He bumped his shoulder lightly against mine. "Surely it has pattered an extra beat of fondness when you are with one of them?"

The only one my heart had pattered harder for was Maxim.

"I can see I'm right." His tone was laced with curiosity. "Which man is he?"

I set aside my parchment and pushed up. "'Tis a riddle. One you must solve." One I wouldn't let him solve.

From below, he studied me. "Very well. And how will I go about finding the clues for this riddle?"

My mind raced. I'd always loved our attempts to challenge one another. 'Twould be entertaining indeed to give him clues he believed related to the twelve chosen men but were about him instead. I'd make sure he didn't discover the truth. But in challenging him, I'd take my mind off the daunting task I had to accomplish before my eighteenth birthday feast tomorrow evening, when I'd make my announcement to the world.

I held out my hand.

He hesitated, looking first at my hand, then down at his own.

"Come hither, O extremely wise one. I shall give

you your first test, and upon completing it, I shall give you your first clue."

He placed his hand in mine. As our fingers slid together, his eyes captured mine. Something fluttery and warm came to life in my stomach, like a butterfly breaking out of its chrysalis.

Maybe this riddle-solving challenge wasn't such a clever idea after all.

As his grin kicked up, the fluttery warmth spread into my limbs. And I didn't want to stop this game even though something warned me that we should.

MAXIM

After hours of following Elinor's clues, she'd led me no closer to a resolution than when we first started. She designed complex trivia questions with the answers spelling out a word that guided me to the subsequent game. She provided mathematical equations calculating how many steps I had to take to the next clue. She directed me on a scavenger hunt across a map of the country with the destination pointing me to an additional puzzle.

I hadn't enjoyed myself so much since I'd spent time with her as a child.

Darkness had long since settled, and the midnight hour had come and gone. When one of her ladies-in-waiting had come to check on her, she'd shoved me out of sight behind the door and let her lady know she wasn't retiring for a while but that they should do so without her.

Now Elinor tugged me down a stone path in the gardens at the back of the royal residence. I knew exactly where she was taking me. To the maze among the tall shrubs.

The night air had dropped below freezing, but we'd donned our cloaks and gloves, and for a reason I couldn't explain, I felt invincible, as if the strongest winter storm could flail against me and I would stand strong. In some small way, that's how Elinor had always made me feel.

I realized now what I hadn't realized as a child, that her presence in my life, her strength, her belief in me, had helped make me stronger so I'd survived the hardships with Rasmus. Without her influence, what kind of man would I have become?

Even with it, I dreaded that too much of Rasmus remained within me.

"You won't be able to stump me with the maze, Elinor." I stopped at one of the arched trellises that marked an entrance. Ivy curled in and out of the ironwork, the leaves already beginning to fade to a pale yellow, another sign the long winter would soon settle upon Norvegia.

"Do not speak too hastily lest you find yourself choking on your words."

I smiled at her quote of an old saying we'd once learned. "I won't choke this time."

"Very well." She made her way toward another entrance a dozen feet away. The high harvest moon shone down on her, revealing her beauty once again, a beauty that had only grown with each passing hour—her eyes sparkling brighter, her cheeks rosier, her enthusiasm contagious. "Since you are so quick at solving mazes, let us race to the center."

"You have the advantage in having already been through the maze. How many times?"

"This is a new design. I asked the gardener for it should I have need of the maze this week."

All throughout our childhood, the head gardener had regularly formed differing patterns just for Elinor's delight. I wasn't surprised he was still creating mazes for her.

"So, have you?" I asked, tamping down the jealousy again. Even though she'd assured me she didn't secretly fancy anyone, she had revealed that her heart beat a little harder for one of the noblemen. All throughout the riddles she'd plotted for me, I'd tried not to think about the man. But here, at the maze, I was reminded all over again that she was destined to belong to someone else.

"Have I what?"

"Had need of the maze this week for the man who makes your heart beat with fondness?"

She studied the trellis as though contemplating her answer.

My muscles tightened.

"I have not needed the maze"—her tone softened—"until tonight."

My breath snagged. What was she saying? That I was the one who made her heart beat with fondness? Surely not.

We were childhood friends. And could be nothing more. But even as I inwardly chastised myself, my blood pumped faster.

"Are you ready?" She stared straight ahead, refusing to look at me.

Was she doing so to hide the truth of her feelings?

Yes, I'd already acknowledged that fondness existed

between us. It always had. But now that we were both adults, the fondness was taking on a life and breath of its own.

"Go." She gave the command without waiting for my reply and started forward.

I couldn't go, couldn't think about the maze in the garden when all I wanted to do was figure out how to navigate the maze separating us.

She lurched to a stop several feet in and tossed me a glare. "Do not even think about allowing me to start ahead of you. If anything, I should be the one giving you the advantage."

I couldn't admit I was pathetically staring into space thinking about her. So I took a step under the trellis. "We'll see about that, won't we?"

In the next instant, we both raced ahead, the lure of the maze irresistible. We shared a competitive spirit which, during our early educational years, had pushed us both to labor harder. Once again, the thrill of vying against her thrummed through my blood.

The heavy scent of evergreen hung in the air. The juniper, dwarf spruce, and boxwood closed in about me. In their glazed clay planters, the shrubs, like the round stones that formed the pathway, could be moved to create new mazes.

Ten feet in, I heard Elinor's footsteps nearby on the opposite side of the evergreens. In the darkness, I could only see the faintest outline of her feet and long skirt. She was near, and yet the maze would soon take us in opposite directions. Was that the way of life? Wishing to stay on the same path but unable to prevent the divergence?

At a T in the path, I calculated the options first for the

left and then for the right. Most people would probably choose the right, but I'd learned in solving puzzles that usually the most obvious clues led a person astray.

When I heard Elinor's footsteps nearby, I knew her process of elimination had been the same as mine. I hastened, memorizing the turns and the corresponding directions just in case I needed to backtrack.

I calculated each step steadily until I reached the opposite side, the edge closest to the castle wall. Normally, the maze didn't wind so far back. Had I miscalculated?

Pausing, I listened for signs Elinor was nearby. But the only sound was the distant call of a fox along with my breathing, the cool air making it more labored.

I studied the area and mentally retraced my route, looking for another path I might have overlooked. Then, with a shake of my head, I continued forward. If Elinor had the maze designed for the noblemen, then she'd likely instructed the gardener and the Sage who helped him draw the maze to increase the level of difficulty, especially if she wanted to test the men. Had she hoped they would get lost? So that only the worthiest would find his way through?

If she needed a method for determining worthiness, then perhaps the Sword of the Magi would help her. Perhaps Rasmus's plan was for the best. And perhaps my part in it was justified. I could prevent her the distress of having to choose one of the noblemen for herself. She could leave it up to the sword to select the best man for her—if the sword could truly do such a thing.

I pushed forward, still counting my steps. As soon as the trail took an inward direction, I picked up my pace, knowing my intuition had been accurate and that I was moving in the correct direction.

The path wound tighter and became narrower. My pulse surged with a strange burst of anticipation. I was almost there. I could feel it.

At the sight of an opening, I jogged the last few steps and found myself in the center of a circle of approximately fifteen feet in diameter.

Elinor stood at the midpoint, facing my entrance and wearing a triumphant smile. "Three minutes, seventeen seconds."

I'd been keeping track of my time and knew she was stating mine. "And yours?"

"Three minutes, one second."

"Very well done."

"Are you surprised?" The moon once again shone down upon her, like a beacon upon a prized treasure. She'd tossed back her hood, and her hair fell over her cloak in long golden waves, freed from the usual constraints and swirling in a magical dance.

While I wanted to go on admiring her, her expectant eyes waited for my answer.

"You need no reassurance from me, Elinor. For surely you recognize by now what an intelligent woman you are."

Doubt flickered across her face as she studied me, as though testing the sincerity of my compliment. "What if I am not worthy to be queen?" The whispered question rose on the puff of a white breath.

Platitudes crowded my mind. The proper response was to reassure her that she was worthy, that she'd make a fine queen someday, and that she had nothing to fear. It was the answer any other man would have given her, especially those participating in the courtship.

However, I'd never told Elinor what she wanted to hear, only what she needed. And though flattery would serve me well in this instance, drawing her affection further from the chosen noblemen and onto myself, I couldn't make myself speak superficially. I'd never been good at that.

I headed toward the stone bench the gardener had always placed in the middle of the maze. I sat and waited for her to do likewise.

She stood rigidly for another moment before she lowered herself beside me.

I let the seclusion and the peace of the maze settle over us before speaking. "When you become queen, I cannot promise you'll never make any mistakes. I cannot promise you'll know everything. Nor can I promise everything will go smoothly."

She released a small sigh.

I took hold of her gloved hand and squeezed. "What I can promise is that you'll be an honorable, sacrificial, and good queen. You'll do the best you can. And that is all that matters."

As I began to pull my hand from hers, she grasped it tighter. "Thank you, Maxim. I hope when the time comes for me to take the throne, you will have completed your training and become a Royal Sage so I can draw upon your wisdom."

My imagination soared into the future, to a time when we were both older, when she was queen and married to someone like Torvald. As earlier, the prospect of her being with one of the noblemen—or any other man— unleashed jealousy, and it was metamorphosizing into an invisible tormentor I could no longer keep locked away.

"Please tell me you will never willingly leave me again."

Her voice dropped as though she sensed my conflicting thoughts.

I swallowed hard. As a child, I'd always pictured myself as her Royal Sage, standing behind her or walking near her right hand as Rasmus did with the king. I'd imagined her spending countless hours with me as we continued to challenge one another to learn and grow.

But after I was sent away, I gave up that dream. Instead, I made my ambition to become the best Sage in the land, to someday exceed everyone else in my wisdom so no one could compare to me. Then King Ulrik would realize his mistake and regret sending me away. And once Elinor was queen, she'd have no choice but to seek my counsel.

Now that I was back and had learned Elinor had no part in expelling me, that she'd missed me, had tried to write, and was even now still my friend, my aspirations needed to be adjusted.

I still wanted to prove to King Ulrik that I was the best and he'd been wrong to spurn me. And I still wanted to prove to Rasmus that I was better than him, so that someday he'd respect me instead of treating me like an inferior.

But with Elinor . . . while I wanted to be there for her, how could I work closely with her without wanting more? More friendship? More time? More of her?

Maybe if I knew with certainty that she would love her husband, that he was the worthiest in the land, that she would be happy in her marriage, I would be satisfied. I might not be able to keep from wishing for a deeper friendship, but at least I'd be close beside her. I'd make sure I was the one person she could always count on, the one advisor who would always have her best interest at heart, a friend she could always lean upon.

"Maxim?" She pulled away, clearly sensing my inner battle.

I drew her hand back and tucked it into the crook of my arm. "I'll never willingly leave you again."

"I would not coerce you into saying so—"

"I pledge it to you of my own accord and from the bond of friendship we share."

"But your hesitation . . ."

"If I hesitated, 'tis only because of my own selfishness. I'll always long for more friendship and companionship from you than you'll be able to give me—"

"I shall always have time for you."

"Once you are betrothed and married, 'twill be unseemly for you to spend time with me alone." Like this. Though the cold nipped at us, the hedges provided a shelter from the breeze. I would be content to sit with her for hours on the bench if she allowed it.

She tucked her hand in deeper. "If you are my Royal Sage, who can oppose it?"

"Your husband." Saying the word unleashed the tormentor inside me again. It slashed at my chest, leaving me nearly breathless with a pain I had no wish to feel.

"Then I shall make certain whomever I choose understands our friendship is important to me."

I could only pray her betrothed would understand it. But if I were her husband, I wouldn't like her being friends with another man. Not in the least.

Chapter 10

Elinor

With Maxim by my side on the turret, the sunrise was more beautiful than any I'd witnessed in years. It was as if the sun had decided to bestow upon us a gift, the perfect ending to the glorious night we'd spent together.

I stifled a yawn as I finished writing down the time and the angle of the sun.

Maxim scanned my notes. "I'd say it's more like thirty-six degrees at 6:25 a.m. instead of thirty-five at 6:26."

I examined the sun's position again. "You are correct." I crossed out my notation and wrote the right numbers.

"'Tis a good thing I'm here to keep you in line, Your Highness."

"Yes, 'tis a very good thing, O extremely wise one." I bumped my shoulder against his, and he did likewise to me.

We'd stayed in the center of the maze until we'd

grown so cold that we needed to get up and race around the maze to warm our limbs. When finished, we sneaked into the castle kitchens and attempted to raid the pot of warm mead simmering on the hearth. Thankfully, we only woke one of the scullery maids, who graciously aided us in our task.

With the mugs of mead in hand, we'd gone back to the schoolroom and talked through the wee hours of the morn. Maxim shared in more depth about his time away, speaking fondly of Father Johann at St. Olaf's, his sincere faith and trust in God, and how the man had been like a father to him.

Maxim had asked questions about all I'd done since he left. Although my life hadn't been nearly as exciting and as adventurous as his, I'd visited various parts of the country in preparation for becoming the queen. I'd even once traveled to the Frozen Wilds, appreciating the untamed beauty of the far northern land with the beautiful Northern Lights.

We'd talked endlessly about everything and lost track of the hour. By the time I realized dawn was approaching, we rushed to the turret and made it just as the first rays climbed above the horizon.

Now we gazed out over the city and distant fields for another minute, then I made another notation. Once finished, I handed the leather journal to him. He took it wordlessly and made the next few entries at every minute.

When the sun had risen enough to cast its light through the arrow slits and form the shape of a cross, Maxim was the first to turn and gaze upon the cross of light. "Do you still pray?"

I nodded and knelt. As I bowed my head, I could

feel his presence beside me.

My heart swelled with gratitude and wonder. Only yesterday, I'd lamented that Maxim was back. Now, this morn, our friendship was as solid as if he'd never left, and I prayed we would have many more days together, that nothing would come between us in the future.

As I lifted my silent plea, his fingers at his side brushed against mine. We were no longer wearing our gloves, hadn't been since returning from the maze. At his caress, my prayers fled so that all I could think about was his hand so close to mine. I wasn't sure if the contact was accidental, so I did nothing.

A second later, his little finger looped through mine.

My heart flipped upside down. What did he mean by it? I could safely assume his touch wasn't coincidental. He'd reached out and purposefully made the connection. Did that mean he was feeling what I was? That this time together was indeed special? Something he'd missed while we were apart? Something he didn't want to take for granted ever again?

"In the name of the Father, Son, and Holy Ghost. Amen," I whispered in closing.

"Amen." His whisper was low but sincere.

While he assisted me to my feet, he kept his finger intertwined with mine. When we stood once more, he faced me just inches away.

Somehow the pale light of dawn softened his features, turning his eyes a warm blue. "Thank you for giving me this night. 'Tis one I'll never forget."

"We can have more like this, can we not?"

He glanced toward the open tower door where

Halvard stood hidden in the shadows. Was Maxim worried my faithful guard would overhear us and report our time together to the king? Would the king be upset to learn I was spending so much time with Maxim—time I could be sharing with the noblemen instead?

My heart quavered. If he'd sent Maxim away once, he could surely do so again. I'd need to be careful. And Maxim obviously sensed the threat too. Even so, we need not put aside our friendship altogether.

"We shall watch the sun rise again on the morrow," I insisted.

Maxim swung our hands back and forth a couple of times before he let go. "Have you forgotten what today is?"

"I beg you not to remind me."

"You're turning eighteen." His voice held a gravity I loathed.

I spun away from him, stalked toward the stairway, and rushed to descend, as if in escaping Maxim I could escape the truth.

I heard the door close and then Maxim's footsteps tapping the stone steps behind me. At the landing leading to my chambers, he caught my arm before I could exit.

"Elinor, wait." His plea stopped me more than his hand.

Slowly I pivoted.

Only one sconce lit the flight of stairs, leaving it shrouded in darkness. Yet I could see the power in his gaze, one that made my insides tremble with a need I didn't understand.

"Please do not tell me you cannot spend more time with me," I whispered, glad for the shadows that hid my trembling lips.

"I would watch the sunrise with you every day if I could." He lifted a hand, as if he wanted to stroke my cheek or my hair, but then let it drop.

"If you would, then do not let anything stop you."

He closed his eyes for a moment, and when he opened them, he took a step back. "You will pick your betrothed today. You must focus on that."

The impending task loomed like a mountain I couldn't climb. Nor did I want to. However, I understood the law, that I must choose a Norwegian nobleman so I could officially be named as the king's successor. Such a move ensured the security of the throne and solidified the future of the country, especially with King Canute making his claims for me and the monarchy.

"Maxim, I do not know what to do, who to choose. How can I do this?"

He studied my face, his dark lashes shielding his eyes. He opened his mouth as though he would answer me, but after a second, he clamped his lips together.

If only he could offer me a solution, one I liked. But that was wishful thinking. The truth was, I would have to announce my choice tonight after the feast. I would pray that by then I knew whom to marry.

⚬⚬⚬

MAXIM

Bright sunlight hit my face, awakening me.

With a half groan, I shifted on my bed and tugged the coverlet over my eyes. I'd gone to bed after watching the

113

sunrise with Elinor, but with so scant an amount of slumber in the past forty-eight hours, my body wasn't ready to wake up.

"The princess is on her way to your chamber even as we speak." Rasmus spoke calmly nearby.

The princess was coming to my room? I lowered the sheet and cracked open an eye.

Rasmus stood in his black robe and long black hat, his expression placid but his eyes radiating an uncharacteristic energy. "This afternoon you must take her to the Stavekirche, show her the sword that has been returned there, and explain how it can help her in choosing the next king."

"Your Excellency." A strange foreboding prodded me. I sat up, letting the coverlet fall away altogether. The shutters had been thrown wide open, letting in the light. By the slant, I could see that I'd slept all morn and the early afternoon hour was upon us.

At the end of my bed, Dag was setting out a clean set of garments I'd never seen before in preparation for my grooming. I didn't need to ask to know Rasmus had brought them for me. As a short man with a hunchback, Dag's head hung unusually low, his chin resting on his chest, his gaze perpetually fixed downward. Though he saw little of his surroundings and what was going on, he was keenly aware of more than most. Ten years my senior, he'd become a friend more than a servant.

Rasmus took a step closer to the bed, commanding my attention as he towered above me. "Tell her this is the Sages' solution to her dilemma. Assure her the sword will only pick the worthiest king, that the weight of the decision can now be lifted from her shoulders."

Would the sword or Rasmus make the decision? Once

again, I feared it was the latter and that my cooperation with Rasmus would lead her astray.

"She wants your help. This is how you will give it to her." Rasmus could read the indecision in my eyes. 'Twas why he'd awoken me so abruptly, so he might take me unaware.

"And if she doesn't want to resign her fate to the sword?" Or to Rasmus?

"After your night with her, you've gained her trust. She'll do as you suggest." Just as the king trusted Rasmus and did as he suggested.

It was a form of manipulation. There was no other way to describe it. Before I could analyze my feelings about the tactic, the door to my chamber opened a crack, and one of Rasmus's scribes spoke. "She's entered the adjacent passageway."

Rasmus crossed the room and exited in a matter of seconds, leaving me only the next clue in this riddle without any time to understand it better.

With an exasperated sigh, I swung my legs over the edge of the bed and grabbed the tunic Dag was holding out. "You should have awoken me the moment Rasmus entered."

"I tried by opening the shutters." Dag's muffled reply was contrite.

"No matter—"

The door swung open, cutting me off. Rasmus's scribe—still positioned outside my room—held it wide and bowed his head in the direction of the princess, now gliding into the room. She was already attired in a fresh gown, her hair back in a neatly coiled knot. Already I missed it hanging loose and wild.

I pushed up from the bed, not wanting her to know I'd just awoken.

As she moved past the scribe and caught sight of me, she stopped abruptly and released a soft gasp.

Confusion pressed over me, but only for an instant. When her eyes rounded and roved down my body, I followed her line of vision to find I was bare except for my linen breeches.

"Oh my." Her words came out breathy. Although her cheeks didn't redden with embarrassment, I could see it in her expression before she spun and faced the opposite direction, looking at the wall instead of me. If the scribe hadn't already been closing the door, I had no doubt she would have run from the room.

I lifted the tunic dangling from my hand and positioned it in front of my chest. Too little effort, too late. Nonetheless, I didn't want to make Elinor more uncomfortable than she already was.

"Your messenger said to come right away, that you had good news for me regarding my decision." Elinor lifted a hand and fanned her face, all the while continuing to stare straight ahead.

My messenger? Had Rasmus purposefully arranged for Elinor to arrive in my room just as I was getting out of bed so we might find ourselves in this indecent predicament? What would happen next? Would the king appear any second to discover me unclad with the princess in my chamber?

I motioned at Dag to help me don my garments. "I beg your forgiveness, Your Highness. But I believed I had a moment longer."

"No, 'tis I who must apologize." Again her voice was breathy. "I did not expect to see your chest—I mean shoulders—arms—" She fanned her face more rapidly.

I paused in thrusting my arms through my sleeves.

The sight of my body was rattling her. Did she like what she saw?

I resumed my dressing, a twinge of satisfaction settling inside me.

"I shall wait in the hallway for you to finish." She crossed to the door, but as she tugged the handle, the door remained firmly closed.

Was the scribe in the hallway holding the door closed, ensuring that she had to stay?

I finished pulling on my tunic. "Have no fear, Your Highness. I am nearly fully garbed."

"I did not realize your state of undress, Maxim. I vow it. Or I would not have barged in as I did."

"'Tis my fault entirely." Dag held out a doublet, and I shrugged into it. "I should have been ready but was inevitably delayed."

Without worrying about the lengthy line of buttons up the front of my doublet, I stepped into my leggings. Dag attached them to the fastening cord of my breeches. Once in place, I added the surcoat that fell to midthigh. "There, almost done now."

She peeked over her shoulder, but finding Dag still at work, her gaze returned to the door. "Did you sleep well?" Her voice was unnaturally high.

"Yes. Very." I slid on my belt as Dag held up one of my stockings.

"Good."

"And you?" I asked. "Did you sleep well?"

"Yes. Quite well."

I stuffed my foot into the stocking and started to tie it into place as Dag helped me with the second stocking. I couldn't remember ever dressing so quickly. I'd likely set a record.

"Have you yet to break your fast?" she asked, filling the awkward silence.

"I admit I haven't."

"I could send word to the kitchen to put together fare for us to take on our excursion."

Excursion? Was that how Rasmus had relayed my request to her? I straightened and allowed Dag to button my doublet.

"Or not," she quickly added. "If you'd prefer not to . . ."

She was most definitely rattled. More so than I'd ever seen her before. Breaking free of Dag, I approached Elinor until I stood directly behind her. She cast me another look before she turned. Her eyes were still rounded and filled with an appreciation that sent another jolt of gratification through me. Even if her presence in my chamber was inappropriate, it was showing me how much I affected her.

Of all the reasons why Rasmus had arranged Elinor's arrival to my chamber, this had to be the primary one. To allow me to gain confidence in my ability to bend her to my will.

If only the thought of doing so held pleasure. As it was, the prospect of manipulating her any further than I already had held no appeal. Yet now that Rasmus's messenger had informed the princess of my good news for her, what other choice did I have but to continue down the path Rasmus had mapped?

Chapter 11

Elinor

Inwardly I couldn't stop flushing, especially because whenever I glanced at Maxim atop his steed, I pictured him standing beside his bed, wearing only his breeches.

As though sensing my attention upon him, he slid me a sideways glance and cocked his brow. The look was entirely too appealing, revealing his spell-binding blue eyes and lending him a roguishness that sent a thrill through me.

"Your Royal Highness?" His question hinted at mirth, almost as if he knew I was thinking on his state of undress.

"In your message, you mentioned you had found a way to help me with my choice." I returned my focus to the waterfront as we steadily approached, several guards riding beside and behind us.

Upon leaving the castle, I'd expected some of the noblemen to see me and ask to accompany me. But I'd learned most were in discussion with the king after receiving news King Canute's army was amassing near the Norvegian border.

While I was disturbed by the show of aggression, I was also relieved for a chance to spend a little more time with Maxim before my betrothal ceremony, before things had to change between us. Though he was right in setting boundaries for our future together, I felt a sting of disappointment in knowing our interactions would be limited so soon after renewing our friendship.

I was also eager to discover his means of aiding my decision. "You must tell me of your plan."

"We're almost there."

"Where?"

A grin quirked the corners of his lips. He was enjoying his opportunity to puzzle me.

Was he planning to take a boat to one of the islands in Ostby Sound? Such excursions were popular in the summer when the Cimbrian Strait and White Sea were calm, providing idyllic conditions for birdwatching, hiking, and boating.

Though the sea grew more malcontent the closer we came to winter, the waters would remain mostly safe for another month, until the winter storms turned them deadly. Perhaps the guards could row us out to one of the islands so we could partake of our repast somewhere we could be unhindered to truly be ourselves—like we had been last night—without everyone watching us.

Even now, the shopkeepers and tradesmen stopped their labor to view our passing, the men doffing their hats and bowing their heads and women curtsying.

The sights and sounds of the busy markets had

always fascinated me. The sea-roughened faces of the people, the weather-beaten buildings. The shouts of the incoming fishermen, the flapping of sails against creaking beams, and the squawk of seagulls circling overhead.

Normally I breathed in the salty sea air and appreciated the opportunity to venture outside the castle walls. But today I could think of naught else but Maxim.

Though I'd experienced an undercurrent of panic from the moment I'd awoken on this, my eighteenth birthday, I'd resolved to make the most of the afternoon. "You must give me a clue, Maxim."

"Very well, Your Highness." He rode quietly for several beats before he offered me a riddle. One puzzle led to the next until at last the clues led me to the Stavekirche at the city center near the waterfront. The church was constructed of hewn logs—staves—rising vertically from the ground and interlocking to form sturdy walls. The central building was cross shaped, but arched buttresses and gabled roofs had been built one upon another, adding a loftiness that made the church rise high above the surrounding buildings.

Four carved dragon heads perched upon the main roof ridges, pointing toward the sky. Normally, I didn't think anything of the historical artifacts that helped drain water off the shingled roofs. But after seeing the draco yesterday, my attention lingered on the dragons so similar to the draco.

The priest allowed us entrance, bowing almost all the way to the ground. I passed him into the silent sanctuary ahead of Maxim, our footsteps echoing against the plank floor up to the high wooden ceiling.

"Where to now?" I whispered as we reached the chancel, adorned with but a few silver candelabras and a central cross on the wall above the altar.

Maxim nodded to the altar draped in linen. "The relics, Your Highness."

The Stavekirche, like most important churches, housed sacred holy relics passed down through the ages. I'd viewed them at times over the years when they'd been removed from their resting place underneath the altar and displayed inside a reliquary on a special stand.

The priest shuffled forward and lifted the linen to reveal a set of stone doors. He unlocked one and removed a box draped in black velvet. He placed the box upon the altar, made the sign of the cross, then nodded at Maxim. Clearly, the priest was working with Maxim with whatever plan he'd uncovered.

After the priest disappeared into an anteroom, Maxim lifted the black cloth away to reveal a red cedar box.

"Is it the Sword of the Magi?" My question tumbled out. With the length of the box, it had to be the special relic. I was well aware of its presence here in Norvegia along with a nail and sliver of wood that had belonged to the cross of Christ. While I'd seen the nail and wood from time to time, the sword had always remained locked away in the cedar box.

The few times King Ulrik had asked to have the sword removed, the priests had never been able to figure out how to open its case. Some had even been hurt trying to do so, and eventually the king had stopped asking.

Maxim traced a finger along one edge and pressed

into the crack.

"Careful, Maxim." I placed a hand on his arm to halt him. "'Tis dangerous to open. None have been able to do so—"

The lid clicked and lifted to reveal the ancient sword in all its glory.

I sucked in a breath. Cushioned against crimson velvet, the sword radiated energy and power. Candlelight glinted off the polished silver blade and highlighted the jewels encrusted into a round pommel.

Maxim took a step back, and side by side we admired the relic, my mind reviewing all I'd ever read about the sword.

"I should have known you would have no trouble unlocking the box," I finally said.

"I admit, I've already opened it once."

"You have?" He'd been home such a brief time. When had he come down to the Stavekirche?

"Rasmus has been studying it in his chambers." Maxim seemed to read my unasked question. "He required me to decipher how to open it."

"For what purpose?" As soon as the question was out, I already knew Maxim's answer.

"He's attempting to help you find a solution to your dilemma."

The night of my coming-of-age ball, Rasmus had indicated that he was investigating the laws and texts for other options and that he was close to finding help. Was the Sword of the Magi his assistance? And was he using Maxim to deliver the help?

"Tell me how such a sword will aid me with picking my husband."

"The engraving on the sword is an ancient language

that reads 'For a worthy king.'"

I studied the archaic markings but had never seen the language before. "So the bearer of the sword is worthiest to be king?"

"Of course, Holy Scripture doesn't speak of the sword. But ancient literature from the eastern wisemen says that only the man worthy to be king will be able to pull it free."

"Free from the case?"

"Yes, or perhaps from whatever is confining it."

I reached for the hilt, tugged at it, but the sword wouldn't budge from the box. I was well versed in history and knew about King Stefan, the first Oldenberg king, releasing the sword from its confinement and using it to defeat his enemies. Tradition stated that the sword imparted a blessing that made the bearer more powerful while wielding the weapon in battle.

But I'd never heard it had the ability to determine who was worthiest to be king. Perhaps no one had ever been able to read the engraving until now. "Rasmus would have the twelve noblemen attempt to dislodge the sword. Whoever is able to pull it free will become my husband?"

"Yes."

The workmanship was magnificent, from the rare jewels all the way to the tiny engravings. Was it really blessed by Providence? "What do you think, Maxim? Is this, then, the answer to my dilemma?"

"It could be." Maxim's voice held a note of doubt, one I needed to explore.

"Tell me all the implications of using this test. I need to know every consideration before I consent to it."

Maxim hesitated, as though debating how much to divulge.

"I pray you will hold nothing back. Tell all."

"'Tis possible none of the noblemen will be able to wrest the sword loose, that even after pouring their strength to the weapon, none will be found worthy."

"Or simply not strong enough?"

"Strength of character is more important than strength of body." The ancient words of wisdom rolled off Maxim's tongue.

"If none of my suitors can successfully dislodge the sword, what then? Must I wait to be named heir apparent until we find one who can loosen it?"

"It would be a risk." He paused and stared at the relic as though deep in thought.

I stared at it too. If the sword could decipher the worthiness with such certainty, wouldn't the risk be worthwhile? "If I delay in choosing a husband, King Canute might grow more aggressive in seeking a union for himself."

"But if a worthy man frees the Sword of the Magi, Canute would be foolish to persist in his endeavors. He would surely know the legend of King Stefan's use of the sword and the great victories he accomplished in battle."

"So, this relic might bring an end to King Canute's threat?"

"In the end, 'tis my hope you will wed the best man in the kingdom and remain safe from Canute's wiles." This time, Maxim's tone was filled with a sincerity that told me he truly had my best interest at heart.

"Will the king agree to it? He is eager to see me betrothed and named as his successor."

"If he knows you're yet undecided by the banquet tonight and you propose this challenge, he will comply with your wish to have help in the choosing."

Though I wanted to discount the ancient engraving, what did I have to lose by giving the sword a chance? If none of the twelve could pull it free, then I could always choose one of them regardless. Perhaps I'd give the king the honor of selecting his favorite. Then the consequences of the decision would rest upon his shoulders and not mine.

I stepped away from the sword. The matter was settled. "Let us be on our way." I spun and made my way through the church. I only had hours left of freedom, and I intended to make the most of them.

MAXIM

Something didn't add up with Rasmus's plan to utilize the Sword of the Magi. But try as I might, I couldn't work out the correct solution. Clearly, he intended for the chosen noblemen to fail. But why? As before, I could only conclude he was widening his scope.

I sat next to Elinor on the rocky shore, my feet bare and dangling in the sea. She swung her legs back and forth in the cold water, kicking up a spray that sparkled in the bright sunlight.

The questions had plagued me all throughout the afternoon we'd spent on the small island in Ostby Sound, talking and hiking and eating. Like last night, the time with Elinor had been a homecoming, as if my wandering soul had finally found rest. It had gone by too quickly, and now the guards waiting by our boat were growing restless.

I nodded at one, indicating that we would leave erelong. As much as I wanted to stay on the island and prevent Elinor from going to the feast, I had always put duty ahead of my personal desires and would continue to do so.

But what was my personal desire?

I glanced sideways at her. Her hair was tangled from the wind, her gown bedraggled from the sea and sand, her face uplifted to the sun, taking in the warm rays.

"I followed every lead," she said, "and none ever brought me any closer to understanding what became of them."

She'd been speaking of her mother and sister and the search she'd conducted once she'd been old enough to do so.

"Not that I could do more than you already have," I replied, "but I would gladly examine all the clues and attempt to decipher them . . . if you'd like."

"Would you?"

"Most certainly."

Although I empathized with Elinor's desire to understand her family's fate and wanted to help her unlock the mystery, my mind went back to the sword and the puzzle that needed to be solved.

What were Rasmus's intentions? With his luring the princess to my chamber earlier, with his command that I spend as much time as I could with her, with his undermining her confidence in the courtship process, surely he didn't plan for me to loosen the sword from the case.

If he believed I could become betrothed to Elinor and

stand in as the next king of Norvegia, he surely understood that no one would accept me. I was of common stock, and the law of the land clearly stated that royalty must marry someone of a royal or noble bloodline.

Even so, I would be a fool to ignore all the evidence that somehow Rasmus was plotting for me to take the throne. But what was the law in the hands of a skillful politician but clay to be molded to his benefit?

I didn't know how Rasmus would change the law, but I had no doubt he'd find a way. Did he expect that in putting me at Elinor's side as her co-ruler, I would be his puppet? That he would be able to rule through me?

The very thought sent a shiver of disquiet through me. Of course, what man could deny an opportunity to become a powerful king? If Rasmus indeed pushed me into it, I doubted I would be able to resist. Especially knowing Elinor would be mine and belong to no one else. Although I wanted to deny how much I cared about her—had been doing my best to reject my feelings—the more time I'd spent with her, the more I resented her being with anyone else.

"You are distracted." Her quiet statement cut through my musings.

What should I tell her? My suspicions? And what if I was wrong? What if Rasmus had another plan entirely? I swirled my foot in the water lapping against the moss-covered stone. "I cannot keep my thoughts from dwelling on what is to come this eve." It was the partial truth.

She pressed her lips and gazed back to the shoreline of Vordinberg, the Stavekirche at the pinnacle of the tall, colorful buildings along the waterfront and hills, all bowing to the castle where it sat in a majestic throne above the city, like a benevolent parent watching over a beloved child.

"I pray for God's will to be done," Elinor said softly.

I feared Rasmus's will would be accomplished and that I had become his unwilling aid.

She shifted on the rock. "You will come tonight, will you not?"

"I haven't been invited—"

"I invite you to sit by my side and give me counsel."

"'Tis not a matter so easily decided."

"I am the princess. I want you there. What more is needed?"

"The king's permission."

"And you fear he will dismiss you?"

"When he learns of how I have monopolized your time for the past twenty-four hours, he might send me far away again."

She skimmed her foot upward and sent more water into the air. "Then you think the king will disapprove of the bond forming betwixt us?"

"I think he will have nothing to fear after you are betrothed. But until then—especially if you decide to invoke the power of the sword—yes, I do believe he'll worry about where you're placing your affections."

She stilled. "My affections?"

"Of course, we're friends and nothing more." But were we only friends? What about Rasmus's instructions to make her fall in love with me?

"Of course." She climbed to her feet, and I averted my eyes. As children, when we dangled our feet in the water, I'd never considered the impropriety of seeing her feet unclad. But now . . . I couldn't give in to the desire to look at her. 'Twould do no good for this increasing pull I was feeling.

She stood and lifted her wet hem, clearly not having

the same concern as me, giving me a view of her feet and ankles.

My blood heated. She was exquisite.

Without another word, she swiped up stockings and boots and walked away, her back stiff, her chin level—the sure sign my words had offended her.

I scrambled up, gathered my discarded footwear, and rushed after her. The path, though laden with sand, also contained many rocks, slowing her. I caught up to her easily and took hold of her arm.

I could feel the eyes of the guards upon us. Were they under the influence of the king or Rasmus? To whom were they reporting back? As I hesitated, they turned away, gazing off into the distance. In that instant, I gained my answer, because the king's soldiers would have continued to observe my interactions with the princess.

A sliver of guilt mingled with embarrassment. Rasmus had likely informed them that the princess and I were enamored and to allow us privacy to be together if we so desired. Now, if I didn't take advantage of this moment, Rasmus would learn of my negligence.

Elinor jerked and freed her arm from my grasp, starting forward again.

"Wait, Elinor."

She continued on.

"I'm sorry." I followed on her heels, reviewing what I'd said or done to cause her grievance, but even with my extensive education, I was lacking when it came to interpreting the ways of women.

She halted and swung to face me. "Exactly what are you sorry for, Maxim?"

I studied her face, trying to find the answer therein. But her eyes regarded me coolly, and her delicate features were taut with frustration. Even so, she was beautiful beyond my imagination, and I couldn't keep from lifting a hand to her cheek and brushing off a smattering of sand crusted there.

At the touch of my fingers, she drew in a quick breath.

I needed to end the contact, but at her equally rapid exhalation, my attention shifted to her mouth, to her lips. I'd never once thought about what it would be like to kiss her. But suddenly I could think of nothing else. What would happen if I bent in and stole just one kiss?

"Your apology?" came her whisper.

I glanced up to see that she was also staring at my mouth. Was she wondering what it would be like to kiss me? With the interest she was exhibiting, I had the feeling she wouldn't push me away, that she might even welcome the kiss. No doubt the kiss would be sweet and gentle.

It would be the perfect way to facilitate more between us and give the guards something to report to Rasmus to keep him content.

But did I dare?

Her long lashes fluttered lower, shielding her eyes. "Are you insinuating I have affection for you but denying the same for yourself?"

"No." Was that why she was upset? Because I'd placed the weight of affection upon her instead of taking it upon myself?

"I know you are too intelligent to believe we have only friendship betwixt us and nothing more." Her low voice did strange things to my insides. "Or perhaps you believe I am a fool and cannot sense that something else is there."

"You're not a fool—"

"Then what am I?" Her lashes lifted, the move

sweeping me back and taking me off guard. I found myself peering into the depths of her eyes, the green warm and welcoming.

The only way forward with her was with honesty—or at least as much as I could afford. "I don't deny something else is there. But I fear speaking of it, since it will do neither of us good and perhaps bring heartache."

She reached up and brushed at a strand of my hair that had come loose from my leather hair cord. The soft caress stole my breath. "I would have you speak of it, Maxim." Her fingers made a trail to my cheek, this time stealing away my rationale.

"Elinor . . ." She wanted to know how I really felt. And I couldn't deny her the truth. I'd never been able to deny her anything.

"If I am to bind myself to a man I do not care about tonight, I would have this one small pleasure with a man I do care about today."

I hesitated yet leaned into her touch and dropped the items I was holding. "You are more than just a friend."

She waited, searching my face while she fingered another strand of my hair. If I'd wanted to keep my relationship in the friendship realm, her touch broke down my ability to do so.

"You are my everything." The whispered words slipped out before I could censor them. 'Twas likely the most honest thing I'd said to her thus far. And yet it was far too private and scared me more than I wanted to admit. What if I lost her again? This time forever? I wouldn't be able to survive it.

I started to back away, but her fingers skimmed to my neck. She rose on her toes, wrapping her other hand behind my neck. In the next instant, she lifted her face to mine and at the same time guided my head down until our lips collided.

The touch of her mouth, the warmth of her breath, the firmness of her hold sent my pulse into a thundering gallop. For a moment, I could think of nothing but kissing her back, pressing in, and letting our lips mesh together in a blissful few seconds.

Just as quickly, I pulled away, releasing her and extricating myself. Before I gave myself any reason to grab her and kiss her again, I spun and paced several feet away.

My heartbeat thudded so hard I could barely hear the waves breaking against the shore. What was I doing? Nothing good would come of kissing Elinor. I couldn't lead her to believe more could exist between us. Could I?

But what harm was there in sharing another kiss? Or two?

A bolt of heat charged through my blood with the need to gather her and kiss her completely senseless. I folded my arms across my chest to keep from doing anything, especially from turning and reaching for her.

I waited for her to say something, to make a witty remark about her last taste of freedom or something like that.

But when she brushed past me a moment later, her expression was somber, even sad. Was she coming to understand, just as I had, that giving way to any feelings developing between us would only lead to heartache?

Elinor and I had never been destined to be together. I'd learned that lesson already, along with the fact that I could never trust Rasmus. The quicker Elinor and I could accept our fates and learn to live within the parameters established for us, the happier we'd be.

Chapter 12

Elinor

I'd kissed Maxim. I'd really kissed him.

I wanted to bury my face in my hands and hide, but I forced myself to sit as regally as I'd been trained in my chair at the head table of the feast. Maxim was nowhere present in the room that I'd observed, or perhaps I would have gone through with hiding.

If I was honest with myself, I'd been hiding since running away from him after the kiss. I hadn't spoken to him on the boat trip back to Vordinberg. I'd ridden ahead of him during the climb through town to the castle. Once at the stables, I'd rushed to part ways and hadn't seen him in the few hours since.

Of course, all the while my maidservants had helped me don another one of my best gowns and coil my hair into an elegant knot, I'd done little else but relive the kiss. How had I been so bold as to initiate it? What had gotten into me?

On the other hand, what woman could have resisted him after he uttered the most romantic words

I'd ever heard: *"You are my everything."*

Even now, amidst my mortification, his words reverberated through my mind and pulsed through my blood, stirring a strange, sweet longing for him. The simple truth was that I'd loved every minute we'd spent together last night and today, and I didn't want our time to come to an end.

I'd gained my friend back with all the qualities I'd always loved about him. But I'd also gained something else I was still trying to understand, something that had to do with how handsome and muscular and chiseled and darkly tanned and roguish he was. . . .

I nodded politely at the nobleman seated beside me in response to the conversation, but I had no interest in him or the others. It was clear now—none of those chosen for me could compare with Maxim. Not now and not in a century of tomorrows.

Perhaps all these years Maxim had occupied a piece of my heart. And now that he'd returned, I could see how my devotion to him had been holding me back and preventing me from caring about another man.

My insides heated again at the memory of the way I'd thrown myself at Maxim. At the time, I'd felt justified, telling myself I deserved to kiss him before I was relegated to kissing forever someone I didn't want. But in kissing Maxim, in the moment of having his lips upon mine, of having him respond, of having his fullest ardor, of having his deepest devotion, I'd realized just how much I wanted to kiss him again. And again. And again.

I wasn't satisfied with just one kiss and one moment of pleasure. I wanted a lifetime with him. But both of us knew such a thing was impossible. Utterly impossible.

That's why he'd held himself at a distance, why he'd used caution, why he was reluctant to cross any boundaries. He'd known doing so would fan flames yearning for what could never be and make us discontent with the friendship we'd resumed.

I fidgeted with the spoon in the silver bowl in front of me, stirring the pudding but unable to force myself to take a bite.

The mood in the great hall was decidedly reserved. Word had reached us that King Canute and his army were marching toward the Valley of Red Dragons, one of the only level areas between the mountains connecting Norvegia to Swaine. The possibility of war with Swaine was all everyone was talking about. Earlier in the day, the king had sent missives throughout the land to the nobility of the southern realm and the clan chieftains of the north, alerting them of the need to rally their forces.

Despite being distracted by thoughts of Maxim, I'd tried to listen to the speculations. As the future leader of the country, I needed to stay abreast of the issues. I wanted to understand why King Canute wanted Norvegia, what he stood to gain from invading and attempting to force a union with me.

Some mentioned the Swainians were discontent over the mining rights in the Snowden Range, believing they should have been allotted more land after the boundary lines had been redrawn as a result of the last border skirmish.

Others discussed the dry conditions and a poor harvest in Swaine, speculating they were attacking with the hope of gaining the provisions they needed to survive the upcoming winter.

Whatever the cause of the aggression, I had the potential to stop King Canute if I invoked the power of the Sword of the Magi. With the threat of so mighty a sword at our disposal—even if yet unleashed—perhaps King Canute would hesitate to push forward into Norvegia. If the legends held true, once the worthiest man held the blade, we would surely defeat King Canute and his army.

Yes, Rasmus and Maxim were wise to suggest the use of the ancient relic. If only I could gather the courage to suggest it.

From a side table with the other Royal Sages, Rasmus stood and approached the king. As he neared the head table, his gaze connected with mine, and he gave a slight nod, as though he'd read my thoughts and wanted me to follow through with the plans.

A tremor started in my stomach and rippled out to my limbs. The feast was finished. We'd finally come to the end of the weeklong courtship. It was time for me to take my stand in front of everyone and announce my choice of a husband. Once I did, we would proceed with a betrothal ceremony and the declaration of my succession as the next ruler of Norvegia.

If I suggested using the sword to do the choosing, we would have to postpone the betrothal and succession ceremonies at least another day. My request would likely irritate the king, especially since he'd wanted me to make my selection days ago.

What should I do?

The master of ceremonies also approached the head table. It was the cue that the time had come. I could no longer wait. I stood, and upon my rising, the noblemen also stood out of respect.

As the king and queen crossed to their thrones at the center of the dais, silence descended over the room. Once they were seated, I made my way toward them, a slow beat of dread tapping within my chest. As much as I'd wanted to avoid this part of the week, time had a way of moving us toward the destination regardless of how much we resisted.

I went through the customary procedure of bowing and kissing their hands before I turned and faced the noblemen who had gathered in front of the dais. The rhythm of dread inside only pounded harder. The same question I'd faced all week now shouted at me. How could I possibly choose the right man?

At a movement near the entrance of the great hall, I glanced beyond the sea of noble faces and the tables of courtiers and staff.

There, in the passageway just outside the great hall, stood the one I truly longed for.

Maxim moved just inside the doorway on the periphery. His attire was disheveled and his expression disgruntled, as if he hadn't wanted to be here but had forced himself.

I didn't allow my sights to linger upon him, lest I draw undue attention his way. Even so, a forceful knocking started up again inside, this time a protest— one that hurt, one that demanded my honesty. I couldn't single out any other man tonight. Maybe not ever.

I couldn't deny that among my deepest secrets, those I hadn't even allowed myself to consider, resided the hope that one day Maxim and I could both be Royal Sages. Together. Side by side. I couldn't give up my dream yet. I now had a valid means of giving myself more time.

"Your Royal Majesty, after a week of seeking to find the worthiest of these noblemen to be my husband and the future king, I have decided . . ."

I wished I could glance again at Maxim to gauge his reaction. Was he hoping I would postpone so we might find a way to be together? Or would I find resignation upon his countenance?

The king straightened, his expression alight with expectation, and the queen smiled at me as benevolently as always.

Had I been a natural-born child of theirs, defying them might have been easier. But after making my entire life an exercise in pleasing them, I didn't want to hurt them now.

Rasmus stood beside the king at his right hand. Though he didn't nod again, his dark eyes seemed to assure me I had every right to defer this decision to a relic that could take the weight of the choice from my shoulders and place it upon Providence Himself.

"Your Royal Majesty." I infused my voice with confidence. If I came across as tentative, the king would deny my request. "I do not have the wisdom to choose the future king for myself. Thus, I humbly beseech you to allow the Sword of the Magi to decide upon my future husband for me."

At my declaration, voices arose, and the great hall erupted into confusion.

The king sat forward, his forehead furrowing and his voice bellowing with consternation. "What is the meaning of such a request?"

I had to explain myself quickly before he squelched the idea. "Your great-great-grandfather, King Stefan the Worthy, was the last king to free the sword. He wielded it with such power his enemies could not defeat him."

King Ulrik's response stalled.

Rasmus bent in and spoke calmly. "Your Majesty, the princess is correct. The Sword of the Magi can give the bearer the strength to defeat the unjust, the unfaithful, and the untruthful."

As my declaration, along with Rasmus's, began to penetrate the room, the protests fell away. Rasmus straightened and beckoned toward the door. Two priests moved forward carrying a long case draped in black velvet. Maxim followed at a measured distance.

Silence descended, this time so heavily that each pound of my heartbeat echoed in my head. Had I made this decision wisely and for the well-being of my country? Or had I done so selfishly, with ulterior motives?

As Maxim drew nearer the dais, I wished for him to look up and reassure me as he had earlier at the Stavekirche that this was indeed the right path to take. But he kept his focus on the sword, once again securely locked in the case.

He'd masked any and all emotions so that whatever I'd witnessed on his face moments ago was gone. He was as unreadable as a blank parchment.

When the priests reached the front of the room, a servant waiting in the wing rushed forward with a pedestal table. The priests carefully pulled away the velvet covering and arranged the red cedar case on the narrow table before stepping away. Maxim positioned himself beside it and bowed to the king.

One thing was clear. Rasmus had expected my

declaration to use the sword and had been well prepared, which meant Maxim was working closely with his father. Should that concern me? Did they truly long to help me, or was this something different altogether?

Part of me wanted to analyze their partnership in this effort. But the other part of me needed the sword and the promise it seemed to be holding out.

King Ulrik stood, descended from the dais, and circled the case. "While I cherish this sacred relic, it has remained an enigma to our country and church these many years since the time of King Stefan the Worthy."

"It has indeed been an enigma, Your Majesty." Rasmus didn't move from his position next to the throne. "That is why I have prioritized studying it these many years as your Royal Sage, so that should such a time as this arise, I would be ready with wise counsel."

The king bent and examined the long wooden box. "No one has succeeded at opening the case in my lifetime. If we cannot open it, how can the sword do its choosing?"

Rasmus nodded at Maxim. "It took me many days to solve the mystery of its opening. But Maxim discovered how to unlock it in two minutes, eighteen seconds."

The king paused in his perusal of the case to regard Maxim. "Can you open it now?"

Maxim bowed his head. "Yes, Your Majesty."

The king stood back and waved at the case. "Then I give you leave."

With another bow, Maxim stepped up to the cedar

box. He fingered the edge as I'd watched him do at the church. Seconds later, the lid lifted.

Murmurs and gasps filled the air.

The silver sword with its jeweled pommel rested against a faded crimson. It glinted with an aura of mystery, as though it had yet to reveal what it wanted us to know.

The king gazed upon it as though viewing the Christ child himself, and the queen joined him, standing by his side. Finally, the king spoke to Rasmus. "The engraving on the blade? Have you translated it?"

"Yes, Your Majesty. It's an ancient language, no longer spoken or written. While I made a study of the language over months, Maxim learned it in four hours."

My pride in Maxim only increased with each new revelation. He was a genius. I'd already known that. But his intelligence was exceeding Rasmus's. That should impress the king.

King Ulrik cocked his head at the relic. "Maxim, I give you leave to read it to us."

Maxim made a show of looking at the engraving, although I was certain he had it memorized. "It reads: 'For a worthy king.'"

"Please explain for us what that means."

Maxim straightened. "The sword will not come loose, not until the man worthiest of becoming king takes hold of it. Only then will it free itself to allow the bearer to defend himself from those who would do him ill."

I half-trembled at the prospect of such a man coming forth and being able to wield the blessed sword to protect us against our enemies. Who would be able to accomplish it? Was the feat another riddle to uncover, or would only the worthiest truly wield it?

The king was silent a long moment before narrowing his eyes upon Maxim. "Since you know so many secrets about the sword, perhaps you should be the first to endeavor to free it."

My muscles tensed with a sudden keen longing. If anyone could uncover the means of freeing the sword, Maxim could. He'd already opened the case and read the engraving. Maybe he was the worthiest.

Oh, if only he could pull it free. Then we could be together without any more boundaries. He'd be mine. I would be his. And we'd never have to worry about being torn asunder again.

Maxim backed away from the sword. "I regret I must decline, Your Majesty."

I hadn't realized I'd been holding my breath. But at Maxim's clear and unwavering statement, a whoosh of air slipped past my lips. Protest swelled in my chest along with a demand that he should at least try. But what if I'd misinterpreted his declaration from earlier today? What if he hadn't meant I was his *everything* in the way I'd taken it?

After all, he'd turned his back on me after the kiss. Maybe he was just as embarrassed by it—or more— than I was.

"I am but a humble man of humble origins," Maxim continued. "The princess must marry a Norwegian of royal or noble blood. The law prohibits royalty from marrying commoners."

Of course. He was right. I stuffed down my disappointment. Or at least attempted to, even as sadness settled over me.

For a heartbeat, Maxim held the king's gaze before lowering his head. After a moment, the king nodded. "Very well, then we shall begin with all haste the process of testing. Each of the twelve noblemen will attempt to take up the Sword of the Magi first. If they are unable to do so, we shall invite every nobleman in the kingdom to take a turn."

"Every?" I squeezed the word past my constricting throat. "Do we have the time for such a search?"

The king grazed the jeweled pommel. "With so powerful a weapon on our side, we must take the time. Then you will not only have a worthy husband and king, but Norvegia will be assured a victory against King Canute and Swaine."

Chapter 13

MAXIM

BY DAWN, THE LINE OF NOBLEMEN AWAITING A TURN AT FREEING the sword stretched through the great hall, down the passageway, and out into the inner bailey. The number of men arriving to Vordinberg and the royal residence was multiplying exponentially by the hour. Soon the line would stretch out of the castle boundaries and extend into the city.

I'd stood beside the Sword of the Magi all throughout the night, giving each man a turn to dislodge the relic from the case—no longer than three minutes, the fair amount of time determined by the Royal Sages.

I wasn't sure why I'd been given the task of overseeing the process of finding the worthiest king. But since Rasmus had assigned me the role, he had an ulterior motive. He always did.

From the corner of my eye, I glimpsed him speaking with the two newest Knights of Brethren near a side doorway. I still hadn't figured out why Rasmus had related my accomplishments to the king regarding how quickly

I'd opened the case and learned the ancient language. Again, he'd done it for a reason. If only I could rationalize his motivation.

After the long days and little sleep of late, my mind wasn't as sharp as it normally was. Was that Rasmus's intention? To weaken me to more readily do his bidding?

The sunrise was brightening the high, narrow eastern windows filled with thick opaque glass. Elinor would be standing in our turret making notations, but without me today. Or any day.

My heart squeezed with the need to be with her, our faces to the east, the glow of dawn in our eyes, and the cool sea breeze blowing our hair.

When she left the hall last night after the twelve had failed to remove the sword from the case, her expression had been etched in resignation. Perhaps she'd expected one of the Knights of Brethren to succeed—Torvald, Kristoffer, or Sigfrid. Perhaps she'd simply wanted confirmation of their worthiness.

Whatever the case, she hadn't expected the king to invite every nobleman within the kingdom to attempt to free the sword. But King Ulrik clearly hoped to gain the sword to deter Canute. If not to deter, then to defeat. The king would evaluate every eligible nobleman of marriageable age—no matter his birth order.

And what would the king do if every nobleman from the White Sea in the south to the Tundra Sea in the north took hold of the sword only to fail? What then? Would he acknowledge the truth: that the sword would pick the worthiest man to be king, no matter his bloodline?

When the king gave me leave to test the sword, I'd been mightily tempted to try it. But the truth had held me back—the truth that I wasn't worthy. My heart was too stained, my ambitions too selfish, my motives too full of lies.

Nevertheless, I'd given the excuse the king had wanted, the reasoning he'd used that long-ago morn when he sent me away. From the flicker in his eyes last night, he'd recognized my use of his own words. With Elinor standing nearby, he hadn't dared to acknowledge them. But I suspected my small act of defiance wouldn't remain unpunished, either by Rasmus or the king.

"Three minutes have elapsed." I spoke the words for the 182nd time. How many more noblemen would fail?

If I had three minutes to figure out how to free the sword, would I be able to do so? Of course, I had the unfair advantage of having studied every angle of the sword most of the long night.

Nothing visible was holding the sword to the case—no iron clasp, no unbreakable twine, no visible screws, no residue of tar adhesive. The sword lay unhindered against a thin silky red cloth and the cedarwood box.

Most would speculate that the sword was somehow enchanted. But from my extensive study of raw elements drawn from the earth, I guessed that an impossibly strong but thin magnetic layer was embedded into the wood and that the designer had crafted the magnetic layer to shape the sword in an unbreakable bond.

The question that had plagued me all throughout the night was, how could a magnetic hold be broken? Ordinary strength alone wouldn't suffice. Something else was necessary to sever the energy field. But what?

I'd gone over every possibility including heat, fire, ice, water, herbs with special properties, chemicals extracted from one life form or another, and more. But in the hours of analysis, I hadn't come up with a viable prospect.

Had Rasmus?

As the next nobleman stepped up to the pedestal and took hold of the hilt, I glanced toward Rasmus. In that instant, he looked my way. His brow was slightly raised, as though to question whether I'd yet uncovered the answer to this newest riddle of how to separate the sword from its case.

Was that why he'd placed me next to it all night? Would he keep me in this position until I had the answer?

Forcing my expression to remain as placid as possible, I stifled a weary sigh. All I really wanted to do was race up to the turret and stand beside Elinor as the sun finished making its appearance. When the rays broke through the cross-shaped arrow slit, I wanted to kneel next to her in prayer. And then when she stood, her face serene and filled with anticipation of the day to come, I wanted to pull her close and kiss her again.

My mind went back to the kiss she'd given me on the island, to the warmth of her lips against mine, the delicate pressure, the sweetness of her taste. Just the memory made my blood pump faster.

When I proposed marriage to her at age ten, I hadn't even known what kissing was. My offer had been from simple heartfelt devotion. Of course, during my days as a Sagacite as I'd begun to grow and mature, I'd wondered if Elinor was also changing, had imagined her turning into a graceful and attractive woman.

But sharing such an intimate act as a kiss with a princess? Unthinkable. It was something I hadn't dared to dream about, not even in my wildest fantasies.

Now shared, I couldn't keep it from influencing all my thoughts. The very touch had seeped deep into my being, down into my soul, awakening me to the need for her I hadn't known was so consuming. While I couldn't kiss her again, I would keep the memory of this one tucked away where I could relive it forever.

Shouts rang from outside the great hall. The noblemen standing in line murmured among themselves. Some left their places and jogged out of the room. The gravity of their expressions and the urgency of their departure sparked a warning inside me. Something had happened, most likely further threats from King Canute.

As another three minutes ended, more of the noblemen conversed, the hum of distress filling the air.

A messenger approached Rasmus, bowed, and spoke tersely. I strained to hear, but the courier was too distant. A moment later, Rasmus and the other Sages retreated from the great hall in a flurry of rustling robes, their hasty pace only tightening my gut.

"What is the news?" I asked the next nobleman who stepped forward to take his place in front of the pedestal table and the sword.

The young man paused, his hand ready to grip the hilt. "King Canute and his fighting men have crossed the border over the night. They are making their way toward Vordinberg even as we speak."

Elinor

I stood beside the queen in the inner bailey along with the rest of the ladies of the court. The king and the Knights of Brethren mingled together, ready to join the army amassing along the waterfront. Together they would set sail for the Valley of Red Dragons, where they would intercept King Canute.

I could only pray that King Ulrik's superior forces and his fierce knights would be able to stop King Canute's march to the capital.

The queen reached for my hand, her fingers trembling against mine even as she remained poised and projected an air of assurance as we bade our good-byes.

The king drew near on his steed, his knights remaining a short distance away to give him a moment of privacy. As he reined in, so grand in his armor, I peered up at him. The clouds now obscured the morning sun I'd watched rise a short while earlier. Their dark underbellies hinted at rain, and I prayed the king and all his men would remain safe, not only from the enemy but also from the elements that could often turn deadly in Norvegia.

I took the king's gloved hand and kissed it. "Before you leave, shall we choose the man of my betrothal, Your Majesty?" I didn't want him to worry about my succession while he was gone. If the matter were settled, he'd be able to ride away and face danger with more peace about the future, wouldn't he?

The king glanced at the line of noblemen winding out a side door of the castle and into the courtyard. Men continued to arrive through the gatehouse, dismounting and leaving their horses to the tending of grooms while they joined those who hoped to free the sword from its case.

"Your betrothal is important, Elinor." His eyes were as kind as always. "You were wise to invoke the power of the sword. We must unfetter the ancient weapon and make use of its great power in the upcoming battle."

Before joining the ladies in the bailey, I'd glimpsed Maxim still inside the great hall. Since he'd been the one to unlock the case, he'd been given the honor of overseeing the Sword of the Magi. But he'd been at his duties for hours without a break. Surely someone else could supervise while he slept.

As soon as the king left, I intended to approach Rasmus and request that Maxim be allowed a respite.

The king squeezed my hand tenderly before he let go. "I have instructed my Sages and the Noble Council to conduct the betrothal and succession ceremonies the moment the sword is freed. Vow you will accept the sword's choice and make the arrangements with all haste?"

My heart quavered. Could I accept the sword's choosing? Or would I find myself coming up with excuses to delay my betrothal again, just as I had this past week?

I swallowed my resistance. This was my duty. My destiny. I had to go forward with it, no matter how difficult. No matter how much my heart might protest.

"Please, Elinor?" The king's voice dropped to a whispered plea.

How could I say no to this man who had so lovingly raised me? "I vow it."

The king nodded, then shifted his attention to the queen, his eyes softening. "Hopefully, this confrontation will not last long."

The queen kissed his hand as I had, her eyes filling with tears. Earlier, she'd beseeched the king not to go, to let Sir Ansgar lead Norvegia's army against King

Canute's. The Knights of Brethren, especially Ansgar, had encouraged the king to allow them to go ahead and determine the magnitude of the threat.

But the king had protested staying behind, had wanted to lead his knights. His Sages had agreed the army would benefit in seeing their king in charge. He would show his prowess and strength, sending the message that he wouldn't allow anyone to trifle with him.

With a final farewell, the king steered his horse in the direction of the gatehouse. Ansgar took his spot at the king's side. As their horses' hooves clattered against the stone path leading away from the castle, a battle was waging in my heart.

I wanted someone to free the sword as soon as possible to aid our army in defeating Swaine. But I also hesitated, my heart protesting much too loudly the prospect of being with anyone but Maxim.

Chapter 14

MAXIM

TWENTY-FOUR HOURS. I'D STOOD AS OVERSEER OF THE SWORD OF the Magi for exactly twenty-four hours before Rasmus sent one of the Royal Sages to take my place. The line of noblemen continued to remain steady as more arrived from their family estates in the Richlande Lowlands as well as other port cities along the coast.

With the news of King Canute's army marching into Norvegia, most of the nobility came with their retainers and villeins, ready to join King Ulrik's forces straightaway after their detour to the royal castle for a chance to free the sword.

As I stumbled exhausted into my chamber, Dag met me and led me to my bed before I collapsed. I fell asleep forthwith. But as tired as I was, my sleep wasn't restful and was filled with strange dreams about freeing the sword and using it to slay anyone who opposed my ascent to the throne.

When Dag shook me awake hours later, I realized I'd been allowed exactly twelve hours of slumber—likely by

Rasmus. Only he operated with such precision. Dag laid out another new outfit from Rasmus—given in an effort to make me appear more important and wealthier than I truly was. I hastily began to dress, fearing Rasmus would send Elinor to my door again. All the while, I peppered Dag with questions about what had transpired over the past hours.

He informed me that no nobleman had yet been able to free the sword from its case. Also, word had just arrived that the king and his army had set up camp near the Valley of Red Dragons with the hope of blocking Canute and his army from drawing any closer to Vordinberg.

Before I finished donning my attire, a knock sounded on my chamber door.

"Hurry, Dag," I whispered, slipping into my final shoe even as Dag attached my stockings.

Although I didn't know for certain, I suspected Rasmus intended for me to free the sword and stand by Elinor's side as her betrothed. He would therefore expect me to continue spending time with Elinor so that she would eagerly accept me even though I was a commoner. No doubt Rasmus would use her affection for me as a catalyst to change the law—or at the very least make an exception this once, convincing everyone that a man of my lowly status should be eligible to marry her.

The knock sounded again, this time louder.

My pulse kicked a punishing beat against my chest. It would be all too easy to continue doing Rasmus's bidding and step in as Elinor's husband. Because I wanted her. Desperately. I couldn't deny it even if I tried.

My words to her came rushing back. I'd told her she was my everything. And that was the truth. I hadn't spoken the words to win her affection and bend her to my will. Rather, the words had tumbled out without thought to ramifications . . . because somehow, in the process of spending time with Elinor, every single wall I'd erected to protect my heart had crumbled, leaving me defenseless.

She was and always would be the sunrise in the dark shadows of my life.

I swallowed a groan that needed releasing. The simple truth was that I cherished her too much, and I couldn't use her any longer. No matter how that might infuriate Rasmus. And no matter how that might interfere with my future aspirations.

The other simple truth was that I'd allowed myself to become entrenched in Rasmus's web of deceit. Somehow, I needed to find a way to extricate myself from his web before it became impossible to do so.

As Dag opened the door, I straightened my doublet and then quickly combed my fingers through my hair. At the sight of one of Rasmus's scribes holding a scroll, I let my hands drop, unsure whether to be relieved or disappointed Elinor wasn't waiting for me.

I hadn't seen her since last eve when she'd approached Rasmus in the great hall and exchanged words with him, the second time that day. Though I hadn't been close enough to hear her on either occasion, her body language told me she was angry.

I surmised she'd complained to Rasmus of his refusal to allow me a break, had perhaps even threatened him. That's when Rasmus had permitted me to go back to my chamber. The princess might have believed she'd influenced Rasmus's decision, but no doubt he'd been testing her to see how much she cared for me and putting her affection on display for everyone to see.

The servant handed Dag the scroll. "His Excellency would like Maxim to translate and study this scroll. In two hours, he should report to His Excellency's chambers and be prepared to discuss the contents."

I wanted to refuse, to tell the servant to report back to Rasmus that I was finished, that I didn't care about my punishment. He could put me in prison for insubordination or send me to the Frozen Wilds to live out the rest of my days in solitude.

But I clamped my mouth closed and resisted. I would visit Rasmus in two hours and tell him myself that I was putting an end to whatever role he had carved out for me in his scheming.

I'd already betrayed Elinor enough with my dishonesty. And I wouldn't do it any longer.

Elinor

At the patter of footsteps descending the stairwell, I jumped back into the hallway and flattened myself against the wall. I didn't want anyone to see me heading into the Sage's wing of the castle and guess I was on my way to visit Maxim. Surely such a rumor would cause a scandal for both of us.

After the footsteps passed by, I slipped into the tower. The low clouds and steady drizzle of rain added to the darkness of the passageway.

As I wound up the narrow stairway and entered the wing where Maxim's chamber was located, my heart sped. Had I allowed him enough time to sleep? Though he'd masked his weariness well last eve, I'd seen it in his face and heard it in his voice.

I now regretted showing my anger with Rasmus in my demand that he find a replacement for Maxim. But the Royal Sage hadn't seemed perturbed in the least and had promptly sent Maxim to his chambers.

I knocked tentatively.

A moment later, Maxim's door swung open, and I found myself peering past Dag's hunched head toward the bed. I certainly wasn't hoping to catch Maxim half-clad, was I?

"Your Highness, Maxim has just left to visit Rasmus." Dag spoke in a muffled tone, but the message was clear enough.

Stifling my disappointment, I started down the tower stairway. I needed to return to my own chambers and attend to the matters at hand, which included making sure the castle was well provisioned in the event King Canute made it all the way to Vordinberg and laid siege.

But at the same time, I couldn't abandon Maxim to the wiles of Rasmus again, could I? What if Rasmus punished Maxim in some other cruel fashion?

As I turned a final corner, I glimpsed Maxim entering Rasmus's chamber. I picked up my pace. Rasmus had always been too hard on Maxim, often pushing him to the limits of his mental endurance. Last eve had been the perfect example of that.

What benefit did Rasmus gain in being so harsh with Maxim? Of course, the strictness had challenged Maxim, likely making him more intelligent than anyone else. But why did Rasmus want Maxim to excel at such a punishing cost?

With my feet already bare in an effort to silence my footsteps, I approached the door without a sound. Lifting a hand to knock, I hesitated. I'd only been in Rasmus's chambers once, when I was a girl and had gone with Maxim. It had been dark and crowded and the air laden with incense. Even now, the spicy mixture of rare frankincense lingered in the hallway.

"I pray twenty-four hours was sufficient for your study of how to free the sword?" Rasmus's voice was faint but clear.

Maxim was studying how to free the Sword of the Magi? For what purpose?

"It was more than sufficient." Maxim's reply was low and even, the way he'd always spoken to his father, as though he needed to be perfect.

I dropped my hand to my side. Eavesdropping was impolite, but in this case I sensed something malicious was occurring, something that made my skin crawl.

"While we await word back from the chieftains, you will continue to enamor the princess and make her fall in love with you."

My breath snagged in my chest. Maxim was attempting to make me fall in love with him?

Silence stretched, and I held myself absolutely still even as my mind raced. What was Rasmus insinuating? Why was he instructing Maxim to make me fall in love with him? Was I some kind of challenge for Maxim, so he could learn to excel in the art of winning women?

Hurt welled up within me. After the past couple of days, I'd formed the belief that Maxim and I had cleared up the past hurt and confusion. That we'd renewed our deep friendship. I'd even come to believe something more was developing between us—an attraction that went beyond friendship.

But if what Rasmus was saying was true, then Maxim had set out in a calculated effort to win my heart and was spending time with me to purposefully make me love him.

Before I could rationalize everything, Rasmus spoke again. "Tell me why the missives needed to be sent to the chieftains."

Again, I silenced my thoughts and waited, needing desperately to understand what Maxim was doing and why.

"If all fifteen chieftains request a change in the law and all seven Royal Sages agree to the change, then the Noble Council must take a vote."

From the precise nature of his statement, Maxim likely had the entire book of law memorized.

What law exactly did Rasmus hope to change?

I remained frozen in front of the door.

"Based on past votes," Maxim continued, "the confidence interval for an odds ratio of twenty-two men agreeing contains an interval of .61 and 3.18, which still must be transformed by finding the antilog—"

"When you free the sword, they will agree." Rasmus's voice boasted such confidence that I couldn't hold back a shiver.

Maxim intended to free the sword himself? Had he discovered a way that had nothing to do with Providence? Perhaps there was nothing special about the ancient relic after all.

"Based on past votes of the Noble Council," Maxim said, "the odds are even riskier—"

"The sword holds great sway."

"Even if the law is changed, the king must approve of the union." Maxim's tone remained unruffled. "The king has his heart set against me. He'll dispute the match of a commoner and royalty and influence the Noble Council to do the same."

A bitter sickness roiled through my stomach as the information finally took form. Maxim *was* planning to free the sword, feign worthiness, and change the law—the one prohibiting royalty from marrying commoners. No doubt he believed by winning my affection, I would champion the change of the law, too, so we could be together.

I'd believed he genuinely cared about me, that I was his everything as he'd claimed. But all along he'd been collaborating with Rasmus to gain my love so that, ultimately, he could take the throne.

"You will have no need to worry about opposition from the king." Rasmus's voice dropped a notch, almost so low I missed his statement. "The danger in battle shall be grave indeed."

I cupped a hand over my mouth as horror raced through my blood, turning it to ice. Rasmus was insinuating that the king would soon face death in battle. From within or without the ranks of his army, I did not know. But one thing was certain. I'd uncovered a plot to murder the king. And the man I'd thought was my best friend, a man I'd quickly developed affection for, was involved.

A trembling began inside and worked into my limbs. Within seconds I was shaking with enough force I was afraid I might collapse in the passageway in front of Rasmus's door. Then when Maxim exited, he'd find me there and realize I'd overheard their plans.

I had to go. Had to get away from this part of the castle. Had to act like nothing was amiss when it seemed my entire world had suddenly come crashing down upon me.

I retreated from the door as silently as I'd come. My bare footsteps hardly seemed to touch the floor as I flew down the passageway. By the time I reached my chambers, I knew what I had to do.

Chapter 15

MAXIM

RASMUS'S SCHEMES WERE WORSE THAN I'D BELIEVED POSSIBLE.

As I stood near his desk, the darkness of the rainy day slithered around me, invading my soul and threatening to overwhelm the flickers of hope still burning there.

Everything Rasmus had just revealed had been systematically laid out in a careful progression, one statement upon another like the building of a pyramid, until he'd added the capstone—the revelation that he planned for the king to face demise in battle. Was that why he'd insisted the king go into battle against Canute? Perhaps he'd influenced the other Sages to agree with him, so unbeknownst to them they were sending the king to his death.

If I raised charges of treason against Rasmus, he could easily deflect accusations. He'd left no trail of evidence that could incriminate him. Rather, it would point to me as the one making plans to become the next king. In the end, 'twould be my word against his.

I didn't need to ponder long to know everyone would

believe Rasmus and shun me. Especially once word spread about my offer to marry the princess when we'd been but children. Rasmus would lead everyone to believe I'd always had aspirations for the throne and that's why the king had sent me away in the first place.

From the calculated glint in Rasmus's eyes as he studied the scroll upon his desk, I could almost believe he'd planned my leaving Vordinberg those many years ago. Perhaps he'd instructed the tutor to stir Elinor's young emotions over the courtship issue, then encouraged the king to send me away, intending to use my mistake later to control me.

I struggled hard to keep my expression from revealing the disgust and frustration rioting within me. I'd come into Rasmus's chambers to inform him I could no longer deceive the princess, nor could I free the sword. But somehow, over the past few minutes, instead of freeing myself from his web of deceit I was firmly wrapped into it like a fly in spider silk.

My muscles tightened, cutting off my breath. I had to find a way out of his trap. Surely I could analyze every angle of his plot and find a crack. But until then, I had to convince Rasmus I was his willing pawn.

The light coming from the stub of wax left in the candleholder revealed more of the ancient cuneiform on the parchment spread out before him, a piece of the ancient writing likely giving away more secrets of the Sword of the Magi.

Over the past two hours of studying the scroll Rasmus's scribe had delivered to me, I'd finally uncovered the method of freeing the sword from its case. The severing of the bond required sacrifice by blood, although exactly how, I didn't know.

Rasmus ignored me, likely sensing my inner turmoil and giving me time to accept my fate. But I wouldn't, no matter how long he made me wait.

After precisely one hour, he broke the silence. "Fourteen days."

The inner workings of my brain began to spin, calculating fourteen days. A fortnight would give the chieftains time to receive and reply to their missives regarding changing the law. A fortnight would also provide enough time for the fight with Canute to commence and for the king to face mortal danger.

"Having needed only two days to entice the princess to kiss you," Rasmus said, "you will have no trouble convincing her to marry you in fortnight."

Though I'd suspected word about my kiss would get back to Rasmus, I'd wanted to keep it private, sacred, cherished. But with Rasmus, my life was an open scroll, a blank story he was determined to author.

Words of protest pressed for release. But I had to keep Rasmus from learning of my objections to every part of his plan if I had any hope of thwarting him. With the great reservation I'd developed during my past interactions, I simply bowed my head.

"You are dismissed." He flicked his hand.

I measured my steps to the door with caution, not wanting to give Rasmus the satisfaction of knowing just how eager I was to leave his presence. Once the door closed behind me, I continued with the same pace and kept my head and shoulders straight even as my emotions raged within me.

If I defied Rasmus, I'd lose my chance at going to the Studium Generale. I'd never be eligible to become an Erudite, Sage, or Royal Sage. In fact, Rasmus would probably feel the need to eliminate me altogether in order to ensure that I'd never speak of his treachery and undermine him in any way. He'd accuse me of treason, and I'd have to spend the rest of my days on the run.

But if I went along with Rasmus's plans like I always had, never standing up to him, never saying no to his schemes, then I'd continue to allow the darkness into my heart, staining it blacker with deceit, ambition, and selfishness. Maybe I'd eventually become greater than Rasmus. But in the process, would I lose my heart and soul altogether to total blackness and evil, the same way Rasmus had?

There was only one option. Deep inside, I'd known it all along. Even if it came with terrible sacrifice, I could do nothing less.

I refused to cooperate with Rasmus to entice Elinor any further. And I refused to convince her to marry me within two weeks. If my unwillingness to conspire with Rasmus led to my death as a traitor, so be it.

Regardless of the outcome, I had to find a way to stop Rasmus from harming both the king and the kingdom.

I wanted to seek Elinor out right away and confess everything. But if I did so, she would surely be angry, and Rasmus would know I'd told her about our schemes. At this point, I couldn't chance Rasmus discovering I was working against him, not until I made sure both Elinor and the king would remain safe.

Instead, I retired to my chambers and worked on equations for foiling Rasmus. I knew first and foremost, I needed to deliver news to the king of his danger. I calculated the risk of sending a secret message with someone trustworthy. I had to do so without alerting Rasmus, but that would be difficult since Rasmus would be watching me carefully.

Knowing I at least had to pretend to follow Rasmus's instructions on enticing Elinor lest I draw his suspicions, I set out to find her, looking in all the usual places to no avail. I inquired among her maidservants and even with her ladies-in-waiting, but their answers took me on a futile search. Clearly, Elinor hadn't wanted to be found and had given her closest companions and servants information to lead them astray.

Had she known I would seek her out? Was she making her disappearance a riddle I must solve?

I broadened the scope of my hunt from the interior of the castle to the exterior but found no clues, not even from the gatekeepers. She'd not passed by them all day for an excursion into the city. My query to the guard by the secret side door revealed the same information. She hadn't left the royal residence.

With eve fast approaching, my pulse took on a new rhythm, one that warned she wasn't playing a game. She'd vanished too completely.

With the number of noblemen coming and going all day to test their worthiness with the sword, perhaps one had secretly stolen her from the castle. But who? And with what motivation? What about Canute? I trembled at the prospect that the neighboring king had sent a spy to abduct her.

As I queried the guards standing at the entrance of the great hall, Rasmus approached. Something in his unhurried step was different, more determined, less controlled. He motioned me, and I followed him to a private antechamber used by the king when he met with his knights or Sages. The room was dark and musty, the patter of rain against the closed shutters adding to the gloom.

When the door closed behind me, Rasmus leveled a severe gaze upon me. "Where has she gone?"

I had no reason to pretend I didn't know who he was talking about. Apparently, he'd discovered the princess was nowhere to be found too. Since he had spies everywhere, I was surprised he was asking me for the princess's whereabouts.

"Your Excellency, I have looked everywhere but have not located her yet."

Rasmus pursed his lips tightly. He likely already knew that. Did he think she might have given me information she hadn't revealed to anyone else?

Mentally, I went over every one of her favorite places, even some of the new reading nooks she'd told me about. But, as before, I could find no trails.

"She has left Vordinberg." Rasmus stated the fact as though I should already know.

"Her horses are still here. And none of the guards saw her leave."

"Two horses in the stables are unaccounted for. And one of her guards is also gone."

My pulse gave a hard lurch. "Who?"

"He is an older guard. Halvard."

The image of the older man immediately came to mind—the same guard who watched her on the turret in the mornings. He'd been one of Elinor's personal guards for years and wouldn't hurt a hair on her head. He would, in fact, die for her if need be. At the very least, I could take comfort in knowing she was safe with Halvard, wherever she might be.

"Where has she gone?" Rasmus repeated the question, this time unable to keep the irritation from his tone.

I was at a loss. I knew of no reason for Elinor to sneak away from Vordinberg, which was what she'd done if the guards hadn't seen her leave. She'd either disguised herself and Halvard or hidden in a cart or some other conveyance to go undetected.

"Can we trail her?" I asked.

"I have already sent trackers out to try."

Why had she left without speaking to me first? Without telling me where she was going or what she was planning?

She'd seemed to trust me again, to genuinely care about me, and to want to renew our friendship as much as I had. What had happened to change that?

I froze.

What if she had sought me out earlier in the day? What if she'd come to my room and discovered my absence? And what if Dag had informed her I was visiting Rasmus's chambers?

Dread pumped through my blood—slow, steady, and certain. I'd oft complained about my disdain for visiting Rasmus. She was aware of Rasmus's severe discipline. And after confronting him last night, perhaps she'd thought to rescue me again.

Rasmus was studying my face, likely seeing a change in my expression, perhaps in my eyes. "You have figured out where she has gone, haven't you?"

I nodded, the dread pulsing harder. She would have had no reason to leave unless she heard the worst part of Rasmus's plotting . . . his plan to put the king in grave peril.

She'd left to warn the king.

Chapter 16

Elinor

Heavy darkness pressed upon us. Yet we urged our horses onward through the shrubs and sparse forest that ran alongside one of the many freshwater lakes within Norvegia. The thud of our horses' hooves and the crunching of twigs and leaves would alert anyone nearby of our presence. But in our mad race to reach the king, speed was more important than stealth.

"How much farther?" I tossed the question to Halvard on his mount beside me.

From beneath the hood of his cloak, the thickly muscled guard glanced to the eastern horizon across the lake. Though the rain had ceased, the sky remained overcast, preventing us from using the stars to guide our path. "I would surmise six hours, Your Highness, if not more."

I released my grip on the reins, my fingers stiff. Bringing my hands to my mouth, I breathed into my leather gloves, hoping for some warmth.

After hours of riding in the cold rain, my entire

body was frozen. My oiled cloak had kept me mostly dry, but I hadn't been able to prevent some dampness from seeping in. When night had fallen, the temperature had steadily dropped. Now, with dawn only a few hours away, I was feeling the effects deep in my flesh.

"The horses will need a rest soon, Your Highness." Halvard bent forward and patted his mount's neck.

I recognized what he was doing. He was feigning interest in the creature's well-being to convince me to stop and warm myself. I forced my teeth to stop chattering before I answered. "We can slow our pace if need be, but we cannot rest."

Halvard bowed his head and said nothing more.

I had no doubt he'd try again soon. Of all my servants and guards, I trusted him more than anyone. He only had my best interest at heart and was worried about my well-being.

But what was my suffering in comparison to the threat the king would soon face—if he hadn't already?

Sharp pain stabbed my heart, as it had since we'd ridden away from Vordinberg. Maxim had betrayed me. All along, he'd been rebuilding our friendship so he could enamor me and make me fall in love with him. The time we'd spent together, the kiss we'd shared, the closeness we'd rekindled—it had all been part of his scheming. He'd meant none of it beyond what he could gain from a union with me.

How had I been so blind? Why had I listened to him? In my vulnerability, he'd convinced me the Sword of the Magi could help me pick the worthiest king. I'd believed him, believed he wanted to help me.

But he'd only wanted to help himself. To the throne.

Oh, how he'd fooled me. He'd certainly become much more skillful at subterfuge than he used to be. He was more intelligent than he'd let on. In fact, he was a mastermind, and everything within me regretted I hadn't seen past his charade to the fraud he was. As it was, my gullibility had been a grave mistake.

I wanted to scream out into the night the frustration and anger pounding against my chest. But I had to stay shrewd if I hoped to succeed in reaching the king in time to warn him of the peril.

I blew again into my gloves, then shook first one hand rigorously and then the other with the hope of regaining some feeling.

If only I could go back in time to the last night of my courtship week to the final feast. Instead of deferring to the sword, I would have chosen one of the noblemen, perhaps Torvald, and I would have gone through with the betrothal ceremony. Doing so would have effectively squelched Maxim's plans to gain the throne.

Perhaps even then, he—with the help of Rasmus— would have discovered another way to introduce the Sword of the Magi into the choosing process, whereby giving Maxim the unfair advantage of being able to loosen the sword—not by Providential means but by sheer cunning that came from reading ancient texts.

Whatever the case, I blamed myself for not discovering their evil ambitions sooner. I should have sensed something wasn't right with Maxim, that the feelings developing between us happened much too rapidly and too strongly to be genuine.

And now they wanted the king out of the way so they could not only change the law about royalty marrying commoners but also avoid his objection to such a union.

If the king died, I would hold myself accountable. And if he lived, I would still blame myself for causing so much trouble. I had to accept what I'd known all along—I wasn't worthy to be the next queen of Norvegia. I wasn't strong or smart or savvy enough to lead this country.

If—when—I found the king and saved him, I would tell him what I should have all along, that he must find a new successor, someone better and more worthy than me.

Maxim would never be such a man. Never. And I would do everything within my power to make sure the king learned of his deception. In fact, I wouldn't rest until I saw Rasmus and Maxim punished for their treason.

But first I had to make it to the king.

I leaned in closer to my horse, urging it faster and hoping to feel its heat.

At the touch of Halvard's gloved hand against my shoulder, I glanced his way. He pressed a finger to his lips to caution me to silence, then pointed in the direction of the lake. For a moment, I didn't see anything. Then I glimpsed the wide wingspan of a bird.

The darkness obscured the creature. Was it an owl out hunting? I prayed it wasn't a draco. The closer we rode to the Valley of Red Dragons, the more encounters we risked, since dracos were known to make their homes in isolated mountainous areas.

Halvard made a motion for me to follow him, then veered his horse away from the lake.

I took one more glance, taking in a smaller and

more pointed head. It was a hawk. And since hawks generally weren't nocturnal, Halvard's warning became much clearer. Someone was using the hawk to hunt for me, most likely a tracker sent out by Rasmus and Maxim.

From the moment Halvard and I had walked out of the castle gatehouse disguised as a father-daughter merchant pair, I'd estimated we would have only an hour or two's lead before someone noticed we were gone and sent out a search party.

I'd been surprised when the hours had passed without any sign of being followed. Now that someone was closing in on us, we would have no time for a respite to warm up even if I'd wanted one.

Halvard led us deeper into the woodland. However, we kept up a punishing pace since the growth wasn't dense like forests farther up in the Snowden Mountains. The overgrazing and the use of timber for fencing, buildings, and firewood by area farms had reduced the woody vegetation and replaced it with coarse grasses and bracken.

We pushed our horses to the limit, but even at the brink of dawn, the hawk circled in the sky overhead. Somehow, we had to evade the bird, divert it from our trail, especially before the new day broke and the light revealed our position and tracks more distinctly.

"Ahead." Halvard nodded toward what appeared to be a dilapidated fence, likely bordering the outfields of a farm. In the summer, farmers used the outfields for pasture and for securing additional feed for their livestock. The tunet, or farmyard, was in the infields, where the farmer grew his grains and maintained his buildings, including his house.

Was Halvard hoping to take shelter on this farm?

As the sky began to lighten, the outline of a low barn came into view. Made of cut logs, the barn was unpainted and the roof covered with tufts of thick grass. The sod held the birch-bark shingles in place and provided extra insulation during the harsh winters, keeping the animals from freezing to death.

In addition to the barn, several other outbuildings formed a central square yard with a traditional lofthouse taking up the southern side. Like the other structures, it was made of logs and the roof of sod. But it was two stories tall with a smaller ground floor used for storage and a larger second floor for the living area.

The farm was quiet, the air peaceful.

As our horses thundered nearer, the short arched front door of the lofthouse opened, and a gray-haired man ducked outside, a candle in hand.

From the barn, another person stepped out.

We reined in, the hawk not far behind us.

"We require the use of your barn," I said, slipping from my mount. As my feet touched the ground, the numbness of my limbs and the pain in my frozen feet nearly sent me to my knees. I grabbed on to my saddle to keep from buckling.

In the next instant, Halvard was scooping me up. "Quickly," he said to the man holding the candle. "Put our horses amongst your livestock to mask their scent."

He didn't wait for the man's compliance and instead carried me to the barn. As he neared, the person in the door moved to block it.

"Who are you and what do you want?" The voice was distinctly feminine and filled with distrust.

"We are on an urgent mission for Princess Elinor to the king." Though I didn't want to deceive her regarding my identity, I would remain safest if I kept up my pretense as a commoner. "He is in grave danger, and there are those who would not wish our message to reach His Majesty."

Dark shadows concealed her face, but I could sense her studying Halvard, then me. As Halvard glanced again at the sky and the hawk, she tilted her head and followed his gaze. Then, without another word, she backed into the barn.

Halvard wasted no time entering after her. "We need a hiding place."

The glow of a lantern lit the interior, revealing a tidy but earthy structure. The faint light also showed the woman to be young, perhaps my age. She wore a simple homespun garment and a cloak that covered her head. But even so, I could see that she possessed pretty features along with fair hair with a hint of red.

She crossed to a stall, swung open the door, and motioned inside. "The sheep are the smelliest. If you lie with them and cover yourself with their hay, your pursuers won't be able to track your scent."

Halvard brushed past her into the pen, and the sheep began to rise from their warm beds, some bleating at the interruption.

The young woman pressed into their midst, comforting first one, then another, until they quieted under her touch. If my circumstances hadn't been so dire, I might have asked her to share her secret for calming the sheep so quickly. Instead, Halvard lowered me, and I tried to help him as best I could with my frozen fingers, rubbing myself with the hay.

Already, after just a few minutes inside the shelter, I was beginning to warm up. The sweetness of the freshly cut long grass filled my nostrils along with the damp woolly odor of the sheep.

"Go on with you," the young woman spoke to Halvard. "You hide too."

"I'll help with the horses first."

"No, my father is already tending to them. You must cover your scent and stay hidden with the princess."

I stilled. This woman had guessed my true identity. Clearly, I hadn't played my role as a merchant's daughter well enough. Or perhaps she was more perceptive than most. I regretted that I was putting her and her father in danger.

Within minutes, Halvard was covered in the hay pile on the opposite side of the sheepfold. With a few more gentle commands from the woman, the sheep lowered themselves, returning to their rest as if they'd never been disturbed.

The woman closed the stall door and then she was gone. For long minutes, I relished the warmth of the barn and the reprieve from the hard riding. We were scarcely safe, but I closed my eyes anyway, exhaustion overtaking me.

I must have dozed, because the pounding of approaching horses awoke me. My eyes flew open to find that the barn was still shrouded in darkness even as faint light filtered through cracks in the shutters covering the windows.

As far as I could tell, the sheep remained at rest around us, which meant I hadn't slumbered long, less than half of an hour. Our pursuers had been closer than I'd realized. From the staccato of horses' hooves, I deduced only two riders. And at the bark of a dog, I guessed they were using an elkhound to track us in addition to the hawk. Both riders dismounted, and though I couldn't distinguish what they were saying, I could hear the accusation in their tones.

Seconds later, the distant lofthouse door slammed open. They were searching the premises. It was only a matter of time before they came into the barn. What would they do if they discovered me in the hay? While I didn't fear for myself, I regretted the danger I was bringing upon Halvard.

Should I give myself up now and save him?

But if I couldn't deliver my message to the king, what would happen? The fear I'd been harboring since overhearing Maxim and Rasmus pushed up into my throat, constricting it. I had to stay on course and make my way to the king. Somehow.

Voices and footsteps drew nearer. When the barn door opened, I sucked in a breath and held myself motionless. The dog's bark rose into the early morning air. Had it already caught our scent? Elkhounds made perfect hunting dogs because of their expert sense of smell. They also, apparently, were good for tracking a runaway princess.

"All the buildings," came a gruff voice. "Check everywhere. The hawk wouldn't keep circling the tunet if the princess wasn't here."

I squeezed my eyes shut. All around me, the sheep grew restless, some rising to their feet, others bleating their unhappiness and worry as the hound snuffled and yipped ever closer.

"Open all the stalls." The gruff command had likely

been given to the young woman.

I tried not to tremble. If the dog came inside this pen, it would have no trouble finding us, even if we were masked by the scent of the sheep.

"Your dog better not attack any of the livestock." The young woman's reply was belligerent and much too bold. Again, I regretted putting this family into danger, that they would likely be punished severely for coming to my aid. But what other choice did I have?

The stall hinges squealed open, and the animal noises all around grew more frightened. The chickens squawked, the cows bellowed, and the sheep continued to bleat with growing alarm. At the very least, the elkhound wouldn't be able to hear my pounding heart above the clamor.

A shriek rang out above it all, a piercing screech that turned my blood cold. I'd heard the sound only days ago, a sound I'd recognize anywhere now. A draco.

The image of the burning pieces of canvas from the pavilion disintegrating and collapsing filled my mind. What if the draco breathed on the barn and set it afire? We would have no choice but to reveal ourselves lest we burn to death in an inferno.

As if also sensing danger, the commander called to the elkhound. While I couldn't see what was going on, I guessed they were hovering near the door, taking shelter and staying out of sight but prepared to bolt if anything should happen to the barn.

The minutes passed in agonizing slowness, and though I wanted to rush off and find a safe place to hide—like a rock cleft where I'd hidden with Maxim—I forced myself to remain under the hay.

"The draco is chasing after the hawk," the commander shouted, finally stepping out of the barn. "We need to go now before it comes back."

A moment later, the pounding of hooves moving onward told me the trackers had searched enough of the farm to conclude I wasn't there. Or at least for now, they'd decided to seek shelter.

As soon as silence descended over the farm, I pushed up from the hay. Halvard did likewise. We exchanged a glance, one that confirmed just how lucky we'd been to have the draco show up when it had, almost as if it had planned to intervene.

"Where to now?" I whispered.

"I don't suppose you'd listen if I suggested we wait until dark to leave?"

My thoughts turned to the day stretching before us and to the king maybe even now preparing to head out to battle. "We cannot. We have to leave at once."

Halvard nodded solemnly. I'd told him of the threat to the king. I'd speculated about the danger but still had no idea exactly what Maxim and Rasmus had planned. Were they paying one of the Knights of Brethren to betray His Majesty? Had they planted other warrior knights to injure him during the height of battle, making it look like an accident? Or perhaps they were even working in conjunction with King Canute.

Even though I would be safest from the trackers and draco if I waited for a while, I simply couldn't delay.

We stood, brushed the hay from our garments, and then made our way out into the tunet. The young woman was watching the sky and whispering, her eyes narrowed. She almost seemed to be talking to herself. At our approach, she whispered one last statement. "Kill it." Then she turned toward us, her face again shadowed.

What exactly did she want to kill? Should I yet remain cautious with her? As soon as the thought came, I shook it off. She wasn't a threat. If she meant me harm, she wouldn't have so readily put her life in danger for me.

"Thank you . . ." I started, hoping she'd supply her name.

"'Tis Lis, Your Highness." She dipped her head.

"Thank you, Lis. You took a great risk in hiding us. I shall see that you and your father are handsomely rewarded."

She straightened. "No need. If the king is in danger, I would do my duty to save him in any way I can."

The father exited the lofthouse carrying two mugs, steam rising from them. As much as I wanted to sip the warm brew, I couldn't waste another second.

As if sensing my urgency, Lis cocked her head toward the stable. "We'll tend to your horses while you warm yourselves with mead."

I hesitated but a moment before nodding. "You are very kind."

As I took off my gloves and then lifted my hood away, she paused to examine me. Suddenly self-conscious, I brushed at my hair, tied back in a long braid. In the rapidly growing morning light, I likely appeared so disheveled that I could frighten the scales off a lizard.

With a limping gait, the father hastened toward us and handed me the mug. "Your Highness."

Nodding my thanks, I wrapped both hands around the clay vessel, letting the heat seep into my flesh.

Before I could manage to lift the mug to my lips, a familiar voice came from near the stable. "Princess Elinor. I was hoping I would find you here."

I spun to find Maxim standing in the shadows. His black cloak and hood shielded him. But I didn't need to see him clearly to recognize him. Several soldiers stood behind him, their weapons at the ready.

My heart sank. I should have known if Maxim was involved in the chase, he'd find a way to outsmart me.

Chapter 17

MAXIM

THANK THE SAINTS IN HEAVEN ABOVE I'D FOUND ELINOR.

Though she'd had a significant lead on her way to the king and the frontline in the Valley of Red Dragons, I'd calculated each path of my race to intercept her, mapping out the shortest routes until at last I'd spotted the hawk circling in the dawn sky and surmised the bird had located its prey—the princess.

I'd picked up the punishing pace, praying with each pounding hoofbeat that I'd reach her in time to keep Rasmus's trackers from whisking her away.

Upon arriving at the clearing of the tunet, a draco had swooped in, snapping and screeching and slapping its red wings. I'd waited for it to set fire to everything, but it had held back, only charging at the trackers' horses and terrorizing them before it spotted the hawk and chased after it.

When a maiden had stepped away from the barn and watched the draco fly away, I'd had a strange sensation that she was somehow communicating with the creature.

In studying ancient dragons, I'd learned they could form bonds with humans if raised from infancy. I wasn't exactly sure how that bond worked, had never seen it in action. But I speculated that the dragon looked to the human as a mother figure of sorts and shared an affinity that carried over into adulthood. Perhaps the draco, as an ancestor of the dragon, could form bonds with humans too.

Once the flying lizard had gone, I'd held back, hoping Elinor would crawl out from wherever she was hiding, clearly a place that had sufficiently shielded her from the trackers and their elkhound.

It had taken less time than I'd estimated for her to step out of the barn. I'd expected her to be more cautious in anticipation of being waylaid. But she'd even tossed aside her hood. Clearly, she wasn't thinking rationally and needed help if she had any hope of making it to the king.

She lifted her chin haughtily and glared at me. "Go back to Vordinberg, Maxim."

"I can't do that, Your Highness." I had to play my role carefully, at least until I could figure out a way to lose the three guards Rasmus had sent along. Of course, I knew as well as he did that we wouldn't need three soldiers to seize Elinor and hold her prisoner for the ride back to the capital. No, the real reason Rasmus had insisted on three was because he'd deduced my hesitancy to his scheming and wanted to prevent me from taking Elinor and fleeing. One guard to hold her as a prisoner and two to force me to comply.

I held up a hand to the guards to command them to stay where they were, and then I made my way across the tunet toward Elinor, Halvard, and the occupants of the farm.

"Do not come any nearer, Maxim." Elinor's expression tightened, as though she was afraid of me.

Regret pierced my heart. Regret that I'd caused her pain. Regret that I'd lost her trust. Regret that I hadn't been honest with her from the start.

Nevertheless, I continued with slow but steady steps toward her.

Halvard unsheathed his sword and moved in front of Elinor. "Listen to the princess, sire. Stay back." His tone radiated a menace that told me he'd defend Elinor to the death.

His loyalty earned him my respect, yet I still didn't stop. I was betting my life on Elinor's compassionate nature. She wouldn't allow Halvard to harm me, no matter how frustrated with me she might be. When I was but a foot away, he swung his sword toward me. From the angle, I knew he only meant to scare me. When he ended by pressing the tip of his blade into my chest, I finally stopped.

I heard the almost-imperceptible clink of Rasmus's soldiers readying to cross and rescue me. Without turning to look at them, I held up my hand again to halt them. Portraying a calm demeanor and unflinching bravery would convince them I had the special powers many people believed Sages had.

After my opening of the sword's case, the rumors about my abilities had spread. I had no doubt that was part of Rasmus's intention, to demonstrate I was powerful well beyond my years and training.

My ease in finding the princess so quickly had also added to my aura. And now, I needed to keep up the charade, using every skill I possessed to control the guards.

"Your Highness," I said, even as Halvard's blade punctured my skin. "I beg of you to give me a final chance to speak to you privately."

I allowed myself a flinch, hoping my acting was convincing and that she didn't already hate me and wish me dead.

Her gaze flickered to my chest. She pressed her lips together, the sign she was attempting to resolve herself to my demise.

"What you overheard," I continued, "'twas a misunderstanding. If you'll let me explain, you'll come to the same conclusion."

I let the sword press deeper, drawing a gush of blood instead of a trickle. Again, I forced myself to show a moment of pain, though it went against everything within me to display my emotion.

"I loathe you."

"You have every right to do so."

As the wet spot of blood darkened my cloak, her gaze invariably dropped to it. Her expressive eyes widened, and she stepped toward Halvard, tugging on his arm. "As much as I would like to kill Maxim, I shall keep him alive for now."

"Very well, Your Highness." Halvard dropped his sword, now tinged with my blood.

"If you would be so kind," she spoke to the maiden and her father, "I would use your home for but a few moments to speak with Maxim."

The two bowed their heads in acquiescence.

With that, she spun on her heel and strode in the direction of the lofthouse.

I'd gotten what I wanted. Privacy with her, away from the listening ears of Rasmus's soldiers. I also knew she was in a great hurry to reach the king and wouldn't delay her mission for long. Especially not for me.

She stepped up through the lofthouse door, three-quarters the dimensions of a full-sized door. I bent to enter behind her, then closed it and lowered the beam to keep intruders out. Even then, I suspected Rasmus's soldiers would congregate outside and attempt to listen to our conversation. They'd likely been instructed by Rasmus not to allow me out of their sight for any reason. I wouldn't be surprised if one of them insisted on leaving the door open or even joining my conversation with the princess.

With the low ceiling of the storage room, I couldn't straighten all the way. Even if I could, bunches of herbs drying in clusters from the rafters hung in my way, the aromas tingling my nose and urging me to identify each spice.

But instead of giving way to the challenge, I crossed to the hearth and stood beside Elinor. She held her hands out to the low flames and stared straight ahead, the muscles in her jaw tensing.

I had a minute, maybe less, before I lost this opportunity to speak the truth. "I am not working with Rasmus." I kept my voice to a low whisper.

"You have always done his bidding without question, and clearly that hasn't changed." Her whispered reply was terse.

"He's attempting to make me do his bidding, but I won't let him succeed this time."

"You are his pawn, and he is playing you to his advantage."

"I will foil him."

"So far, he has foiled you."

"No. I have no intention of allowing his men to take you back to Vordinberg. We'll find a way to escape them, and I shall ride with you to warn the king."

"I don't want your help. I don't want to see you ever again." Her low response was harsh.

I turned toward her, wanting her to see the desperation and truth in my eyes. "I didn't mean to hurt you."

She stared straight ahead. "You didn't mean anything."

I took hold of her arm and twisted her, forcing her to face me. I had to make her understand the truth. Now. Before we were interrupted. "I meant everything."

She shook her head. "You were following Rasmus's orders—"

"Every second of every minute I've spent with you the past few days is because I'd rather be with you than any place else on earth."

The door handle rattled. Rasmus's men were closing in. I leaned in, and thankfully she didn't back away. Instead, her eyes regarded me with pain—pain I'd caused her.

"I want you."

"You want me?" Some of the pain in her eyes dimmed.

"You're all I've ever wanted." I didn't have time to temper my words. "'Twas what made leaving Vordinberg difficult as a child. And 'tis what made coming back difficult. Because I want you and know you're not mine to have."

She opened her mouth to respond but no words emerged. Instead, she scrutinized my countenance as though she could find the answer there.

Someone pounded on the door. "Sire, His Excellency

gave us specific orders to accompany you and the princess at all times. For safety purposes."

I glanced at the door. We had only seconds left.

"I admit," I rushed to say for her ears alone, "I've had a difficult time denying Rasmus control over my life." Perhaps, deep down, I'd hoped to prove I was worthy, make him proud, or earn his love. Yet nothing I'd done had ever brought me closer to having a father who cared about me. I finally had to accept the truth that I'd never gain his approval, and I needed to stop trying.

Elinor stared at the door and then me.

"But I no longer care what Rasmus wants." My whisper came out harsher than I'd intended. "All I care about is you."

I'd do anything for Elinor. Even die for her.

Chapter 18

Elinor

The blood on Maxim's cloak was dark and spreading wider. His wound needed tending.

The knock sounded again, louder. Maxim didn't move to answer it. From the hardening of his jaw and the dark defiance glinting in his eyes, I sensed he wanted to let go of the hold Rasmus had on him. But could he truly accomplish it? Or was this another ploy to bend me to his will?

Maxim could manipulate a person's thoughts more superbly than anyone else. Even now, how did I know he was speaking the truth and not simply telling me what I wanted to hear?

"I do not know how I can ever trust you again," I whispered.

"I'll prove to you that you can."

Could he? The unspoken question hung in the inches that separated us.

"I vow it." His expression turned earnest. But again, he was an expert at reading people and assessing their weaknesses. Was he trying to play upon my weaknesses?

"Sire, open the door." The wood frame rattled.

I broke our connection and strode to the door. I threw it wide open and glared at the soldier. "Please assemble supplies so that I may doctor Maxim's wound."

The guard bowed his head. Although he was working for Rasmus—of that I had no doubt—he would still do as I commanded. I was, after all, his sovereign. And I wouldn't let him or the others forget that fact.

I left the door wide and returned to Maxim, guiding him down onto the stool. "Take off your cloak."

He hesitated. "'Tis but a surface wound."

"We shall make our escape plans as I bandage your wound."

With a nod, he shed his garment, revealing the blood-soaked tunic underneath. Before I could speak again, Lis ducked inside. "I'll get you a salve and linen strips."

Her father came inside after her and was followed by one of the guards, who took one look at the low ceiling before he backed out and stood outside the door. He was close, but we'd have some ability to communicate without him interfering.

I didn't want to trust Maxim after the way he'd betrayed me. But at this point, I needed help if I had any hope of reaching the king.

I caught Maxim's gaze and raised a brow. Did he have a plan for breaking us free from the soldiers? And if so, what was it?

He cocked a brow back at me. Then he glanced overhead to the dozen or more bunches of herbs. I could see him jump from one to the next, silently naming and assessing the properties. His attention halted on a small bundle in the corner.

Valerian root.

The plant was known for its sedative abilities. Was Maxim considering giving the soldiers some? If so, how?

"A tonic of Valerian root mixed with various percentages of monkshood or belladonna or another similar herb you have will do nicely to ease the pain." Maxim spoke casually, but it was direct enough that Lis halted in her rummaging through a cabinet.

The young woman must have understood Maxim's meaning. She shot a glance in the direction of the guard waiting outside the door before she focused on the cabinet. "I have just the thing."

Maxim had no need of a painkiller. But if we laced the warm drinks for the guards, then we might be able to disable them.

"I'll heat more mead." Lis's father limped toward a cask. "Then you can warm yourself while you're waiting."

I wasn't sure if he'd also understood Maxim's intentions, but he busied himself with drawing more mead and setting it to heat above the hearth. Meanwhile, Lis clipped some of the Valerian and placed the herbs in a mortar. She added a pinch of several other herbs from crocks within the cabinet. With a pestle, she ground the mixture into a fine dust. Then she crossed to her father and offered the mixture to him.

They made a show of adding some to a mug of steaming mead before Lis handed it to Maxim. All the while, they slyly divided the rest into several other mugs before adding mead.

Maxim pretended to sip his as I finished staunching the flow of blood and then cleaning his wound. Maxim had been right; it was nothing more than a surface cut. He was clever enough to ensure Halvard's sword sliced his flesh to cause profuse bleeding but not deeply enough for stitching.

While a part of me was aware of his tunic pulled up to reveal his chest, another part was too anxious over the circumstances to give his physique more than a passing thought. After I bandaged the spot, Maxim lowered his garment, then grimaced, making sure the guard at the door took full note of his discomfort.

"How much longer before the herbs dull the pain?" Maxim asked.

"Soon," Lis answered. "Perhaps a few minutes." She had finally discarded her hood, giving us a view of her features, and she was elegantly beautiful, with golden red hair and green eyes. I felt as though I'd seen her somewhere before, although I knew not where.

I swept my gaze over the room, searching for another exit, even a window. If the tonic didn't work on the guards, we needed another plan.

Lis cocked her head toward a ladder that rose into the upper loft of the house, the living quarters. Was she suggesting we leave via the upstairs room if need be? Perhaps climb out of an upper window?

I nodded. This woman and her father had proven themselves trustworthy so far. "I cannot thank you enough for your hospitality."

"I'm honored to serve you." The older man added several more cords of wood to the fire, and the flames sparked to life. "I only wish my dear wife were here to see you, a princess, in our humble home."

"I am sorry to have missed her."

The man stood back from the hearth and placed a hand over his heart. With his gray hair and weathered face, the man appeared old enough to be Lis's grandfather. "She's been gone nigh five years, and we miss her every day. Don't we, Lissy?"

"Very much." Lis crossed to her father, took his hand in hers, and squeezed it.

The guard outside the door tipped up the last of his cup of mead, swallowing the warm brew. Perhaps he hadn't been as cold as I'd been. But he'd relished the chance to chase off the chill remaining from the cold night.

He wobbled slightly and braced himself on the door frame.

Maxim was busy donning his cloak and appeared oblivious to the guard. But he was never oblivious. He saw every nuanced detail as if it was painted across a bright sky in dark ink.

"Are you nineteen years, Lis?" Maxim asked casually.

"You're correct."

"Your mother was quite a bit older than you, a few months shy of forty years difference?"

"Yes, good guess."

I wanted to tell Lis that Maxim never guessed, that his observations were empirically grounded. I didn't know how he'd surmised Lis's mother's age, but apparently he'd had enough clues to do so.

"Your farm is quite secluded." Maxim eyed Lis's father, who was poking at the embers. "You likely have very few visitors."

"An occasional neighbor," Lis answered before her father could.

Before she or Maxim could make further conversation, the guard at the door grabbed the frame and tried to steady himself. But his knees buckled, and he slid down. An instant later, he was sprawled out in front of the doorway.

The thuds of the other guards hitting the ground came a moment later.

Maxim sprang toward the door, and I raced after him. I needed no instructions to understand this was the moment we'd been waiting for. We stepped over the guard to find that Halvard was already leading our mounts out of the stable.

"Secure the soldiers onto the backs of their horses," Maxim called over his shoulder to Lis and her father, who had followed us out, "and lead them away as far as you can go for one hour to the south."

"Then you think 'twill be safe for us to stay here?" Lis's question chased us.

Maxim didn't slow his stride. "They'll have a challenging time locating your farm without the aid of the hawk. But to be certain, head up into the Snowden Mountains and remain there for three days."

Before I could formulate an apology for disrupting their lives, Halvard was beside me, waiting to assist me into my saddle. "We must go, Your Highness."

From the urgency in his tone and expression, I knew we couldn't waste a single second in our escape.

Once in my saddle, I had no time but to issue a brief nod and thank you before kicking my horse after Maxim, who was already riding away. As we charged into the outfields surrounding the tunet, I offered a plea that Providence would show his favor upon the farmer and daughter for their aid, and I prayed I would soon be able to return and reward them myself.

Maxim pushed through the forestland with a speed and confidence that left me breathless. It was no wonder he'd been able to catch up with me. He seemed to know exactly where to go, as if he'd ridden the route a dozen times. More likely, he'd spread an invisible map out in his mind and was navigating the shortest and most direct route. At least, I hoped he was, instead of leading me into a trap.

While I wanted to believe the sincerity of the words he'd spoken in the lofthouse, I guessed the battle between good and evil still raged in his heart. He might care about me as he'd claimed, but was his loyalty to me enough to outweigh the influence Rasmus held over him?

We galloped at full speed, and the morn passed in a blur. The closer we drew to the Valley of Red Dragons, the higher the mountain peaks rose on the horizon until at last they loomed above us, topped with white caps of snow that had already fallen—or had perhaps never melted from the previous winter.

The land grew more rugged, slowing our pace, until at last Maxim reined in.

I urged my horse up the rest of the incline and halted next to him to find that we were on the edge of an expansive hillside that dropped away into craggy cliffs below. A waterfall fell over a rock outcropping, cascading a hundred or more feet into a pristine river, one of the many tributaries that poured into the Atlas River.

The sight would have been enthralling had not the urgency inside my chest been pounding harder with each passing hour.

"The Valley of Red Dragons." Maxim's narrowed gaze swept over the low, open land below connecting Norvegia to Swaine. The rest of the border between the two countries was lined with the Snowden Mountain Range, running from the Tundra Sea in the north all the way to the White Sea in the south. The high, rugged mountains functioned as a natural wall, separating the two nations.

I'd visited the area once several years ago, but the route by ship was shorter and smoother than traveling by land, and we'd sailed from Vordinberg through the Bay of Fire and up the Atlas River. This vista, looking down on the valley spreading out for miles from east to west, was one I'd never seen.

The bright crimson, yellow, and orange of the changing leaves of the hardwoods in the valley contrasted with the evergreens that populated the mountains. Across the wide expanse, another waterfall gushed from a rocky wall amidst the greenery.

Maxim pointed to the east. "There."

Halvard had reined in beside me and now released a whistle. As my gaze came to rest upon the open eastern valley, I understood his reaction. A brutal battle was underway, knights upon horses as well as foot soldiers clashing swords and pikes. Norvegia's royal-red flags with intricate dragon heads upon them, the same heads that graced the four corners of the Stavekirche, filled the Norvegian half of the field. Slithering white serpents wound through the black flags of Swaine on the opposite part of the field.

It appeared that the black flags were making an inroad into the red. Bodies on both sides lay unmoving on the ground. Although we were too far away to identify anyone, my heart shot into my throat at the prospect of King Ulrik even now deep within the battlefield and vulnerable.

"Tell me what you know of the plot against the king," I demanded of Maxim.

Maxim stared at the battle, his handsome features hardened with severity. "I've been contemplating Rasmus's plans since I left Vordinberg yesterday."

"And . . .?"

"And I believe he must be colluding with the two newest of the Knights of Brethren, bribing them with more power and prestige . . ."

"To be given to them when you become king?" I finished his sentence, unable to keep the note of bitterness out of my tone.

"I don't want to become king." He turned his eyes upon me, the blue a soulful, sorrowful pit I could drown in. Again, I didn't know whether to trust what I was seeing. Was this another act, or was he genuine?

"To prove it to you, as soon as we inform the king of the assassination plot against him, I intend to leave for the north and never return again."

I didn't have time to question him. At the moment, all I could do was trust that he wanted to help me save the king. After all, he'd brought me this far.

"How do we reach the king from here?" Halvard shied sideways on his horse and glanced over the jagged cliff and steep drop.

Maxim tugged on his reins and veered his horse back the way we'd come. "There is one path, not known to many."

How, then, did Maxim know? Likely he'd read an obscure paragraph in an ancient battle story that told of the route. Or perhaps he'd studied old military strategies.

I trailed him as he led us to a deep ravine and a narrow footpath hidden among rocks and trees, one only wide enough for our horses. Even though we were in a hurry, we had no choice but to dismount and lead our horses down the zigzagging trail. As we neared the bottom, Maxim glanced back at me, our eyes meeting, his assessing me with a concern too intense to be false.

His confession from the lofthouse sifted through my mind, as it had several times during the past hours of riding. *"I want you. You're all I've ever wanted. 'Twas what made leaving Vordinberg difficult as a child. And 'tis what made coming back difficult. Because I want you and know you're not mine to have."*

A place deep inside longed for his confession to be true. Even if nothing could come of it, I still wanted to know he cared, truly cared about me, not for what he could gain but because of the bond we'd once shared.

"She's your sister," Maxim said.

"What?" The weariness from the long night and even longer morn was heavy upon me, and I didn't have the energy for riddles.

"The maiden from the farm." Maxim's tone assured me this was a riddle he'd already solved on my behalf. "She's your lost sister."

Chapter 19

MAXIM

I'D FIGURED OUT THE IDENTITY OF THE MAIDEN AT THE REMOTE farm almost from the start. But I'd spent the past hours of our ride—when I wasn't navigating—piecing together the details to present to Elinor.

I'd also debated the right time to tell her. This mission to save the king was of the utmost importance, and I didn't want to distract her. But we were nearing the end of our journey together. After we reached the valley floor and remounted our horses, we would set off at full speed to the Norwegian encampment. Once there, Elinor would search for a faithful messenger to ride out into the fray to deliver her warning to the king.

With everything I'd done to contribute to the king's danger, I planned to be that messenger. Elinor didn't trust me yet, might never trust me again. She certainly wouldn't put her faith in me to take a dire message to the king. But I aimed to go, even if she sent another man.

The truth was, I could very well die this day, quite possibly in the next hour, and I needed to tell Elinor everything I'd deduced about her lost mother and sister so that when this battle was over and the king was safe, she could pursue discovering more.

"Lis is my lost sister?" Elinor fumbled over her words. "Whatever do you mean?"

"Lis is nineteen, the right age for your sister. She wasn't born to the farmer and his wife, although from the farmer's hesitant body language, I could tell he and his wife allowed Lis to believe she was their child. When they came upon her, they were already old and had likely given up hope of having any children of their own."

"That does not make her my sister." Though Elinor's response was quick, it contained a note of hope.

"Your sister's name was Elisbet, and Lis is a nickname oft derived from Elisbet. Somehow the farmer and his wife knew her name, which means Princess Blanche was involved in placing her with the couple. Not only that, but Lis shares similar features to your mother and you. She shares a resemblance to your mother's portrait, particularly the reddish tint of her hair."

Elinor paused and then nodded. "Yes, she does indeed share a likeness."

I'd seen the portrait of the late Princess Blanche several times during my childhood. It had graced the wall of Elinor's chamber since she was but a child. Queen Inge had moved it there after the searching failed to find the lost woman and her infant daughter.

"The isolation of the farm and the lack of connection with neighbors or a community kept Lis from anyone who might draw a conclusion regarding her true heritage." Although I'd easily connected all the information to figure out who Lis was, I hadn't yet begun to understand why Blanche had left her with the farmer and his wife. What had motivated her to do so?

The crunch of our horses' hooves and our steps echoed in the narrow ravine. A shower of gravelly rocks cascaded down as Halvard stumbled on the path above us. But he steadied himself and continued silently. If he'd heard our conversation, he gave no indication of it—the sign of a true and faithful servant.

"Please, Maxim." Elinor's voice was low, desperate. "Please tell me you are certain of this."

I caught her gaze. Her eyes glimmered with a lifetime of questions and a need for a family she'd never known. I wished I could have another lifetime to look into her eyes, but I would have to take this moment, likely one of the last.

"The color of her eyes is identical to yours." I returned my focus to the path ahead. Though we were nearing the bottom, the way was still precarious.

"Eye color is not proof enough that she is my sister."

"Surely your mother left Lis something she could use to verify she is of royal blood." Unless Blanche didn't want Lis to know.

"And if she did not leave anything?"

"I have every faith you'll find a way to prove her true identity."

Though we'd had no more rain, a damp chill lingered in the air. And a strange silence, one that had begun to set me on edge more with every passing moment.

"Then you really are leaving for the north?" Her question was soft, tentative, as if she hadn't meant to ask it.

If I lived through the battle ahead, Rasmus would never stop searching for me. If he didn't kill me for my rebellion against him, he would bend me into doing his will somehow, someway, likely by threatening to bring harm to Elinor. I couldn't let that happen.

"I will bide my time until Rasmus is gone. Perhaps then I'll be able to return." Since Rasmus only seemed to be growing in power, I might have to wait for years. 'Twas the very real possibility I might never be able to return.

As though she sensed the same, we were both quiet the rest of the descent, and when we reached level ground near the river's edge, we remounted and began the wild dash to Norvegia's camp.

With each pounding step we drew nearer to the fighting, the harder I prayed that I would be able to reach the king in time. As the first tents of the Norwegian encampment came into view, I nudged my horse alongside Elinor's. "We must be wary of everyone until we know who is working for Rasmus and who remains loyal to the king."

Her face was pale, likely from cold or weariness or both. But her eyes radiated determination. "I intend to deliver the message directly to the king myself."

"No." The word came out strong and harsh.

She flicked me a look and arched one of her delicate brows.

"No." I gentled my tone, but only with great effort. "If Canute realizes you're here, he'll stop at nothing to capture you and will marry you on the spot. Besides, 'tis much too dangerous to ride into the midst of the battle. If something should happen to the king, you must stay safe."

"I have not yet been named the king's successor."

"'Tis only a matter of time."

"Perhaps. But I shall end up being wed to the man of Rasmus's intention, not the sword's. Any man who chooses deception to better himself will forfeit his greatest asset, his honor."

She was quoting an old Norvegian saying, one I knew well but hadn't wanted to consider. A man's greatest asset was his honor. And I'd lost that with Elinor. Once lost, it might never be found.

"You must think about Norvegia," I insisted. "If you die trying to save the king, then you'll give Rasmus more control."

Elinor hunched lower against her horse. Her hood had fallen, and her hair tangled in the breeze. From the hard set of her chin, I knew I hadn't yet convinced her to stay back.

"You must remain strong, Elinor." My declaration rose above the pounding hooves. "You may be Norvegia's only hope against falling into darkness."

Holy Scripture in Proverbs cautioned: *"Keep your heart with all diligence. For out of it spring the issues of life."*

Letting down one's guard came with a little compromise here and a little there. The darkness would creep in, subtly and unnoticed at first, until too late it pervaded one's soul and crowded out the light of goodness. The darkness of the soul then spread its influence, seeping over into the nation itself.

As we darted past the first of the tents, Elinor tugged on her reins. "You know I have never wanted to be Norvegia's hope."

"But you will do your duty. You can do no less." I slowed my mount. I would also do my duty, for I, too, could do no less. And if I needed to tie Elinor up and hide her in a tent, then I would.

The camp was more crowded than I expected, with craftsmen feverishly at labor: the blacksmith repairing a pike, tapping the red-hot metal against his anvil, the swordsmith sharpening a blade, the sparks flying against his wheel, the armorers patching broken pieces of plate mail, grooms doctoring wounded horses.

The farther in to camp we rode, the harder it became to navigate through the injured and dying, having been pulled back from the battle, now clustered outside of tents. Several priests moved about, comforting and praying with the men, but moans permeated the air, and the scent of blood and death hung heavily.

The din of battle continued to escalate—the clashing of swords, the terrified neighing of horses, the cries of the wounded. At last, within sight of the fighting, Elinor halted, her eyes wide upon the destruction unfolding before us.

She swallowed hard before beginning to dismount. Halvard hopped off his horse and was at her side in an instant to assist her. Once she was standing, I caught the slight tremor of her hands before she clasped them together in front of her and assessed two wounded knights limping away from the battlefield, both leaning heavily upon their squires.

"Where is the king fighting?" she called.

One of the knights collapsed to his knees, blood running in rivulets down his face from what appeared to be a head wound. The other stared at Elinor blankly, as if he couldn't remember where he was or what was happening.

"I have come with an urgent message for the king," she persisted. "You must direct me to him."

A priest paused in his ministrations and straightened to look at Elinor.

"Remember to use caution, Elinor," I murmured. "We

don't know whom we can trust."

The priest bowed his head and made his way toward us. Even as he did, one of the squires who was drawing closer with his master called out, "The king and his knights are fighting on the frontline." He pointed to the northeast. "At least half a mile that way."

Elinor followed the line of his direction. She broke free from Halvard and reached for her mount, clearly intending to ride there. Her servant was quick to move between her and the horse, blocking her access. "Your Highness, I pray you'll let me take the message to the king in your stead."

The gravity on Halvard's face told me I had an ally in him, that he didn't want Elinor riding into the heart of the fighting any more than I did.

"I'll be the one to go," I stated, hoping Halvard read the sternness in my gaze and could understand he needed to stay and restrain Elinor.

She pinned me with a glare that contained the bitterness from earlier. "How do I know you are not bent on going to the king and plunging your dagger into his heart as you make a pretense of warning him?"

"I vow to protect him, Elinor." How could I make her trust me? What reason did she have after I'd been unfaithful thus far?

"I shall take the message." She tried to sidestep Halvard, but he blocked her again.

"Please, Elinor." I had to make her see reason. "You must stay alive to discover more about Lis." I was manipulating her by reminding her of this newfound possibility, something she'd longed for her entire life. She wouldn't risk losing a connection to her family, would she?

She hesitated for a moment, staring between Halvard and me, and then she nodded curtly. "Very well. You may take Halvard."

And then who would be left to guard her? "Halvard must stay and look after you."

"No—"

"I know I'm not worthy of your trust, but you must know by now I would have taken you back to Vordinberg if I'd remained loyal to Rasmus."

"You have more cunning and intelligence than Rasmus and the other Sages combined."

Did I really? At the whiz of an arrow that landed only a dozen paces away, I wrapped the reins more securely around my gloved hand. I needed to go now. I could delay no longer.

With a nudge of my boots into the horse's flank, I started toward the battle, my mind making a mental path, one that was not only the quickest to the king but also the safest.

"Please, Halvard," the princess pleaded behind me. "I must be the one to deliver the message."

"No, Your Highness. We cannot stay here so close to the fighting." The firmness to Halvard's tone reassured me that he would take care of Elinor.

"Godspeed, Maxim!" she called.

I shifted in my saddle so I could take a final look at her, perhaps my last. She stood amidst the chaos like a lone flower in a fading field. As our gazes connected, my heart squeezed painfully with the truth I'd tried to deny for so many years. I loved her. Definitively. Deeply. Desperately.

While on the brink of sacrificing my life for my king and country, I wanted her to know my feelings went beyond simple wanting and yearning. It wouldn't hurt to tell her now, would it? Even if I lived, I'd ride away from this battle and never see her again.

"I love you," I called to her. "I always have, and I always will."

I didn't wait to see her reaction, didn't want to subject myself to her rejection. Instead, I kicked my horse forward and plunged into the battle.

Chapter 20

Elinor

Maxim had declared his love for me.

My entire body and soul down to my marrow quavered with the need to race after him. But he'd been swallowed up among the fighting, his proud bearing and black cloak no longer visible.

Even if I'd been able to spot him, Halvard's grip was unyielding. He led our horses and guided me alongside him. Though I wanted to resist, I couldn't deny the wisdom in moving away from the fighting. If the tide shifted, if King Canute's main force broke through the front, Maxim was right. I would be in terrible danger. King Canute wouldn't stop at simply capturing me. In his quest for Norvegia's throne, he'd force me to be his the moment he laid hands on me.

"I love you. I always have, and I always will." Maxim's words cut through the confusion I'd been feeling since overhearing his conversation with Rasmus. Deep inside, I knew Maxim had spoken the words of love from his heart, that he hadn't been manipulating me,

and that his declaration went beyond friendship. His tone had been too raw and his eyes too full of love to be anything other than genuine.

Maxim loved me.

A strange warmth opened within me. Like one of the hot springs high in the Frozen Wilds, it bubbled amidst the cold, thawing the truth I'd let stay frozen for so long. The truth was, I'd always loved him too. Even when we were young, my love had been real and consuming, though it had been childish and untested.

Now that we were adults, my love was different. More mature and charged with physical attraction. Even different, it was still just as real and consuming. Perhaps that was what scared me so much and why trusting him was difficult. I was afraid I'd lose him again . . . just like he'd been afraid he'd lose me.

"Oh, Maxim," I whispered. We both had insecurities. If we didn't learn to face the doubts haunting us, we'd never have confidence to give ourselves freely in a relationship.

I shook my head, forcing my attention forward to aid Halvard in our safekeeping instead of impeding him. 'Twas foolish to ever believe Maxim and I could consider a future together, since the law forbade royalty from marrying a commoner. Even if Rasmus convinced everyone to change the law, Maxim insisted he didn't want to become the next king, that he was leaving for the north and would never return to Vordinberg.

My thoughts stalled, and I drew to an abrupt stop. Maxim's declaration of love had been his farewell.

Panic burst through me.

"Your Highness." Halvard tugged me. "Please, we

need to retreat farther."

I strained to see Maxim through the clashing swords and thrusting pikes. He wouldn't have declared his love if he'd had any intention of returning to me. No, he expected to die. Today. Out there.

I jerked my arm free from Halvard and began striding back toward the battlefront. I had to go with Maxim. And Halvard needed to come too. The three of us would be safer together as we sought the king.

"Mayhap we should retreat to the ravine." Halvard fell into step next to me. "We don't know who we can trust here."

A shriek came from a distance, from the direction of King Canute's camp—the kind that belonged to a draco, the kind that made the hairs on my arm stand up.

I searched the sky but saw nothing, not even a faint wisp of campfire smoke. Halvard, too, peered up at the cloud cover, his aged face creased with concern.

Perhaps I was wrong. I prayed the shriek had come from a dying or wounded soldier instead.

We continued forward more cautiously, but a moment later, another shriek filled the air, louder and more distinct. This time a red-and-black draco broke through the clouds and swirled above the battlefield.

The noise of the fighting subsided as the men lowered their weapons and broke apart, staring at the sky. King Canute's men were running in retreat.

The creature flapped its wings harder and faster, circling low enough that I could clearly see the checkered design of its underside.

Was this the same draco we'd previously encountered? Maxim would have been able to tell right away. I prayed it wasn't, but my intuition told me we were in grave peril.

As the draco swooped down, my heart plummeted with it, especially as I realized where it was headed. The northeast area of the battlefield. Directly where the king and his knights were fighting. And directly where Maxim had gone.

Shouts erupted nearby from commanders calling for archers to ready their arrows.

But it was too late. The draco released another of its skin-crawling cries, and a moment later, the heat of its breath swept over the army, setting on fire and burning everything in its path.

Arrows whizzed through the air. But the draco shot upward out of range, leaving billows of fire and smoke in its wake.

"Please, not the king. And not Maxim." Yet even as I prayed, I suspected the draco had attacked that area specifically, almost as if it had been told to do so.

With the Ice Men having a history of capturing dracos, it was possible King Canute had hired them to utilize a draco as a weapon. Although I didn't see any of the fierce-looking warriors on the battlefield, I surmised they were nearby and able to command the draco.

The Knights of Brethren could keep the king safe and surrounded during a land battle. But how would they be able to shield him from a draco when they had no place to run or hide from its fierce, fiery breath?

My mind spun back to everything I knew about the flying lizards. Was there any way to stop them? In ancient times, what had the people done to protect themselves and their livestock from being decimated?

I scoured through my memories of all the history I'd learned, the tales I'd read, and I rapidly pulled to the forefront a story where villagers had shot flaming darts at an attacking dragon, scaring it away, giving themselves enough time to find safety. Would that work now?

We had to try.

My insides were twisting tight with the need to do something—anything—to stop the draco. As a flaming arrow shot upward from the northeast region of the battlefield, my pulse tripped over itself. Maxim was alive. And he'd come to the same conclusion.

"Shoot fire into the air to scare the draco," I called to the nearest soldiers. "It will give us a chance to take refuge."

But where? We were in the middle of the valley without a tree or stone to use as shelter. The nearest safe places were the Snowden Mountains to the north or the hills and cliffs to the south. I rapidly gauged the distance back to the ravine we'd recently traversed. It was too far, even by horse. The draco would easily catch up and incinerate us.

My attention caught the Atlas River. Though I couldn't see the longboats, I knew they were moored there, the dragonheads upon their prows fierce and stately. With the threat of the draco, would the king and his army be able to retreat by boat?

At the very least we could douse ourselves, and the water would protect us from the draco's fire. It would be frigid, but it was the only way. I prayed Maxim was even now instructing the Knights of Brethren to make their way across the battlefield.

"The river!" I shouted above the din. "We need to

get to safety in the water!"

Several soldiers nodded, and a nearby commander took up the cry, shouting my new instructions. Within moments, soldiers raced toward the river while the archers continued to shoot fiery arrows into the sky toward the draco.

Halvard motioned urgently at me. "We must go now too."

The draco glided overhead, just out of reach of the arrows. It was waiting for a break in the firestorm. And then it would attack again. We had minutes left. Halvard was right. We had to go.

As a groom handed us the reins to our mounts, my attention fell upon the tents behind him and the wounded men lying out in the open. These men had served Norvegia bravely. They deserved our compassion and aid.

Even as I scanned the camp for pallets, litters, or any means we could use for the transport, helplessness seeped into my soul. There were too many wounded, some severely. Dragging them to the river would likely result in more pain and injury. But leaving them behind would doom them to death.

"Your Highness." Halvard grabbed the reins of my horse. "Please."

"The tents." As I stalked away, I unsheathed my knife at my belt. "We shall cut up the tents and use pieces to transport the wounded to the boats."

The priest straightened from where he'd been praying over a moaning soldier.

Without waiting for his permission, I approached the nearest tent, stuck my knife into the thick oiled canvas, and tore it. I made another cut, then ripped the piece downward until it came loose. I tossed it toward the priest, who laid it out on the ground and shifted one of the wounded onto it.

We might not be able to evacuate all the men, but we could save as many as possible.

Halvard stepped up next to me. I half expected him to hoist my body over his broad shoulder and carry me away. Instead, he thrust his knife into the tent and slit it downward. Others began to do likewise, and within minutes, priests, tradesmen, and knights alike were hauling the wounded with them toward the river.

I labored without stopping, moving from tent to tent, shredding the material as fast as I could.

"The archers are running out of arrows!" came a shout from a commander. "We must get the princess to the river! Now!"

Before I could complete the slash I was working on, Halvard finished it and laid the canvas on the ground. "You've done all you can, Your Highness. Now you must think about the rest of the country. Norvegia needs a good and honest and self-sacrificing princess like yourself to stay alive and out of King Canute's control."

I was breathing hard from my exertion, and I wiped my cloak across the perspiration on my forehead. From what I could tell, most were on their way to the river. The remaining men lying about the camp were silent and still.

"Very well, Halvard." I sheathed my knife. I wasn't sure I agreed with his assessment, similar to Maxim's, that Norvegia needed me, but I could leave now, knowing I'd done all I could to help.

A young page waited with our horses. His face was

gritty from the dust of battle, the whites of his eyes wide with fright. Once in my saddle, I leaned down and held out an arm to the boy not more than ten years of age. "Come up with you now." The boy started to shake his head, but I thrust out my arm again. "We have no time to argue. You must obey me at once."

As he took hold of me and scrambled up into the saddle behind me, the shriek of the draco reverberated in the air. Fresh dread coursed through me. Our archers had exhausted their supply of arrows. Our respite was done. The race for our lives to the river had begun.

Chapter
21

MAXIM

"THIS WAY!" I SHOUTED TO SIR ANSGAR AND THE OTHER KNIGHTS of Brethren. The path through the battlefield was riddled with fire and fiends. But with each step and turn, I'd steered the knights clear of immediate threat, and now the edge of the mayhem was in sight.

If only we'd been able to go faster. But even with the archers working frantically to keep the draco at bay, the king's injuries hampered our escape, forcing us to proceed with caution lest we harm him further.

From the fewer flaming arrows rising into the sky, I guessed we had mere minutes, perhaps only sixty seconds, before the archers reached the limit of what they could do. After that, anyone lingering on the battlefield would be at the mercy of the draco and his fiery breath.

"Make haste!" I quickened my pace into a jog, hoping the knights would do likewise behind me. Only eight of the ten knights remained. Four carried the king and four surrounded the entourage for protection. Sir Ansgar, however, had enough courage and strength to make up for the two we'd left behind, the two who'd colluded with Rasmus to murder the king.

Of course, I had no proof they'd taken bribes from Rasmus for the dirty deed. Rasmus was too wise to leave any trail of evidence that would point back to him. Even so, I'd known from the moment I arrived and witnessed the king wounded and down upon his knees that he'd been betrayed. And that I was too late.

In the midst of fighting off a horde of Canute's fiercest warriors, the other knights hadn't witnessed the king fall, had assumed he'd been injured by the enemy.

I'd leveled my accusations against the two newest knights to prevent them from further harming the king, knowing they would need to be restrained. But the Swainians had chosen that moment to send their draco against us.

If not for the knights forming a barrier above us with their shields, we would have perished under the attack. As it was, while crouched, one of the treasonous knights attempted to finish killing the king.

The final wound was only superficial, but at the inflicting of it, Ansgar and several others had eliminated the traitors in their midst.

Thankfully, Ansgar had taken my word more seriously after that. He'd followed my orders for the shooting of the fiery arrows to hold the draco at bay, and he'd accepted my help in leading the group toward the river.

As we broke out into the open, the draco screeched again. While it was still gliding in a perfect circle out of the range of arrows, it had dropped its head, searching for its prey. I had no doubt it had been commanded to seek out King Ulrik. And I had no doubt King Canute was working with the Ice Men to weaponize the draco.

The patterns of its checkered markings on its underbelly proved it to be the same draco from the hunting party. I'd assumed the creature had sought after Elinor then, but perhaps it had been gaining recognition of the king so that it could kill him now with certainty.

I paused but a moment to take in the scene that met us, the soldiers fleeing toward the river's edge. Those straggling behind were trying to save the wounded, some dragging bodies on canvas and pairs carrying the disabled on the canvas between them.

At the sight of a maiden on horseback galloping away from the camp, her long blond hair streaming in the wind, my pulse crashed to a painful halt. I'd expected Elinor to be at the river by now. Why hadn't Halvard taken her there?

A young boy rode on the saddle behind her, clutching her and casting fearful glances at the draco. Clearly, Elinor was aware the arrows had diminished and that she needed to get away. But why hadn't she left sooner?

As much as I wanted to rush to her and keep her safe, sheltering her body with mine, I needed to save the king. If the draco caught sight of him, it would pour out its deadly breath. The knights might be able to provide a defense of the king another time or two, but erelong the fire would crack their shields and leave them completely exposed.

A dozen ideas pinged through my mind. Only one settled there. "Cover the king with my cloak," I shouted to Ansgar.

With a flick of the clasp, I released my cloak and tossed it toward the knights. Without slowing their pace, they threw the garment over the king, shielding his body and face from the draco. It would only buy us another minute. But we needed each second we could get.

With every passing moment, my admiration for the Knights of Brethren grew. The task of hauling the king in his armor and under such duress would be taxing to even the fittest of men. But they moved forward as one unit, undeterred by the betrayal of two they'd counted as brothers.

Sir Ansgar had indeed proven himself worthy of his title as Grand Marshal. If I'd ever regarded him as too young or untested, I no longer did.

"How much time before the draco attacks again?" he called to me from the forefront of the group, holding the king's head as steadily as he could even as he charged forward, his armor clanking with each step.

I took in the angle of the draco's head and its line of vision. It was still searching for the king and hadn't yet discovered we'd concealed him in my black cloak. "Forty-five seconds."

With the visor of his helm raised, Sir Ansgar's face was speckled with blood and lined with sweat. But he set his face toward the river with determination and picked up his pace.

Was there anything more I could do? Or was I helpless to stand by and watch the king die after all?

***

Elinor

Among the soldiers fleeing toward the river, my sights had narrowed upon the Knights of Brethren and the figure of the king they were carrying. He was injured.

They were less than a hundred paces from the river. I wanted to give way to my relief at seeing Maxim sprinting alongside them. But I couldn't. Not when King Ulrik was in such danger. With the draco drawing nearer, it was clear the creature had had its eyes on the king and had every intention of destroying him.

My spine stiffened. No. I wouldn't allow it. Maybe we'd arrived too late to save the king from harm. But I could still save him from death.

I leaned back and spoke to the boy behind me. "I want you to keep riding away as fast as you can. Do not stop for any reason. Do you understand?"

"Yes, Your Highness." His voice was hollowed out with fear.

I slowed my mount, then swung out of the saddle. I was airborne for but a moment before I landed in the grass. I attempted to stay on my feet, but the momentum was too great, and I fell to the ground. I braced myself with my forearms, but the jolt knocked the air from my lungs. For a dazed moment, I struggled to draw in a breath. I almost panicked as my airways refused to open. Then with a swoosh, air filled my lungs, and I expelled my relief in a half cry.

I had so little time to act. Though pain shot through my arms, I pushed up, scrambling to untangle my legs from my skirt. The flying creature now circled directly over the king, as if its demon-eyed underbelly could see everything. Although it hadn't started its dive downward, I sensed it would at any second.

I needed to gain its attention. In my recent studying of dracos, I'd read somewhere that those who attempted to tame dracos used various patterns of shrieks and calls. In addition to keen eyesight, the draco had an unusual ability to hear. If I imitated its warlike cry, would it seek me out? I could only pray so, at least long enough to allow the knights with the king to reach the river.

Cupping my hands around my mouth to project my voice, I released a piercing shriek. When the draco didn't veer from its path above the king, I let out another, this one louder and more authentic.

The draco turned its head in my direction. Another flap of wings passed and then it shifted, swirling around and flying in my direction.

Exhilaration shot through me. I'd accomplished it. I'd saved the king. Now the knights and Maxim would have time to reach safety. With the flap of the draco's translucent red wings drawing nearer, I spun and ran as fast as I could. A glance over my shoulder told me the creature was gaining ground and would be upon me in a matter of seconds.

Strangely, fear fell away and a quiet resolve filled me. I would die today to save the king. I could ask for no more noble death than that.

Behind me, I could hear the knights shouting and Halvard calling out warnings. Above it all, I heard Maxim's anguished, "No, Elinor!"

With death but a breath away, I had only one regret—that I hadn't told Maxim I loved him. The undeniable truth was that I loved him with my whole body, soul, and spirit. If only I'd had the chance to let him know . . .

Chapter 22

MAXIM

I SPRINTED AFTER THE DRACO. I DIDN'T KNOW HOW I WOULD STOP it from attacking Elinor, but I had to try. I'd wrestle it with my bare hands if I could reach it.

"Elinor, drop to the ground!" I shouted. "Cover your head." At least then she might only sustain burns to her back. The very prospect sickened me, and I wished I could magically trade places with her.

As the draco flapped lower, I unsheathed my knife. The blade would do no good against its hard scales, but if I could aim it for the underbelly, I might be able to wound it enough to send it on its way.

Halvard was galloping at a punishing speed to reach Elinor, but he would be too late.

The creature released a piercing cry and then dove.

My heart slammed hard against my chest, and I readied to throw my knife. "No!"

Elinor dropped and covered her head as I'd instructed, clearly aware that the draco was about to breathe upon her.

The creature opened its beak-like mouth. But another shriek a short distance away filled the air. The new pitch was different, but one I'd heard previously. Before I could place the sound, a second draco broke through the clouds in the west, flapping its wings and screeching in fury.

Canute's draco soared over Elinor as if it no longer saw her, its attention tuned in to the draco drawing near.

In the distance, a cloaked and hooded rider was advancing from the direction we'd arrived. I didn't need to see the rider to know who it was.

Lis. And she was bringing her draco.

It dropped lower and chased after Canute's draco, snapping and shrieking as though scolding it. As I paused to watch the retreat, relief welled up inside me so intensely that I wanted to weep.

I'd been right. Lis was bonded to the draco and could communicate with it. She'd likely sensed our danger and ridden after us. Or perhaps she'd felt a connection to Elinor. Whatever the reason, she was here and had saved Elinor.

Lis's draco was smaller. From the number of checkered rings on its underside, I surmised it was yet a juvenile, perhaps ten years of age, unlike Canute's, which was much older, closer to fifty years.

The younger would have the advantage of speed and agility, but Canute's would have more experience. Eventually, it would turn on Lis's draco. But for now, we had gained more time.

I bolted the rest of the distance to Elinor, reaching her at the same moment as Halvard. She hadn't moved, was frozen to her spot on the ground.

Kneeling beside her, I wanted to draw her into my arms and never let her go. But I had to get her to safety first. We had no time to waste. "Elinor, we must go to the river."

She lifted her head and peered up at the sky and then back toward the river. "The king?"

I followed her gaze and gauged the distance left to the river for the Knights of Brethren. "He's almost there."

She nodded, her shoulders sagging. Her efforts, although foolhardy, had almost certainly saved the king.

"You need to go to the river too," she said, her voice trembling.

Halvard had dismounted and was kneeling on the other side of her. Gently, he assisted her to her feet. She didn't resist as we helped her up onto Halvard's horse. Only when the guard was positioned behind her did she hesitate. "What about you, Maxim. Where is your mount?"

My horse had bolted at the first sight of the draco on the battlefield. I had no hope of finding him now amidst the chaos of men and beasts fleeing to the river.

"Go. I'll be there in no time." I met Halvard's gaze, silently communicating to him that he needed to take the princess away regardless of what happened to me.

He gave me a curt nod before digging in his heels and urging his horse away from the open grassland. Elinor shouted a protest, but thankfully, Halvard continued regardless.

I assessed the two dracos, the younger one still in pursuit, chasing the other toward the Snowden Mountains. How long did we have before they circled back around and posed a threat again? Would we be able to start down the river toward the bay? And even then, how long would Lis's draco be able to protect the retreating Norwegian forces?

A thousand thoughts raced through my mind. If Rasmus had plotted the king's demise once, what would prevent him from trying again? If I didn't go through with his plans to release the sword and marry the princess, who would he pick in my stead?

Already my heart protested the prospect of any other man being with Elinor—even a good and honest man. But how could I run away and hide for my life while Rasmus married Elinor off to another man of his choosing, maybe a man with a heart as black as his?

Yet how could I possibly stop Rasmus? He was too powerful, too important, too crafty. I'd never be able to show myself in Vordinberg without gaining swift punishment.

Perhaps I could foil Rasmus by sharing the secret of the Sword of the Magi with a worthy nobleman, one of the Knights of Brethren. At least then an honorable man would pull the sword loose and marry Elinor, a man who could hopefully stand strong against Rasmus and put an end to his scheming.

"Maxim!" Lis was riding in my direction, her arm outstretched. "Hop on behind me!"

I eyed the distance separating us and positioned myself for the best angle to grab her and hoist myself up. She slowed a little, latched on to my arm, and helped swing me behind her. She was riding bareback, and I had to hold on to her to keep from sliding off.

We galloped for several beats of silence. "Thank you for saving Elinor."

"The draco did, not me."

"He obeys your commands."

Lis didn't respond except to veer her mount in the direction of the river.

Of course Lis wouldn't want anyone to know she could communicate with a draco. In ancient times, such people had been considered witches and had been hunted down and burned at the stake. It was possible people would still consider such a skill the sign of witchcraft.

I calculated the distance and time left with Lis. I had no time to waste in speaking the truth. "You saved your sister."

Her body stiffened. "I have no sister."

"Ask your father. He'll tell you the truth."

"He'll tell me I am his daughter."

"You're the firstborn child of Princess Blanche, sister of King Ulrik."

"You speak blasphemy, sire."

"She disappeared eighteen years ago with her one-year-old daughter Elisbet, and the two were never found."

"Sharing a name doesn't mean I share a family."

A hint of doubt tinged her voice, one that told me I'd successfully piqued her curiosity. She was a strong maiden and wouldn't be satisfied now until she pursued answers for herself.

Ahead, Halvard and Elinor were nearing the river, and I released a breath.

"You love the princess." Lis spoke as if it was an obvious fact. Was it? Had I allowed my emotion to show?

It was my turn to remain silent. I might have declared my love to Elinor on the battlefield when I believed I might die and never see her again, but I didn't want to admit it here and now. Some of the soldiers, certainly Halvard, had heard my declaration. But most had been too busy to pay attention. The fewer people who knew of my love for the princess, the better—and safer—for her.

"I passed the trackers who were at the farm before

you." Lis cast her glance in the direction of the dracos, still headed toward the mountains. "I overheard them speaking of the princess. They were talking about giving her the hermit tonic."

My heart rolled over itself, stirring a sickening feeling. The hermit tonic was made from the rare hermit mushroom. It was occasionally prescribed to calm severely distraught people. But it was known for triggering hallucinations and altering a person's mind.

Why did the trackers intend to give such a dangerous tonic to Elinor?

I only had to toss around a handful of explanations to land on the correct one. Rasmus had ordered it. He not only intended to eliminate the king, but he wanted to weaken Elinor and alter her mind to make her malleable to his control.

Under the influence of the hermit tonic, she wouldn't be able to think clearly and would be easily influenced to do Rasmus's bidding, whatever that might be. Essentially, Rasmus would use her for his own purposes, and she would never know the difference.

My muscles tightened with frustration. Even if I alerted her to the plan, told her to beware and involved Halvard, Rasmus would eventually find a way to control her—if not with the hermit tonic, then with something else.

"The princess will be in danger if she returns to Vordinberg." Lis spoke with a finality I didn't want to hear but knew to be true. And I also knew this was the reason she'd risked so much to come to the battlefield. She felt some connection with Elinor. At the very least, she was doing her duty to the kingdom. "You must hide her and keep her safe until the threats have passed."

How? Again, my mind catalogued every possibility, but none supplied the measure of security I desired for her.

"You'll find a way, won't you?" Lis persisted.

"Yes. Have no fear. I shall protect her with my own life." I had to figure out something. And soon.

Chapter 23

MAXIM

KING CANUTE'S MEN WERE REGROUPING. IT WOULDN'T BE LONG before they chased after our retreating troops.

From where I stood on the riverbank, I had a clear view of the battlefield. The Swainian black flags fluttered in the wind among the ranks of knights on their mounts along with the foot soldiers falling into line.

In the distance, the dracos were nothing more than specks in the sky above the mountain peaks. Whether or not Lis admitted to communicating with the young draco, I'd caught her whispering on two separate occasions, likely giving the draco further instructions.

The king's boat was being readied for his transport. Upon my instructions, the rowers were drenching the interior and the single square sail with water to keep the draco's fire from causing damage.

The Knights of Brethren were standing guard around the king, who was resting on the ground, conscious but weak. Elinor knelt beside him, holding his hand between hers and speaking in gentle tones, while one of the fighting men, who was also a physician, doctored the king's wounds.

All around, the soldiers watched Elinor with reverence and awe, not only for saving the king by drawing the draco's attention to herself but also for how hard she'd labored to rescue the injured soldiers. I'd learned she'd organized the evacuation efforts. Without her ingenuity, the weak and wounded would have been left behind at the mercy of Canute.

She'd earned a new level of respect and devotion. Someday, when the king died, the people would remember her bravery and kindness and would welcome her as their queen. I was proud of her. But at the same time, with Lis's warning uppermost in my mind, I feared for her.

Ansgar hopped off the boat and climbed up the steep riverbank, his keen gaze taking in everything. Not much missed his inspection. All the men respected him. And he'd proven himself to be strong and true and faithful.

I'd already spoken to Ansgar, revealing more about the plot to harm the king. While I had no solid evidence pointing to Rasmus, I urged Ansgar to be on guard against Rasmus's wiles. If Rasmus had orchestrated the demise of the sovereign once, he would likely do it again.

Ansgar passed the king and strode to the grassy embankment where I stood beside Lis. She held the reins of her horse and had positioned herself to keep the dracos in her line of vision. At the same time, I'd caught her studying Elinor with unabashed interest.

As Ansgar approached, Lis regarded him warily. He'd removed his great helm and coif, and his light-brown hair lay flat against his head from perspiration. His face was coated with dirt and blood, and his armor was dented.

Despite the dire predicament, he maintained a calmness and confidence that had transferred to the rest of the army. The fear and frenzy from the retreat was gone, and the soldiers labored efficiently to load the wounded onto the waiting boats.

Ansgar bowed his head at me, his humble acknowledgment of my leadership skills and his submission to my wisdom. A part of me craved such homage and wanted the accolades. My long-held dream of becoming the wisest man in the land, even above Rasmus, prodded me to use this occasion to seek after greater fame and more power.

Was that what had happened to Rasmus? Had the small taste of esteem increased his appetite for more until it couldn't be sated?

"Sire," Ansgar said with nary a glance toward Lis. "Your wisdom and intelligence are greater than any other. I would be honored to have you at the helm of the royal longboat, directing us safely back to Vordinberg."

How could I reject the Grand Marshal's offer? He needed me. Saw my value. Realized my potential. The king would also hear about my daring feats and elevate me to higher honor. I didn't need to worry about Rasmus, did I? Not when I was gaining so much favor.

Was this my chance to rise to fame?

A war broke out inside me. The darkness I'd allowed inside was hungry, almost ravenous, for honor and admiration. But the glimmer of light within my soul begged me to let the craving for praise go unfulfilled. Refusing to feed pride would lead to its starvation and eventual death. I would fare better to let humility swell and grow in its place.

Was I famished for praise because Rasmus had never

given it to me? Or was this another temptation to give way to more darkness, so that one day I would end up just like the man I loathed?

I dropped my gaze to Elinor as she comforted the king. I'd let myself slip too far already into becoming like Rasmus and had hurt her in the process. I didn't want to hurt her ever again. That meant I had to let go of the darkness. Starting now.

Suddenly, I knew what I must do. I had to take her far away and keep her safe until Rasmus was no longer a threat.

"I'm honored, Sir Ansgar." I bowed my head at him, letting him know I respected him just as much as he did me. "But I must decline so esteemed a position and instead offer you the services of Lis." I motioned toward the maiden.

With her hood thrown back, her fair hair was windblown. The beauty and likeness of the sisters was unsettling, and I was surprised no one else had made mention of it. Perhaps, in the midst of the crisis, everyone was too busy to pay attention. More likely, this was another instance where I saw things others didn't notice.

Ansgar shifted his attention to Lis. Though his expression remained kind, one of his brows arched in question.

"I assure you," I continued, "Lis is the better choice. She'll keep you safe on the voyage to Vordinberg."

"Is that so?" Ansgar's tone was diplomatic, without a trace of condescension.

"I'm not going to Vordinberg," Lis said quickly.

"If not Vordinberg, then where?" I posed the question knowing I was trapping her. If she chose to go anywhere else, she would appear selfish.

She glanced at Elinor. I could see the answer formulating in her expression. She wanted to go with Elinor and explore the truth of all I'd revealed about her origins. Although Elinor had been too preoccupied with the king to notice Lis, I had no doubt Elinor would want to have the chance to get to know her sister too.

Lis tore her attention from Elinor and focused again on the dracos. She alone, with her draco, had the power to deliver the king and all his forces back to Vordinberg alive. Without their protection, Canute would send his army to attack time after time, and King Ulrik and all his men would face great peril.

Resignation settled across Lis's features. She'd obviously recognized the same.

"Are you sure I cannot convince you, sire?" Ansgar asked.

"I assure you, in this case you'll be heartily grateful for Lis."

Ansgar hesitated but a moment before bowing his head in subservience.

He was worthy. My pulse sped with the realization. Ansgar was the worthiest man in the kingdom, the one worthiest to become the next king. I'd never met a man like him before, a man who exuded greatness and strength and humility all at the same time.

Did I dare share with him the secret of removing the Sword of the Magi from its case? Doing so would thwart Rasmus's plans to put his pawn onto the throne. If Ansgar became king, he had the strength of character never to bow to Rasmus's wiles and whims.

As soon as the deception crossed my mind, I tossed it out. Such a decision about who should become the next king was no more mine to make than it was Rasmus's. For now, I would have to let the matter rest in God's hand.

Ansgar motioned at Lis's horse. "I'll have one of my squires take your horse aboard."

"No need," she replied. "I can lead it myself."

"As you wish. You may ride at the helm with me, near the king."

"I'll ride in the bow."

Ansgar looked to me as though needing guidance for so strong-willed a woman.

"Allow Lis to do as she pleases," I offered. "It is for the best, as you will soon discover." Although Elinor wasn't obstinate, I could see the resemblance in the strength the sisters possessed.

Once Ansgar was distracted giving instructions for transporting the king onto his longboat, I turned to Lis. "Thank you for agreeing to go with them."

"I'll go to Vordinberg, but I have no intention of staying."

She was a maiden of principle and would remain there as long as she was needed, but I held back my pronouncement.

Lis let her gaze rest on Elinor again. But as Ansgar's commands grew louder and urged more haste, I knew the time had come to go. Canute's army was advancing toward the river, hoping to prevent the longboats from leaving.

How would I be able to convince Elinor to come with me? And even if I did, how would we be able to ride away without the enemy seeing us?

I scanned the river, searching for a way of escape.

Lis inclined her head upriver. "Get into the water and lead your horses upriver for half a league. There you'll find caves on the north side of the river."

Though autumn, the water level was still high and the current swift. The temperature of the river was frigid, and doing as Lis suggested would be difficult. But we couldn't ride away on land. The enemy would too easily spot us leaving and send forces to follow us. We needed the riverbank to hide our escape.

"Go now." She gave me a gentle shove toward Elinor, who was assisting with the loading of the king. "Godspeed."

"Godspeed to you too." Without another moment of hesitation, I motioned at Halvard with our horses and then started toward Elinor. She would demand to stay with the king and accompany him to Vordinberg. I would need to be at my sharpest to convince her to come with me instead.

Chapter 24

Elinor

I backed away from the king as his knights hoisted him onto a sturdy lift. One glance across the grassy field at the approaching army told me all I needed to know. We were in imminent danger again.

Earlier, I'd glimpsed Lis standing near Maxim, and I hoped she wouldn't leave before I had the chance to have words with her. Now I noticed her guiding her horse across the plank into the royal longboat. Did this mean she planned to ride with us to Vordinberg?

I didn't have time now to stop and question her plans. But hopefully, once we were away from the threat of Canute's forces, I would have the chance to speak with her at length and share with her my suspicion that we were sisters.

"Elinor." Maxim approached, his dark hair loose and wavy, his face creased with soot and dirt, and his expression severe.

My heart gave an extra thump. Even in the worst of circumstances, he was starkly handsome, and his eyes pierced me with their intensity, almost as if he wanted me to sense the brewing emotion in their depths. Was it love?

He'd said he loved me, but had he really meant it, or had he only spoken the words because of the distress of battle?

Something radiated from him, that same magnetism I'd felt with him before, and this time it was strong enough to keep my feet anchored to the earth, rendering me immovable. I could only watch his approach, my body leaning toward him with the need to fling myself against him and assure myself he was alive and well.

As he stopped but a foot away, he reached for my hand and clasped it in his. "You will not be safe returning to Vordinberg, as Rasmus intends for you to ingest hermit's tonic so that he might control you."

Maxim's words were low and urgent, leaving me no doubt he was worried. "How did you come to know such information?"

"Lis overheard the trackers speaking of the plans."

My gaze sought out the young woman again. She was inside the longboat now and was gently stroking her horse.

"You must come with me into hiding until we can build a case against Rasmus and rid the land of his threat."

My chest tightened. Go into hiding with Maxim?

"I realize I haven't earned back your trust," he whispered, "but I hope I've proven I'm your loyal subject and owe nothing to Rasmus but my contempt."

I wanted to ask Maxim if he desired to be with me, and not just to protect me. Was he suggesting it because he wanted to do his duty to me and for the greater good of the country? Or did he have other motives that had to do with us? But now was neither the time nor the place to bring it up.

"I promise that when the time is right," he continued, "I'll make sure you return to Vordinberg. But until then, you must vanish so Rasmus cannot find you."

"What about the king?" The knights had started hoisting him carefully across the plank leading into his boat.

"If he knew of the plot against you, he'd urge you to leave with me anon."

I nodded. Maxim was right.

More shouts rose around us, voices filled with urgency. Our time was running out, and my pulse pounded with indecision. I didn't want to abandon my country or the king in their time of dire need. "I do not want to run away from trouble, Maxim. Not if I can be of aid."

"You will be of greater aid to your country if you stay out of Rasmus's clutches." The shadows in Maxim's eyes told me he was speaking to himself as well.

"If the king returns to Vordinberg, will he not also be in danger? What if Rasmus continues to plot against him?"

"I've alerted Ansgar of Rasmus's threat. And Lis knows. We must trust them now to keep the king safe." Maxim's grasp tightened against my arm, and he tugged me away from the longboats upriver.

I didn't resist as he led me down the steep riverbank to the water's edge where Halvard was already waiting with our horses. Packs of supplies were tied upon each of the saddles. Apparently, Maxim and Halvard anticipated a long journey ahead.

Halvard nodded at me gravely, and the reality of the situation smacked me hard in the chest, making my breath catch. They were protecting me so that no one could take the throne from me. I wanted to protest, to shout out that I still didn't want to be the next ruler of Norvegia. It was too much pressure. Too many expectations. And I wouldn't ever be ready for the challenge.

If I survived, I would much rather spend my days advancing my Erudite training alongside Maxim and someday becoming a wisewoman, a Royal Sage. Was that too much to hope for? Or should I leave my secret dreams buried?

Maxim's hand slid down into mine. Though we wore gloves, I could feel his warmth and strength. He squeezed gently, clearly sensing my inner turmoil. When I glanced up, I found him watching me, his eyes reading my thoughts with such keenness.

"You rose to the challenge on the battlefield and showed your inner strength with all that you accomplished." His tone was soft and assuring. "If the time comes for you to do so again, you'll go forward, knowing you have the strength to do anything God asks of you."

My thoughts raced back to helping the wounded and the king. I *had* done much more than I'd believed myself capable of doing.

"God always gives us the exact amount of courage we need to face whatever task he puts before us." Maxim's quote of a wise old saying resonated within me. Yes, God had given me exactly what I'd needed at the right moment. No more, no less. Would he do so the next time? I could only pray Maxim was right.

I released his hand and crossed to the horses. "Where to, Halvard?"

Instead of helping me into the saddle, Halvard handed me the reins, his expression still grim. "We'll be swimming upstream a ways, Your Highness."

"If we stay low"—Maxim waded in ahead of me— "hopefully, Canute's forces won't notice us."

I followed him in, the river water soaking through my leather boots and weighing down my skirts.

Some of the longboats had already launched, and the rowers were digging in deep, attempting to get out of range of King Canute's archers.

Halvard and Maxim plunged in deeper, urging their horses to move as swiftly as they could against the rushing water.

The frigidness of the water nearly robbed me of breath. But I pushed myself anyway, allowing the horse's momentum to drag me forward. "Do we have enough time?"

"Using the distance-speed-time formula, the speed is the distance divided by the time." Maxim detailed his mathematical equations, listing off several approximations. Each one left me with the same conclusion. We needed a miracle if we hoped to get away before someone from among Canute's forces spotted us.

Chapter 25

Maxim

Elinor's teeth chattered. Her skin was pale. And she could hardly move. After only nine minutes in the river, she was already freezing.

Urgency prodded me. We had to find the caves Lis had mentioned. Soon.

I pulled Elinor along more rapidly, my hands and legs numb and prickling with the pain of being frozen. "See anything?" I called to Halvard, who slogged a step ahead of us.

He shook his head.

Elinor stumbled, her legs too cold to help her any longer.

If my calculations were correct, we had less than two minutes left before Canute's army reached the river. It wasn't enough time. Someone on the edge of Canute's line of soldiers would spot us all too easily.

Ahead, the riverbank rose into cliffs. Once we reached the rocky area, we wouldn't be able to climb out anywhere nearby on either side of the river and attempt to outride the enemy. We would be stuck moving upriver.

"Take the horses." I tossed the lines toward the guard, then bent and swooped Elinor up into my arms.

"I'm sorry, Maxim," she stuttered through blue lips.

I didn't waste the energy responding. Instead I lunged forward, pushing my body to obey my mind. I'd learned the technique from Father Johann at St Olaf's, the process of narrowing the scope of concentration, centering on one aspect of the body so intensely that the muscles and nerves would work beyond their capability.

With every step, I focused on contracting and relaxing the muscles in my thighs and calves, sending the message along my nerves to work harder and faster.

I passed Halvard, moving in a direction that would have the least resistance from the current as well as the shallowest water that would still allow me to remain hidden.

Faster, I commanded my muscles. As one minute ticked away, I began to run. From the splashing behind me, I could tell Halvard was doing so too, the power of the horses likely giving him some momentum.

As another fifteen seconds passed into thirty, I cringed and waited for shouts from downriver as Canute's soldiers spotted us. All the while, I pushed my body, knowing the human mind could oft do more than anyone believed possible.

"There!" Halvard's call was filled with relief. "Just ahead."

I needed no urging to swerve into the closest gaping cavern in a rising rock wall. I plunged in deeper, giving Halvard room to enter behind me with the horses.

I grabbed one of the reins and guided the horses farther back. We sloshed through the water, now only knee deep. With the slight incline of the ground, I guessed we had another twenty, maybe thirty feet, before we reached dry ground—at least I prayed we would find dry ground.

As we pushed onward, the passageway narrowed into the shape of a rhombus. But I didn't let the odd angles slow my pace. The shallowness of Elinor's breathing and the sluggishness of her pulse impelled me to keep going. She was faring poorly, more so with each passing second, and I had to find a place to warm her body temperature.

The light from the cave opening guided our winding steps, the way growing dimmer the farther we traversed. When I finally stumbled upon a dry ledge, I dropped to my knees, laid Elinor on the ground, and began to strip her wet garments from her.

My fingers were stiff from the cold and fumbled too slowly. Biting back a frustrated cry, I slipped my knife from its sheath, stuck it into her bodice, and wrenched upward, rending the material.

Halvard pressed past me with the horses, drawing them up out of the water.

"I need dry blankets for the princess," I whispered. "Quickly."

As Halvard rummaged in the blackness through the supply packs, I none too gently finished ripping the saturated clothing from her. Attired only in her shift, I wrapped her into a thick, dry blanket Halvard had dropped beside me. I wound her in another, and then another, making sure every inch of her frozen body was tightly bound. Then I rubbed over the blankets vigorously against her arms, back, legs, and feet. The friction was necessary to create thermal energy and subsequent heat.

I labored without ceasing, kneeling on the ledge

beside her and trying to bring warmth back into her body. All the while, I prayed fervently, beseeching God for mercy, not for me but for her.

Finally, after at least half an hour had passed, she released a long, normal breath. "Maxim, warm yourself now."

I kept rubbing, unable to stop. I was possessed with saving her, needed to make sure she survived.

Halvard had moved the horses farther back into the cavern, and I'd heard him tending to them as well as getting himself out of his wet clothes and into something dry.

"Maxim," she said softly. "Please, you must take care of yourself."

"I can't lose you." My cold, damp garments clung to me. I couldn't feel my toes. My legs ached from the cold. But I didn't care. The only thing that mattered was her. Only her.

She squirmed to loosen the cocoon of blankets that surrounded her, but I kept my hands moving, determined to cause friction and warmth. I'd lost her once in my life. And I couldn't bear to lose her again.

Perhaps the most I could ever ask for was to be her close companion—watch over her, stand by her side, and be there to protect her. While I wanted more—a banquet of loving her for the rest of my life—I would gladly settle for any crumbs she might throw my way. Yes, I loved her enough that I would take even the smallest of crumbs.

"Maxim." Her voice grew stronger.

I only increased my efforts.

She broke her arms free of the blankets, and in the next instant she was grasping my hands in hers, forcing me to halt. When I tried to pull away and resume, she intertwined her fingers through mine.

As she flattened her palms against mine, I could feel her push up from the ground, and the next instant she was kneeling next to me, her warm breath bathing my cheek. "I love you," she whispered.

My internal monologue ceased. My bodily functions halted. My constantly whirring mind lost every coherent thought . . . except one . . .

She loved me. She'd said it. But what did it mean? It couldn't mean that she cared about me the same way I did about her. That was too much to hope for.

Her breathing quickened against my skin, sending a delicious shiver up my backbone.

"Are you going to say something?" Her whisper turned shy, as though her admission now embarrassed her. "Or maybe you did not truly mean what you said earlier when you were riding off to find the king."

What had I said? I tried to make my mind work, but it was sluggish with wonder, amazement, awe.

She started to loosen her threaded fingers, and her warm breaths dropped away from my cheek. I could feel her pulling away emotionally too. And I didn't want her to. I wanted her to stay with me, right beside me, for the rest of my life.

Such a dream was impossible. But I couldn't think of that right now. All I knew was that I couldn't let her out of my reach.

Before I could stop myself, I lifted my hands to her face, cupped her cheeks, and guided her back. This time, I wasn't content to feel her breath upon my cheek. I wanted her breath upon my lips. I paused for several heartbeats, let her soft gasp welcome me. Then I closed the distance and fused my mouth with hers.

At the touching, heat charged through me, moving through my body into my limbs, warming me faster than friction or even a fire. When she pressed in and met me eagerly, hungrily, I angled so I could feast for as long as she would allow it.

Her hands found my cheeks. Her fingers grazed the stubble over my jaw before gliding up and into my hair. As she delved in, her kiss turned more passionate. I responded in equal measure, hoping I left her with no doubt about how much I loved her.

A sharp prod to my back stopped me short, and I broke the kiss.

The prick belonged to Halvard's knife.

Elinor's swollen lips brushed mine, and her ragged breathing beckoned me to kiss her again. But another sharp prod of Halvard's weapon kept me from doing so.

"Release her." Halvard's voice was low and stern.

Slowly, I lowered my arms. The darkness wasn't so dark anymore. My eyes had adjusted to the cavern, lit only by the faint light coming from the distant opening, enough light that Halvard had witnessed our kissing and was angry about the intimacy. And rightly so. He was tasked with protecting Elinor and keeping her safe, even from ardent men who loved her, like me.

"Please, Halvard." Elinor released me too, her eyes widening at the sight of Halvard's knife against my back. "Do not harm Maxim."

"I don't intend to harm him." Halvard didn't shift his blade. "As long as he vows he won't touch you again . . ."

Could I vow such a thing?

"But, Halvard." Elinor's tone contained censure. And disappointment?

"Nary a touch. Until you are wed."

"Wed?" This time Elinor's voice rose with surprise, and dare I say hope?

"You'll stay away from her"—Halvard bent in and spoke to me—"until the priest declares you husband and wife. Do you understand?"

"Yes."

"If I find you so much as lay a finger on her before then, I'll tie you up and leave you that way until your wedding day."

Halvard spoke as if our marrying was a foregone conclusion. Was it?

Chapter 26

Elinor

Marry Maxim?

Next to me, he stiffened and shook his head. "No. I cannot marry Elinor."

As confused as I was about Halvard's suggestion, I certainly didn't want Maxim to object to it right away. Didn't he want to be with me? Wasn't he willing to find a way to be together?

At Maxim's declaration, Halvard finally backed up and sheathed his knife. While the cavern was tall enough that the horses could rest comfortably out of the water, the jagged ceiling made standing difficult for a large man like Halvard. Though he resumed grooming the horses, he remained nearby, clearly intending to follow through on his word to tie Maxim up if he touched me again.

"I'm not aspiring to be king," Maxim stated quietly. "I have no wish for it."

If I'd ever believed Maxim was using me to gain power and become king, I could safely set those thoughts from my mind. He was fighting an internal battle to free himself from his father's control. Though he might have made some mistakes, ultimately, he was the kind of man who wanted to do what was right.

"I know your heart, Maxim. And you are a noble and good man."

"The darkness within me battles with the light. Light might have won the battle this time, but what about the next?"

"Holy Scripture says that the light shines in the darkness, but darkness does not overcome it." The simple fact that Maxim wanted to fight the darkness meant he was already on the path to victory.

He was still in his wet clothing and needed to get warm and dry. I started to peel away one of my blankets to wrap around him, but he wound it back more tightly than before.

I could think of no one more worthy than Maxim. He was kind and tender, and yet he challenged and tested and refined me like no one else.

My love for him swelled in my chest, bringing an ache to my throat. I didn't want to marry any other man, not when I was so thoroughly in love with Maxim. In fact, I couldn't bear the possibility of spending my life with anyone but him. "I must choose a husband, and I choose you."

He held himself rigid before dropping his head and letting his shoulders slump. "The law forbids a royal princess or prince from marrying a commoner."

"The missives to the chieftains will bring about a change in the law."

"We don't know for certain. And we don't know what Rasmus is capable of doing once he hears of my disobedience. I suspect he will accuse me of treachery, turn the court against me, and hunt me down."

I shuddered. While my limbs and body had warmed up because of Maxim's efforts, I was suddenly cold again at the prospect of the danger Maxim would face. "All the more reason for us to get married. As my husband, what can Rasmus do to you?"

"Rasmus is clever and conniving. If he wants to destroy me, he'll find a way, whether I'm your husband or not."

"You are more intelligent than him. And you have me. Together, we shall come up with a plan to destroy him first."

Maxim's head was still bent, his jaw rigid. "Until we discover a way to thwart him, I'll have to live in hiding, always in danger. I cannot put you through that."

He hadn't spoken of his love to me again in words, but his kiss had contained his ardor. It left me with no doubt of his love, that what he felt for me was real and true. Now it was because of his love that he wanted to shield me from the threats and danger Rasmus would perpetrate. I admired his desire, but I had no intention of giving in.

"If you let your fear determine your steps, you will always falter." It was a wise old saying we'd learned together, and never was it truer than now. "We cannot let fear of Rasmus guide our path. If we do so, we give him the victory."

The lapping of the river against the stone ledge filled the silence, along with a trickling from somewhere deeper in the cavern, likely a spring of fresh water that fed into the river.

The air inside the cave was dank and musty, but

Maxim had saved us. He'd brought us to this shelter just in time, keeping King Canute's forces from noticing our escape. We would have to remain hidden in the cavern for a day or two, or perhaps more, until the Swainian forces withdrew from the area.

In the meantime, we were safe with supplies.

"What if we're not so fortunate the next time?" Maxim clearly sensed the direction of my thoughts.

"I have lived for too many years apart from you. And I would spend the rest of my days by your side, no matter how long that might be."

Finally, he lifted his head. The darkness was too pervasive to see his features clearly, and it would be some time before we could safely light a fire. Even so, I sensed his tender gaze upon me. He reached out as though he intended to caress my face, glanced at Halvard brushing one of the horses only a foot away, then dropped his hand.

"I want to spend the rest of my days by your side too," he whispered. "I can think of no greater joy than that. But I also don't want you to regret your choice. If the marriage law isn't changed, you will forfeit your right to become the next queen."

"'Tis a risk I am willing to take."

"If Rasmus deceives the country by giving the secret of freeing the sword to another, he'll advocate for his choice to become king and the country won't accept me, perhaps not even you."

"We shall find a way to expose his duplicity."

Maxim nodded, but sadly. "I fear our union may create more conflict for the throne, especially between those who will support Rasmus's candidate and those who will remain faithful to the House of Oldenberg."

"We will do all we can to work toward peace." While I still had much to learn, my trials were teaching me that I was stronger and could accomplish more than I'd allowed myself. "However, you must not forget: I am technically no longer the first in the line of succession."

Maxim hesitated. "Elisbet will learn to accept her heritage. But if we never find proof of her bloodline and connection to the royal family, you may yet be the closest heir to the throne."

I inwardly lifted a petition that Providence would find a way to make Elisbet the next queen and not me. But if not, I would take the responsibility and embrace it fully. I could do nothing less.

"Wherever the path, whatever the task, whatever the difficulty, I pray I shall have you by my side both now and forever." My plea rose above a whisper and echoed in the cavern. I didn't care that Halvard knew of my feelings for Maxim. I suspected he'd already guessed my ardor, which had likely led him to suggest that I wed Maxim. If he supported it so readily, surely many others would too. Even if they didn't, I had to follow the ancient wisdom I had just spoken to Maxim. I couldn't let fear determine my steps.

Maxim didn't immediately respond, the sign his mind was weighing every option in an algorithm, calculating the risks by percentage points, and postulating the probability of every outcome. He was a man destined for greatness. I just hoped I would be with him to ensure that Norvegia benefitted from his full potential.

"Elinor." He whispered my name with a reverence that sent warmth spiraling into my innermost being. "I love you more than life. I want to spend all my days by your side, proving my love. Though I tremble at the prospect of becoming your husband, I can ask for no greater honor."

My breathing hitched. Was he agreeing to our union?

He waited, as though he, too, was holding his breath.

"And . . .?" I finally managed.

"And . . . I humbly beseech you to spend your days by my side too . . . as my wife."

"Yes." The word tumbled out containing all my joy.

Through the darkness, I could see his features relax. He reached for my cheek and started to bend toward me.

Did he intend to kiss me again? My pulse raced with anticipation and strange need.

Halvard moved away from the horse and jerked on Maxim's cloak, pulling him back, the collar tightening and nearly choking him.

Maxim broke free and shrugged out of his wet cloak.

"Meant what I said, that's for sure." Halvard glowered at Maxim. "Don't touch the princess. Not until you're married."

"I shall do my best—"

"You'll do it." Halvard's sternness left no room for argument.

"Yes, I'll do it."

Halvard harrumphed and backed away.

Maxim peered upward with that unseeing way of his that told me he was thinking hard. "Twelve days, three hours, and eight minutes . . . no eighteen minutes."

I snuggled deeper into the blankets. Even though I found myself in a desperate place, facing great trials ahead, I'd never been happier. "And what is happening in twelve days, three hours, and eighteen minutes?"

"Our next kiss."

"Is that so?" I couldn't contain my smile.

"It is. We'll be married the moment we arrive at St. Olaf's Abbey."

"Then I shall begin counting the minutes." And I did.

Chapter 27

MAXIM

THE THICK DOOR OF THE IMPOSING STONE ABBEY SWUNG OPEN, and bright light and warmth rushed out to greet us. Just inside, Father Johann stood at the forefront of several monks and bowed reverently toward the princess, revealing his bald head with his circle of gray hair. Behind us, the small wilderness community surrounding St. Olaf's was quiet. With the coming of winter and the diminishing sight of the sun, the hours of light would be replaced by darkness erelong.

A faint dusting of snow covered the landscape, turning the gray of the rocky terrain into a breathtaking wonderland. The mountains rose to the east with daunting cliffs, steep slopes, and white-capped peaks. To the far west, majestic fjords carved out the coastline.

But here in the central landlocked Frozen Wilds, the abbey was isolated, the way of life simple, and the people rugged but generous. I prayed we could find refuge here.

Father Johann rose to his full height, close to seven feet tall. "Your Highness. Welcome. You are our honored guest." The scent of roasting game and the waft of herbs told me we had interrupted their supper hour.

Elinor stood beside me, wearing a white cloak made of polar bear fur. We'd purchased it from a remote trading post in the Golden Plateau near the Snowden Range, along with fur-lined boots and mittens. Except for her rosy face, she was tucked into the layers of fur and remained as comfortable as I could possibly make her in the cold temperatures, which continued to drop every day, especially the farther north we rode.

Her eyes shone brightly. "Thank you, Father Johann. I have heard much about you from Maxim."

Turning to me, Father Johann smiled, his features as warm and welcoming as I'd hoped. "Maxim. I admit, I did not expect to see you again in this lifetime."

"Nor I, you. But I'm heartily glad and pray you'll give us refuge in the days to come."

"You shall always find refuge here."

I bowed to my mentor—the man responsible for shaping most of the good in my character. I was grateful for his influence, one more person who had given me the strength and encouragement I'd needed to become different than Rasmus.

Father Johann regarded Halvard, standing with our horses a short distance away near a low stone barn. Halvard had indeed proven himself loyal the past days of traveling. He'd done everything in his power to hide our tracks and keep us hidden so no one would know of our remote location.

Though I'd inwardly grumbled that he refused to give Elinor and me a moment of privacy, and though he refused to allow me to touch the tiniest hair upon her head, I realized the importance of his presence. He'd kept me from taking advantage of our situation. His strict rules had forced me to utilize every ounce of self-control I could muster. His push to maintain boundaries had kept us chaste while at the same time opening the door for more sharing, talking, and challenging than we'd ever experienced before.

When we broke camp earlier in the day, I'd been almost sad knowing our travels were nearing completion. My feelings for Elinor had multiplied with each passing day until the strength of my love had reached beyond anything I'd believed possible.

Even now, as I stood before Father Johann, my insides quaked with the need to make Elinor mine once and for all.

Father Johann studied my face, likely seeing there just how great was my love for the princess. "St. Olaf's is your home for as long as you shall have need. Same to you, Your Highness."

"Thank you, Father," Elinor said, but with a shiver. The freezing night air was growing bitter, even with our heavy fur cloaks.

Father Johann stepped back, waving the princess inside. "We are honored to have you here."

She hastened into the warmth, but I kicked off the snow from my soles and waited for Halvard before entering the main hall. Fires blazed from two hearths on either side of the rectangular room, accounting for the twin curls of smoke we'd witnessed from a distance as we'd ridden within range of the abbey.

"You are just in time for supper." Father Johann began to close the door.

I stopped it halfway. "Our guard, Halvard. We would like him to join us."

Father Johann paused, his brow rising. The two dozen other monks had already grown silent and were watching us curiously from where they were seated at trestle tables laden with simple fare.

Normally, servants and soldiers of Halvard's rank congregated together in a separate area for meals. But Halvard had become more than just our guard. I couldn't quantify his role quite yet, but after his loyalty to Elinor and me, he deserved to be present for the evening.

"We would like to be married as soon as possible." I met Father Johann's gaze directly, unashamed of my desire for Elinor.

Father Johann already knew of my childhood friendship with Elinor, how much I'd adored her. And now he nodded as if the news of our impending nuptials was what he'd expected all along.

But something else more serious in his expression told me he knew of the importance of our union. Had the monks this far north already heard the rumors?

Although the proclamation of my treachery had come from the king, I'd had no doubt lies about me plotting to overthrow the throne had come from Rasmus. He'd twisted all my good deeds to save the king, casting doubt over everything I'd done. Alas, my running away made me look guilty, and Rasmus was capitalizing on that. Worst of all, we'd learned he was accusing me of kidnapping Elinor.

With such an allegation hanging over our heads, I needed to marry her now in order to prove we were together by choice and not coercion. If twenty-four monks and Halvard acted as witnesses to our willing union, Rasmus would have no basis for his story.

In addition to learning about Rasmus's threats, Halvard had also gleaned news about King Canute.

Thankfully, King Ulrik and the Norvegian fleet had been able to escape back to Vordinberg without more casualties. Canute hadn't been able to stop the retreat. I had a feeling Lis's draco had played a prominent role in keeping the king and his men safe. And now I prayed she'd been able to do so without drawing attention to her abilities to communicate with the draco, especially from Rasmus. If he discovered what she was capable of, I feared what he might do to her and how he might use her.

From what we could tell, Canute hadn't yet made additional efforts to invade Norvegia. With Elinor's disappearance, he'd likely had no choice but to halt his aspirations for Norvegia's throne. At least for now. I had no doubt he would regroup and launch another campaign at some point.

Maybe by the time he did, Norvegia's future queen and king would be secured. If Elinor and I were destined for such a duty, we would humbly take it. But we prayed Providence would provide another way and somehow foil Rasmus's plan to use the Sword of the Magi to put a man of his choosing on the throne.

"We would be delighted to host a wedding," Father Johann said, "and we can do so forthwith."

"Then you will perform the ceremony?"

He nodded, and a sheen of tears glistened in his eyes. "I would consider it one of the greatest honors in my life."

In less than a minute, we shed our heavy outerwear and stood before Father Johann at the center of the hall with the entirety of St. Olaf's monks surrounding us.

Halvard led Elinor toward me, her eyes shining with an admiration that made me breathless.

Halvard bent in to share a private word with Elinor, but his voice was gruff and loud. "Princess Blanche would be proud if she could see you now, Your Highness."

"Do you think so?" Elinor gave him her full attention, his answer clearly important to her.

"Aye, you found your heart match, a man who loves you more than life."

I nodded at Halvard, hoping he knew exactly how right he was.

As Elinor took her place next to me, her eyes seemed to ask if this was truly what I wanted.

I smiled down at her. *She* was all I truly wanted and needed. If only she knew how much. . . .

I'd simply have to spend the rest of my life showing her.

I wanted to take her hand, twine my fingers through hers, and draw her close. But the lesson in self-control these past twelve days was not one I'd soon forget, and after refraining thus far, I could persevere over the next two minutes.

"In the name of the Father, Son, and Holy Ghost. Amen." Father Johann made the sign of the cross.

As he spoke the opening words of the ceremony, my chest swelled with a fresh joy at the realization I was getting to marry my best friend and the woman I loved.

"Wilt thou have this woman to be thy wedded wife, to live together after God's ordinance in the holy estate of matrimony? Wilt thou love her, comfort her, honor, and keep her, in sickness and in health? And forsaking all others, keep thee only to her, so long as you both shall live?" Father Johann paused and nodded at me.

"I will." The words reverberated in the room and down to my soul, promises to this woman I intended to keep no matter what it cost me.

After Elinor recited her vows, Father Johann reached

for my hand and connected it to Elinor's. "Those whom God hath joined together, let no man put asunder."

At the touch of her soft skin, a shimmer of pleasure filled me. Elinor brushed her thumb against mine as though relishing this connection too.

"I pronounce that they be man and wife together." Beaming, Father Johann stepped back.

I glanced at Halvard with a grin. "Am I safe to kiss my bride?"

Returning the grin, the faithful guard patted his knife ensconced in its sheath. "Aye, mighty safe now."

"Good." I shifted to face Elinor and tugged her closer. Then, snaking my free hand around her neck, I bent in. I paused with my lips hovering near hers. "May I kiss you?"

Her lips curled up into a smile, giving way to her dimples. "You must. I command it of you."

I closed the distance and meshed our lips and our lives. Hers was a command I would happily fulfill.

I'd once believed I could enamor her. But 'twas I, indeed, who was enamored.

Take a peek as the real story
of Excalibur continues . . .

Chapter 1

ANSGAR

"The king is not himself." I hunched over the table and kept my voice low. "He has an ailing that goes beyond his injuries."

My five closest companions from the Knights of Brethren were huddled around the table with me, their expressions somber, the overcast morning adding to the gravity.

I glanced over my shoulder toward the door of the antechamber. We oft congregated in the small, private room to discuss matters of the kingdom's safety. However, for a reason I couldn't explain, the meeting place off the great hall no longer felt secure, as if somehow the door and walls were listening to our conversations and conveying them to the entire world.

"He deteriorates more every day," I said. "In fact, the deterioration is happening much too swiftly. We need to determine why."

The king had sustained multiple injuries in the battle a month ago against Swaine, but his chain mail had prevented the assassin's knife from penetrating his innards. While he'd suffered lacerations and severe bruising, which had made movement difficult in the early days of his recuperation, his wounds were healing.

Why, then, was he growing weaker, especially in his mental capacity?

The question taunted me and was clamoring louder with each passing day.

Kristoffer rubbed his smoothly shaven chin, the only one of our group without facial scruff. "'Tis possible his humors are out of balance—too much black bile, leading to this melancholic state." As the most learned among our Knights of Brethren, I could always count on Kristoffer to keep us well informed.

For all his education, Kristoffer couldn't compare to Maxim, the wisest and most intelligent man I'd ever met. If only he were with us. He would diagnose the king's illness and devise a solution all in one breath.

As it was, I hadn't heard from Maxim since we'd parted ways on the bank of the Atlas River during our hasty retreat from the Valley of Red Dragons after the fighting. He'd put his own life at risk by riding to the frontline to inform me of the plot to kill the king. In addition to learning about the king's danger, Maxim had discovered Princess Elinor was in peril and had subsequently taken her into hiding.

At least, that's what I wanted to believe, although I had no proof of where he'd gone or why. I couldn't yet accept the current theory making its way through court that Maxim had kidnapped the princess. Not after the honor and self-sacrifice he'd displayed.

The fact that King Ulrik adamantly blamed Maxim only confirmed the decline of his faculties. The intelligent and kindhearted king who'd earned the name Ulrik the Good had never assumed the worst about people. Previously, he'd waited to form judgment until he had solid evidence.

He'd also accused Maxim of orchestrating the murder attempt against him. Such an allegation was false, even ludicrous. I'd been there in the middle of the combat. I'd witnessed everything, including the desperation in Maxim's expression as he'd warned me of the impending danger.

The truth was, without Maxim's intervention, the king would have suffered more than surface wounds. He would have died. Maxim was a hero, not a criminal.

My efforts at reasoning with the king and relaying facts from that day had only been met with sullen resistance instead of sound judgment. And for the first time since coming to court as one of his elite knights, I'd grown hesitant in speaking to him with my usual frankness.

"Could someone be poisoning him?" I asked, although I didn't know how such a thing was possible since I was testing his food and drink.

"If poison, he would likely already be dead." To my right, Sigfrid fiddled with the fletching of an arrow on the table in front of him. "Perhaps the physicians missed an internal injury."

To my left, Torvald gripped the hilt of his sword, his jaw tight and his lips pressed in a thin line. Across the table Espen and Gunnar sat on either side of Kristoffer, all of us attired simply in dark-brown tunics and hose, leather belts, and calf-length leather boots.

We made up six of the ten Knights of Brethren, the brave group chosen to guard the king in battle and serve as his bodyguards during times of peace. As the Grand

Marshal, the leader of the Brethren, I was cognizant that we shouldn't be meeting without the entire group of ten. But I no longer trusted all the knights, especially now that we'd gained new members.

"Whatever is wrong with the king"—I dropped my voice to a whisper—"we must uncover it."

Gunnar drummed his thumbs on the table. "Perhaps we ought to collaborate with the Noble Council and inform them of our concern." With his older brother on the council, Gunnar had connections to the group of noblemen closest to the king. In addition, Gunnar had an easy way about him that many people liked, making him a natural liaison.

At the slap of passing footsteps outside the chamber, Kristoffer paused before responding. "Do we know if we can trust everyone on the council?"

Torvald gave a curt shake of his head. "We cannot trust anyone at this point."

"I say we come up with a test," Gunnar interjected. "And let's flush out who's faithful to the king and who's not."

"What kind of test do you propose?" I asked.

Gunnar shrugged.

Kristoffer glanced around the table at the others, giving them a chance to voice their thoughts before making another suggestion. "One of us could feign interest in plotting against the king, drop crumbs of malcontent. Those who are already conniving against him will most certainly attempt to gain another ally."

"You're suggesting that one of us spy?" Gunnar's eyes lit with the prospect of being that spy. But such a role would be dangerous, and only someone with a façade of stone, like Torvald, could pull it off.

As if sensing the direction of my thoughts, Torvald sat straighter. "I'll do it."

Before I could respond, the chamber door swung open. At the sight of the king, we pushed back from our chairs and stood.

"Your Majesty." I bowed my head in his direction, but not before I caught sight of others behind the king, including the remaining four Knights of Brethren and Rasmus.

"And what exactly are you men doing in the meeting chamber by yourselves?" The king's voice rose with uncharacteristic anger. A bulky, muscular man, the king had always been imposing, but now, slouched and shuffling, he appeared to have aged well beyond his fifty years. His tunic was stained, his doublet unbuttoned, and his light-brown hair was disheveled as if he hadn't been properly groomed.

The king couldn't have known we were having a private discussion unless someone had informed him, likely in an effort to undermine my authority. The king knew I was a man of integrity, and the best way to manage this situation was to speak honestly. "We believe that your life continues to be in danger, Your Majesty, quite possibly from someone within the ranks of your trusted staff. Thus, we were discussing how we might eliminate the threat."

The room was shadowed, lit by a single candle on the table. The wind rattled the shutters that were battened to keep out the cold draft that had blown in as October turned into November. 'Twould not be long now, ere southern Norvegia was blanketed in snow.

In the dim lighting, the king's face appeared thinner, more haggard, and paler.

I loathed that the king was suffering. And I blamed myself. I was tasked with not only leading the other knights, but with keeping the king safe, guarding his life above my own, and sacrificing myself for him.

Somehow, despite my most rigorous efforts, I'd failed. I'd failed during the battle to see the danger among our own ranks. And I was clearly failing again to protect him from the threat within the royal residence.

Familiar frustration wound through me. I hated failure, and lately it was following me like a hound sniffing its prey.

The king wobbled and pressed a hand to his forehead, as though dizzy. Or truly unwell, as I suspected.

I hastened to the king's side, but one of the new knights reached him first. Gotfred. The dark-haired, dark-eyed knight was tall, well built, and seemed to have the fortitude required of the Brethren. Even so, knights were selected to be part of the Brethren based on valor in battle, and Gotfred hadn't fought in the recent confrontation with Swaine. I doubted he had any fighting experience other than upholding peace among his clansmen.

The young knight had obviously been chosen because he was Rasmus's nephew. As one of the seven Royal Sages, Rasmus had earned his position from years of education and demanding work. I couldn't deny he was wise. But he was also crafty. And if Maxim had been correct, Rasmus was behind the threat against the king in the recent battle.

Though I'd protested Gotfred's selection a fortnight ago, the king had gone forward with the decision anyway, disregarding my opinions on the matter as if I'd never spoken.

At that point, I should have realized something wasn't right with the king, but I'd never questioned the king's decisions, having grown to respect and trust him deeply. I'd assumed the pain of his injuries was affecting his ability to reason. But now, after repeated uncharacteristic behavior, I had to finally admit something more was going on.

Gotfred gently tucked the king's hand through his arm as if he were a son and had every right to assist the king so personally. "Your Majesty, would you like to sit?"

"No." The king glanced around, his eyes filling with confusion as though he didn't know where he was or what was happening.

Rasmus stepped to his other side. In his black scholarly robe and long black cap that hung down into a tasseled tip, the Royal Sage's dark eyes were always shadowed, as if the shutters to his soul were closed tightly. Since the king's return from battle, Rasmus had hovered near the king, like a worried parent with a sick child.

I had the sudden urge to secret the king away from Vordinberg and away from the danger, perhaps to one of his summer estates along the northern coast. Or perhaps I could hide him in an abbey until he was well. Would doing so help him? Or would failure trail after me?

More likely, I'd be accused of kidnapping the same way Maxim had.

Rasmus swept his gaze over the six of us before focusing on me. "We believe the king's life continues to be in danger too, possibly from someone within the ranks of his trusted staff."

I didn't look away. Rasmus was using my words from moments ago against me, twisting them to turn me into a suspect. He was wise enough to know my loyalty to the king was genuine. He couldn't believe I was capable of treachery, could he?

"Yes," the king spoke, his eyes clearing of confusion. "Someone is plotting against me, someone I trust. And I believe we are getting closer to uncovering who." The king narrowed his eyes upon me with his last statement.

My chest pinched. Surely the king didn't mean me. Not after how faithfully I'd served him over the past four years. I'd devoted myself to him and the other knights wholeheartedly, leaving no room in my life for anything else. I'd given myself to the task without reservation.

His Royal Majesty had always praised me for my loyalty. How could he turn against me now?

He glared at me a moment longer, then turned his attention to Rasmus. "You were right as usual, Rasmus. Unfortunately, I do not know whom I can trust anymore."

The Royal Sage was the one the king shouldn't be trusting. But how could I say so when I still had no proof of Rasmus's involvement in the assassination attempt? Not when he'd shifted the blame of every problem to Maxim. The real question was, why was Rasmus undermining me and the other knights who were most loyal to the king? Did he hope the king would eliminate us? And if so, why?

"Your Majesty." I had to try once again to help the king see reason. "I have done everything in my power to remain steadfast to you. I have always spoken the truth and nothing less. And I shall remain honest with you now and forevermore."

Rasmus waved a hand at me as though to silence me. "Sneaking around behind the king's back in clandestine meetings is hardly honest."

"We seek only the king's highest good, Your

271

Excellency." Even as I spoke, doubt remained etched on the faces of the Knights of Brethren standing behind the king and Rasmus. Perhaps our meeting did seem suspect. If everyone else chose not to believe us, I would have to labor all the harder to prove we were faithful.

Gotfred, still at the king's side, regarded us with contempt. "We can escort Sir Ansgar and his compatriots from the royal residence, Your Majesty."

"No." My spine grew rigid at the prospect of leaving the king defenseless. I couldn't let Rasmus cast me out. At the moment, nothing was more important than staying close to the king and exposing the real threat. "The king knows we are more than trustworthy, that we would die for him. He has naught to fear from us." As I spoke, I locked eyes with the king, once again hoping he'd see the earnestness of my declaration.

He wavered, the same confusion as earlier flitting across his features. "You're a good man, Ansgar Nordheim." He spoke and then spun back toward the door. Without another word, he exited.

The others filed out after him, but Gotfred and Rasmus lingered behind, watching the group of us warily. "Should we rid the castle of the lot of them, Uncle?"

The title of address was informal, and I expected Rasmus to rebuke Gotfred and demand the respect due his position. But the Royal Sage's expression remained as impassive as always. If the offense bothered him, he didn't show it. He inclined his head toward me and spoke softly, without a trace of emotion. "Henceforth, if you have concerns about the king, you must come to me in order that we might work together."

Work together? What did he mean? Was this an underhanded means of threatening me to cooperate with him? Since he hadn't been able to eliminate the king at the battle, was he hoping now to make the king his pawn, to control him and rule through him?

I stifled a shudder at the prospect. I didn't want to imagine Norvegia under the control of a man like Rasmus. But from what I could see, his influence was growing as the king's seemed to decrease.

I bowed my head, neither accepting nor declining Rasmus's invitation. My gut told me I would do best to steer far away from Rasmus. But at the same time, if I angered him, I feared he would make sure I never had access to the king again.

As he turned to go, his expression gave nothing away. I could only watch him depart with a strange feeling of being trapped. Gotfred followed Rasmus. Once they were gone, Gunnar opened his mouth, likely ready to spew his dislike for Rasmus and Gotfred. But I cut him off with a curt shake of my head.

We could no longer gather here in the castle. Instead, we needed to have our discussions elsewhere to evade Rasmus and his spies. In the meantime, we would have to pretend to comply with Rasmus.

While I didn't speak the words of instruction aloud, the expressions of my closest companions told me they understood my directive.

As we exited the chamber, one of the castle stewards approached and handed me a small piece of parchment rolled up and tied with twine. "A message, sire."

When the steward strode away with no interest in what was inside, I guessed he—or perhaps Rasmus—had already read it.

"Who delivered it?" I called.

"A street urchin," he replied over his shoulder.

Which meant the writer of the message wanted to remain anonymous. I untied the note and read it aloud. "'I am a secret admirer and would like to meet you. Please come to the Dragon Tavern at high noon.'"

Gunnar and Espen both whistled, grins lighting up their faces. The two had no trouble with the ladies. With how handsome and charming they were, maidens flocked to them.

Torvald, Kristoffer, and Sigfrid were popular among the ladies too, mainly because of their status as firstborn sons and the accompanying wealth and titles. The three had recently participated in Princess Elinor's weeklong courtship in which twelve of the most eligible firstborn noblemen of marriageable age competed with one another to become the next king.

Princess Elinor hadn't ended up choosing any of the men and had invoked the Sword of the Magi for help in finding her husband. The engraving on the sword indicated that the man who wielded the sword would be worthy of being king. So far, none of the noblemen who'd come from all over the kingdom had been able to loosen the ancient relic from the cedar box that held it.

Recently, we'd learned the law was being changed so that any man, whether noble or common, could attempt to pull the sword free, marry Princess Elinor, and become the next king.

A commoner marry royalty? A commoner become the next king? The idea was preposterous. But already the chieftains—including my oldest brother—and the Royal Sages had agreed to amend the law. A majority vote from the Noble Council would make it official. The council had yet to gather, but with the king supporting the change, everyone believed it would happen soon, likely within the next month.

"Are you going to meet your secret admirer?" Gunnar asked, his grin still wide. "If not, I shall go in your stead."

I was tempted to hand Gunnar the note and give him leave to seek out the maiden for me, but I hesitated. Why would a maiden want to meet at the Dragon Tavern? Taverns weren't places women frequented. Why not pick the Stavekirche or city center or even the waterfront?

"Probably a rich young noblewoman trysting without her father's knowledge, hoping to win your heart," Gunnar teased, shaking his head and sending his overlong dark-brown hair off his forehead.

"Soon enough we'll be able to marry those *rich young noblewomen*." Espen clamped my shoulder. Like me, Espen was one of the few Knights of Brethren who wasn't nobly born and instead belonged to the northern clans.

"Even if the law is changed," I said, "the nobility will still guard their status. No baron or earl will give his daughter to a commoner. Tell me I am wrong about the matter."

"You are not wrong," Kristoffer answered. "Though I would gladly give you each my daughters if I had them, most of the nobility will attempt to keep the current boundaries in place."

I nodded. "Laws may change, but traditions will remain the same."

"You are too serious, my friend." Gunnar laughed. "At the very least, go and have fun. You deserve it."

Gunnar was never one to pass up an opportunity to make merry or meet with maidens. He spent most of his free time doing that very thing. But he knew how I felt, that I had no wish to be in a relationship and give a woman false hope of a future together, not when I intended to serve the king for as long as I had life and breath.

But this time, with this note, I sensed something deeper was happening. I couldn't yet put the clues together, but I needed to explore further.

"If you have a mind to meet your admirer," Gunnar said, "I shall go with you. No doubt she'll have a lady companion needing attention."

I couldn't afford to draw suspicion, not when I was already suspect and would likely be followed. Taking Gunnar would add credibility to my journey. "Very well. You may join me."

Torvald's stoic expression registered surprise. He had the same viewpoint I did about getting into relationships. The two of us had oft remained at the castle while the other knights frequented taverns and public houses for the pleasure of mingling with maidens. Torvald and I had played many games of chess while the others were out.

I needed to provide an excuse for why I was reconsidering my position, hopefully one Torvald would be able to see through. I tossed out the first I could find. "If my days are numbered as one of the king's knights, I might have need of a wife soon. I may as well begin the process of meeting maidens." If the doors and walls truly had ears, then my explanation would hopefully sound reasonable enough.

I just prayed I wasn't walking into a trap.

Author's Note

Hi dear readers!

I hope you've enjoyed this first installment of my newest sweet medieval romance. This series is loosely inspired by the legends of Merlin, King Arthur, and the Knights of the Round Table.

The first book, *Enamored*, is based upon the wizard Merlin. But as you just read, Maxim is our hero, and instead of using magic as a weapon, he wields his mind (as does Elinor).

The second book, *Entwined*, centers around Ansgar and Lis and their reckoning with a legendary sword. Then, in the final books, four of the other Knights of Brethren will each get their own love stories for a total of six books in this series.

I hope you'll love reading each of their adventures just as much as I've enjoyed writing them. If you want to stay informed on the release dates for each of the books in this series, please visit my website at jodyhedlund.com or check out my Facebook Reader Room where I chat with readers and post news about my books.

Until next time . . .

Jody Hedlund is the best-selling author of over thirty historicals for both adults and teens and is the winner of numerous awards including the Christy, Carol, and Christian Book Award. She lives in central Michigan with her husband, busy family, and five spoiled cats. Learn more at JodyHedlund.com.

More Young Adult Fiction from Jody Hedlund

The Fairest Maidens

Beholden

Upon the death of her wealthy father, Lady Gabriella is condemned to work in Warwick's gem mine. As she struggles to survive the dangerous conditions, her kindness and beauty shine as brightly as the jewels the slaves excavate. While laboring, Gabriella plots how to avenge her father's death and stop Queen Margery's cruelty.

Beguiled

Princess Pearl flees for her life after her mother, Queen Margery, tries to have her killed during a hunting expedition. Pearl finds refuge on the Isle of Outcasts among criminals and misfits, disguising her face with a veil so no one recognizes her. She lives for the day when she can return to Warwick and rescue her sister, Ruby, from the queen's clutches.

Besotted

Queen Aurora of Mercia has spent her entire life deep in Inglewood Forest, hiding from Warwick's Queen Margery, who seeks her demise. As the time draws near for Aurora to take the throne, she happens upon a handsome woodcutter. Although friendship with outsiders is forbidden and dangerous, she cannot stay away from the charming stranger.

The Lost Princesses

Always: Prequel Novella

On the verge of dying after giving birth to twins, the queen of Mercia pleads with Lady Felicia to save her infant daughters. With the castle overrun by King Ethelwulf's invading army, Lady Felicia vows to do whatever she can to take the newborn princesses and their three-year-old sister to safety, even though it means sacrificing everything she holds dear, possibly her own life.

Evermore

Raised by a noble family, Lady Adelaide has always known she's an orphan. Little does she realize she's one of the lost princesses and the true heir to Mercia's throne . . . until a visitor arrives at her family estate, reveals her birthright as queen, and thrusts her into a quest for the throne whether she's ready or not.

Foremost

Raised in an isolated abbey, Lady Maribel desires nothing more than to become a nun and continue practicing her healing arts. She's carefree and happy with her life . . . until a visitor comes to the abbey and reveals her true identity as one of the lost princesses.

Hereafter

Forced into marriage, Emmeline has one goal—to escape. But Ethelrex takes his marriage vows seriously, including his promise to love and cherish his wife, and he has no intention of letting Emmeline get away. As the battle for the throne rages, will the prince be able to win the battle for Emmeline's heart?

The Noble Knights

The Vow

Young Rosemarie finds herself drawn to Thomas, the son of the nearby baron. But just as her feelings begin to grow, a man carrying the Plague interrupts their hunting party. While in forced isolation, Rosemarie begins to contemplate her future—could it include Thomas? Could he be the perfect man to one day rule beside her and oversee her parents' lands?

An Uncertain Choice

Due to her parents' promise at her birth, Lady Rosemarie has been prepared to become a nun on the day she turns eighteen. Then, shortly before her birthday, a friend of her father's enters the kingdom and proclaims her parents' will left a second choice—if Rosemarie can marry before the eve of her eighteenth year, she will be exempt from the ancient vow.

A Daring Sacrifice

In a reverse twist on the Robin Hood story, a young medieval maiden stands up for the rights of the mistreated, stealing from the rich to give to the poor. All the while, she fights against her cruel uncle who has taken over the land that is rightfully hers.

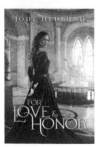

For Love & Honor

Lady Sabine is harboring a skin blemish, one that if revealed could cause her to be branded as a witch, put her life in danger, and damage her chances of making a good marriage. After all, what nobleman would want to marry a woman so flawed?

A Loyal Heart

When Lady Olivia's castle is besieged, she and her sister are taken captive and held for ransom by her father's enemy, Lord Pitt. Loyalty to family means everything to Olivia. She'll save her sister at any cost and do whatever her father asks—even if that means obeying his order to steal a sacred relic from her captor.

A Worthy Rebel

While fleeing an arranged betrothal to a heartless lord, Lady Isabelle becomes injured and lost. Rescued by a young peasant man, she hides her identity as a noblewoman for fear of reprisal from the peasants who are bitter and angry toward the nobility.

A complete list of my novels can be found at jodyhedlund.com.

Would you like to know when my next book is available? You can sign up for my newsletter, become my friend on Goodreads, like me on Facebook, or follow me on Twitter.

Newsletter: jodyhedlund.com
Goodreads:
goodreads.com/author/show/3358829.Jody_Hedlund
Facebook: facebook.com/AuthorJodyHedlund
Twitter: @JodyHedlund

The more reviews a book has, the more likely other readers are to find it. If you have a minute, please leave a rating or review. I appreciate all reviews, whether positive or negative.

CARROLL COUNTY

JAN 2022

PUBLIC LIBRARY

WITHDRAWN FROM LIBRARY

CPSIA information can be obtained
at www.ICGtesting.com
Printed in the USA
LVHW031648191221
706649LV00001B/22

9 781733 753487